Mount Merrion

JUSTIN QUINN

PENGUIN
IRELAND

PENGUIN IRELAND

Published by the Penguin Group
Penguin Ireland, 25 St Stephen's Green, Dublin 2, Ireland
(a division of Penguin Books Ltd)
Penguin Books Ltd, 80 Strand, London WC2R ORL, England
Penguin Group (USA) Inc., 375 Hudson Street, New York, New York 10014, USA
Penguin Group (Australia), 707 Collins Street, Melbourne, Victoria 3008, Australia
(a division of Pearson Australia Group Pty Ltd)
Penguin Group (Canada), 90 Eglinton Avenue East, Suite 700, Toronto, Ontario, Canada M4P 2Y3
(a division of Pearson Penguin Canada Inc.)
Penguin Books India Pvt Ltd, 11 Community Centre,
Panchsheel Park, New Delhi – 110 017, India
Penguin Group (NZ), 67 Apollo Drive, Rosedale, Auckland 0632, New Zealand
(a division of Pearson New Zealand Ltd)
Penguin Books (South Africa) (Pty) Ltd, Block D, Rosebank Office Park,
181 Jan Smuts Avenue, Parktown North, Gauteng 2193, South Africa

Penguin Books Ltd, Registered Offices: 80 Strand, London WC2R ORL, England

www.penguin.com
First published 2013
001

Typeset in 12/14.75pt Dante by Palimpsest Book Production Ltd, Falkirk, Stirlingshire
Printed in Great Britain by Clays Ltd, St Ives plc

A CIP catalogue record for this book is available from the British Library

ISBN: 978–1–844–88301–1

www.greenpenguin.co.uk

For Dave

Contents

1. The New Hospital, 1959   1
2. Confinement, 1968   47
3. Industry and Commerce, 1968   85
4. The Royal Marine, 1974–5   115
5. Lynch-Bages, 1987   145
6. Witches' Night, 1995   167
7. The Dark Fields of the Republic, 2002   193

I

The New Hospital

1959

The county hospital was only a few months old. The nuns and doctors still got lost in its corridors and ended up asking colleagues for directions in loud, humorous tones. The nuns especially seemed to doubt the very feasibility of the building. For them, the place still had the air of an experiment, the ambition of which was too outrageous to succeed. They would not have been surprised to be sent back to the smaller health-authority clinics after a year's trial, leaving the new hospital to rust like an impressive wreck on the wild rocks of the western coast.

The architect, unusually for the time, had used the resources of natural light as much as possible, and the hospital's high windows let in extravagant amounts of it from early morning to late in the day. It came slanting down on the patients lined in rows, illuminating their hair and other features (the broken remainders of their bodies covered underneath the crisply ironed white linen). It was cut in surprising angles by the building's design, suddenly conjuring a square of intense light at the back of a laundry room or bathroom that would disappear minutes later. As it reflected off the volumes of their white habits, it gave to the nuns' faces an angelic aspect that all noticed but none mentioned. They glided humbly but purposefully through their own wards, drawing the patients' gazes after them like guiding stars. If these people had come to them to be healed and depended on their mercy, then their mercy, in accordance with their order's vow, would be great.

The boy, though only twelve, had nearly a man's length in the bed. He couldn't move because his plastered leg was slung up in the air, pointing to the distant corner of the room. For most of the day, he stared at the ceiling; if he twisted his head to look to either side, the movement sent a pain to his leg. He read nothing and the nurses had been instructed by his father not to speak to him in Irish. He hadn't spoken English since first class at primary school and would be ashamed to begin now, in this big, clean hospital, so he did not speak at all.

A large stone had toppled off a wall onto his shin, ripping the flesh and breaking the bone. His father had carried him to the cart and deposited him on the settle, where he had been left for several days, running a fever. He recalled the doctor coming into their house, and his conveyance to the hospital, but little else. His father had been roundly rebuked by both the doctor and the hospital staff, though the boy hadn't heard it. He would have died without the antibiotics that he'd received.

Gradually he had begun to be able to tell the difference between night and day, and to distinguish between the different voices of the nurses. He could understand what they said in English to him, but he felt unable to respond. One had taken pity on him and reassured him, in Irish, that he would be all right now and wasn't to worry. He asked for the glass of water that he'd been dreaming about for the previous five hours but had been afraid to ask for. *Deoch uisce*, a drop of water.

On his third day, a man was billeted in the bed next to him. Arthur could hear the conversation between nurse and new patient. The only place he'd heard English spoken like that before was on the radio. It had the delicacy of a fine lady's linen. He decided to pay the price of pain and twist his neck to see his fellow patient: a man in his early twenties. Slim enough, but strong all the same, with hands that looked like they could do a decent bit of work. The features of the face surprised Arthur – they seemed almost familiar, as though he knew this man's cousins. How could an accent like that come out of such a country face? Was there another man beyond? The eyes were blue and steady as they ranged around the ward, his bed, the nurse as she plumped the pillows, and then settled on his own in an appraising look.

Arthur turned his head back to the ceiling too quickly and pain shot down through his leg. He stifled a cry, but a whimper escaped. He didn't know if the man had heard or was still looking at him.

After the nurse had left, he could hear the man settling in the bed. There was silence for a few minutes.

'So how did you do that to yourself?' the man asked eventually. 'Did one of the famed crocodiles of Connemara sink his teeth in you?'

Arthur was almost sure he understood. The man must be looking at him now. Arthur stared ever harder into the ceiling.

'Or did he get your tongue?'

Arthur didn't move.

'Or did you, my young fellow, take a vow of silence?'

Why wouldn't this man leave him alone? Arthur felt the sweat breaking out slowly from the pores on his forehead, and then a small trickle suddenly run down his temple. The walls were so white, and so smooth also. He would never escape.

Then the man said, 'Oh,' as though he'd just realized something. 'Is it Irish you'd prefer?' the man said in that language. Arthur involuntarily turned his head again. The pain was even greater this time and he cried.

'You seem to be in a bad way there,' the man said.

Though he had the option of his own language, Arthur found himself still unable to speak.

'But you're brave enough, I see, and that'll get you through.'

Arthur managed a kind of nod with his eyes. The face of the man was serious, but there was a kind of sympathy or fun in his eyes.

'This must be a strange place for you to find yourself all the same. I'm from Ardnabrayba, or at least my people are. What about yourself?'

Arthur just managed to say 'Uachtar Ard' in an undertone.

'Sure I know it well.'

A nurse approached them. 'Mr Boyle, this boy's father has asked us to speak to the boy only in English, so I'll be pleased if you do the same.'

'Of course, Sister, I understand.'

The nurse walked away.

'My word,' the man said in a whisper to him, in Irish again. 'It seems like you're a prisoner of war here. We'll have to plan our escape very carefully. Can you keep a secret?'

Arthur nodded.

'Good. Well, tomorrow we'll make our plan. For the meantime, play it cool. And we might even try a bit of English to fool them. Would you be up for it?'

Arthur nodded again.

'Good man. What's your name, by the way?'

'Arthur,' he managed.

The man didn't laugh like the others.

'Well, that's a fine name, Arthur. A king's name into the bargain, even if he was English. I'm Declan. And we're now conspirators.'

§

Declan was sure he had no business in the hospital. A low-grade temperature for most of the summer hardly required hospitalization. He was a little more fatigued than usual, but he put that down to the strain of his finals in early June, followed immediately by the Civil Service examination; after this he'd left Dublin directly on the train for Ardnabrayba to spend the summer helping his grand-mother with the pub and his uncle Joe with the farm work, as he had every summer since childhood. Mamó, his grandmother, haunted by stories she had heard in the parish, eventually dispatched him to the GP.

The examination was peremptory but respectful. The GP enquired after Declan's father and his work in Dublin. He then con-sidered Declan, who was standing naked from the waist up in the middle of the spacious Victorian study, not so much to make a diag-nosis as to assess the career that lay ahead of him in the next few decades. The doctor's bearing, the medical solemnity of his gaze, the manner in which he removed the stethoscope from around his neck, suggested he had a fair idea of what Declan would achieve. The younger man was accustomed to such examinations by his father's important acquaintances and the parents of his school friends – after all, here he was, the son of a Galway boy made good in Dublin. Was he made of the same stuff as his father? they wondered.

'Off you trot for a few weeks to the county hospital,' the GP said. 'I don't like the sound of what's in there, although it's probably nothing. Has there been any blood when you expectorate?'

'I don't have a cough, Doctor.'

'Indeed. In any case, your constitution is at a low ebb, which might be the examinations, as you say, and might be something else. I've no doubt you'll be as fit as a fiddle by the end of the month and ready to take your place in the ranks of the Civil Service to terrorize the good people of Ireland.' The doctor snorted at his own wit. Declan, gazing out the bay window of the surgery at the small fields and stone walls that stretched up the facing hill, thanked the GP as he buttoned his shirt. He left the surgery with his jacket over his arm, the referral folded in his pocket.

He made the journey of thirty miles to the hospital the next day – his grandmother wouldn't hear another word about it. On her insistence too a car was borrowed. Although twenty-three years of age, he didn't wish to enter into a debate with her about the matter. And so he found himself again naked from the waist up as the admitting nurse, a young nun, took his blood pressure.

'The GP measured my blood pressure yesterday,' he said.

'I'm sure he did, Mr Boyle. But we're obliged by regulations to take a measurement for our own records.' She held a card up to emphasize her point, not meeting his eye. Then she put it down and removed the manometer from his arm.

'Stand up, please.'

As he marshalled his body to carry out her instruction, he felt as though he had lead weights attached to each of his limbs. Suddenly the idea of lying in bed for a very long time was attractive. On the wall facing him there was a picture of the Sacred Heart of Jesus. He was familiar with the print from the houses in Ardnabrayba, but here it looked out of place against the bright modern walls of the hospital that still had a scent of paint beneath the odour of disinfectant. The figure gazed at him, hair coming down in effeminate waves

7

to the shoulders. The exposed heart, when he thought about it, as he did now for the first time, was grotesque, as though the man's ribcage had been prised open by surgeons.

'I said you can put your shirt back on.'

'Of course, Sister.'

The young nun closed the door behind her as Declan reached for his shirt. She returned a minute later and instructed him to go to St Dermot's Ward and ask for Sister Imelda. He walked out and she closed the door abruptly behind him. Declan was left facing a choice between three long and seemingly identical corridors, their floors polished and gleaming. He felt a film of sweat covering his body.

As he walked past ward after ward, he could pretend to himself that he still belonged to the healthy world outside. He tried to imagine that he was strolling nonchalantly, but it was hard work. Although he passed several nurses as he went, he resolved to find his way to St Dermot's Ward alone, and in the process take the measure of the new building.

One door was ajar and he caught a glimpse of a white-coated doctor with two nurses attending, all of them moving quickly and methodically around a prostrate patient, who was motionless except for his eyes. One of the nuns saw Declan and closed the door. He continued down the corridor, imagining the same efficient activity behind every door he passed. The largeness of the organization bore in upon him with force, and he realized he'd underestimated it.

§

In his first days in St Dermot's, these initial impressions faded. The limits of the ward became the limits of his world, and he forgot about the larger organization of which it was a part. Arthur gradually began to talk, and Declan discovered that the lad was clever, but scared witless by the hospital. The nurses woke them at half five to insert thermometers and administer medicines. Breakfast followed three-quarters of an hour later.

It turned out that the nurse who had admitted him, Sister Colette, was on morning duty that week in his ward. She had a look of calm determination. He was curious about where she came from and what her family name was.

'Are you from these parts, Sister?' he asked on Wednesday, knowing from her accent that she wasn't. It was his second day in St Dermot's, and he sat in the visitor's chair as she changed his sheets.

'No. My people are from Donegal. Glencolmcille.'

'It's a beautiful part of the world,' Declan said, 'but I think my heart will never wander far from here.'

She paused her work for a beat, weighing up the intent in his remark. Glancing at him quickly, she saw that he was looking out the window. She resumed making the bed, satisfied that he wasn't that type.

'That's true, it is. Now. There you are.' The bed lay before them, immaculate and smooth, the sheets folded with industrial precision. It seemed almost wrong for the patients to defile such perfection with their sick bodies. The starch gave the sheets the stiffness of card, after they'd been tucked in tightly under the mattress. Now this young woman gave them the finishing touch.

'Can I ask who your people are?' he said. 'A school friend of mine came from that area. His name is Cunningham.'

'Oh, the Cunninghams,' she said, her tone indicating that her own caste was lower than theirs. There was no shade of resentment in the way she said this, merely acceptance of the fact that she and her family would enter the Cunningham household, if ever they did, through the back door. 'Everyone knows the Cunninghams.'

'The fellow I knew wasn't the brightest, but he was a decent sort all the same,' Declan countered. He was trying to level the difference that had emerged between them, but his remark had the opposite effect. The young woman appeared mildly offended. Since she herself couldn't make or share such a judgement, she shouldn't be told about it. That was the concern of other people, at other levels, not hers. It was unfitting for him to say it, and he saw how it quietly edged him out of her world. He felt her considering the hinterland behind him: young, educated, interested in new ideas, some of which might be good, others of which might be dangerous.

'So there you are,' she repeated, and turned to go. As she went to Arthur's bed, he realized that he still didn't know her family name.

Only four of the twelve beds in the ward were occupied: the county did not appear to have enough sick people to fill the hospital yet. One man, in his twenties, had undergone an appendectomy and would be going home on Thursday. Another man had cancer and the only activity that could draw him from his torpor was smoking. He reached for the cigarette packet as for a spar that would save him from drowning. The nurses encouraged him in this, saying that the aroma would be good for the others on the ward also – 'Soothe the nerves it will.' The man would sit up in bed for the few minutes it took to smoke the cigarette, and then subside, coughing, into a supine position once more. It wasn't clear whether he was sleeping or looking at the ceiling. Declan didn't know what this man's occupation had been before he'd arrived here to wait for his death. The hands seemed unspoiled by hard labour, but it was hard to imagine him as a hale bank manager or engineer.

'Arthur, we have to find out who Sister Colette's people are.'

The boy nodded, smiling.

'Now here's the game. You say, in English, "My name is Arthur Naughton," and you ask Sister Colette her name. I'll tell her we're practising your English, and she'll be delighted. You say, "My father's name is Joseph Naughton," and then you ask her what her father's name is. She'll never see it coming. Are you with me?'

Arthur nodded happily. But when the time came, Sister Colette said her name was Sister Colette and her father's name was his own business and no one else's. Then she walked off.

'Arthur, I can see that she's been trained by the Gestapo and I don't know if we'll get the better of her.'

'What if we ask one of the other nurses?'

'I can see you've got a good head for this work, Arthur, but it won't fly. I think they're even tougher.'

Arthur turned back to look at the ceiling. It no longer hurt him to turn his head.

'But don't you worry,' Declan said, winking, 'we'll win this one yet.'

§

Two days later, Declan was dozing when he heard two men talking in Irish at the other end of the ward. He opened his eyes and saw a bishop – to judge by the biretta and fascia – and a layman standing in front of a group of nuns. Sister Imelda, the ward's head nurse, was among them, as well as one or two others who seemed to be her superiors. An unsympathetic observer might have described the expression on the nuns' faces as sycophantic. Their faces glowed with admiration, as if two demigods had chosen to come among them, gracing them with their wisdom, illumination and guidance. The only exception to this was Sister Imelda, whose eye was keen, appraising and unconvinced. The grey suit of the layman and the dark cassock of the prelate stood out against the soft white phalanx of nuns' habits behind them.

The bishop talked of the good work that was being done by the sisters and how much that work was enabled by the new building itself. The layman responded that he was glad to see such – what was the word? – devotion in the sisters. The men were uncomfortable in Irish, but persisted in the effort. The words they used did not form a stream of speech but felt stiff and distinct, as though each one had been freshly taken from a dictionary. Declan had heard this type of Irish many times in the past, usually from enthusiasts in Dublin. Some even insisted that the language be spoken by their families; he couldn't imagine speaking to his parents or sisters in such a stilted, unnatural idiom. His father rarely spoke Irish at home in Dublin, because Declan's mother had none, but when he did he was transformed. He'd left Ardnabrayba in his late teens, and so when speaking Irish he reverted to that age, and Declan heard the rhythms and tones of a community very far from the one James Boyle was now a master of.

His father had sent Declan each summer to Ardnabrayba, in part to help his uncle Joe and his grandmother, in part to show him a world beyond Mount Merrion Avenue and in part to learn Irish. James Boyle wanted his son to know about his own native county, not the statelet of south Dublin alone. At the beginning of July, he would drive Declan to Kingsbridge Station and help him load his luggage onto the Galway train. James Boyle would not wait for the train to pull out, but took his leave of Declan with a handshake once he was installed in a compartment, his knapsack beside him and his suitcase up on the rack.

Declan shifted in the hospital bed to hear the two men more clearly. They were performing for an audience, rather than conversing with one another. They both understood this and added grace notes of smiles, demurrals, nods to heighten the effect. Now, however, they were flagging, and switched to English.

'In any case, Mr Devereux,' said the bishop, 'I would have liked to extend our colloquy in the first official language of our republic a little longer, but it would have been rude to our company. We must, with some chagrin, return to the Sasanach's tongue. But perhaps after all that is a better language for doing business in, while Irish should house our souls.'

'Again, I am left with no choice but to agree with Your Excellency.'

Mr Devereux, evidently the architect who had designed the hospital, suggested they visit the chapel and then the kitchens. The bishop inclined his head, and the whole group moved out through the doors that were held open for them by two nuns.

Declan entered another land each summer when he stepped off the train in Galway. This summer he'd been looking forward to the work and the opportunity to strengthen his constitution after all the sedentary days of study. It seemed like freedom also, to be heading into the country, having now left university and not yet entered adult life. He'd arranged the journey to coincide with his uncle's trip to sell his produce at Galway fair. The two would travel to Ardnabrayba on Joe's cart, arriving at his grandmother's in the small hours of the next day.

His uncle would ask, 'And how's Séamus Óg?' His father's name. Not James Boyle SC, the given name redolent of English kings and counsellors; rather Young Séamus, retaining his boyishness deep into middle age. Also, one of a line, a son himself, and not the self-made man of Mount Merrion Avenue, with airs and graces. In the question he felt his uncle brace himself for tidings of the older brother's status and achievement.

His uncle's farm did well. Joe had taken it over when their father died, expanding it and acting as a kind of agent for local farmers with the large dealers in Galway. The name of ó Baoill had grown in Connemara under his uncle's stewardship; but Joe knew he'd never be offered a cabinet seat, as James had. He might be able to slap a minister on the back, if he'd known him as a local TD, but that was the extent of it. Declan was obscurely aware that he himself was a conduit for the brothers' affection, all the long way from one side of the island to the other.

'We've to pick up three lads in Salthill,' his uncle said. 'They helped me drive in some livestock yesterday, and now they're taking their ease in a pub. I don't know what state they'll be in, but they're good lads.'

They pulled up outside a pub and Uncle Joe went in. From the cart, Declan could pick up the smell of porter, a flash of skirt, the churning strength of men barely contained in the dark interior. This pub did not resemble the Two Widows in Ardnabrayba, which had a grocery on one side of the room, the beer-taps on the other, and his grandmother between. This pub was the mouth of hell. Joe emerged from its noisy darkness after a minute or two, driving three huge men before him. They stood swaying on the road while his uncle rearranged the goods in the back of the cart. The smell of animals and tobacco had soaked into the weave of the cheap wool clothing they wore. For a moment it seemed as though they might drift back into the pub, but then Joe was telling them to get on and be sharp about it. They bundled their brawn onto the boards of the cart, and his uncle cracked the whip. The three men talked animat-edly for about fifteen minutes and then quickly fell asleep, leaving Declan and Joe in what now seemed an enormous silence, as the cart made straight for the setting sun, gradually shedding Galway town.

'Quiet enough in O'Connor's still. See what it's like in two hours,' his uncle remarked after a while. 'And what about yourself? Will you be off on the boat?'

'No. I took the Civil Service exams in June,' Declan replied.

'So it'll be your last summer with us,' his uncle remarked neutrally, and lapsed into silence.

The road was awful, but Declan always enjoyed the trip. Over the years he had found out more about his family on these journeys with his uncle than he ever had on Mount Merrion Avenue. His grandfather had returned with money from Philadelphia, married the most beautiful girl in Connemara and hardly talked to her for the next thirty years. His grandmother, Mamó, had done little during those decades. Her husband had wanted to set her up as a woman of leisure to prove his achievement and refused to let her do any work, either in the pub or on the farm. But when Séamus Sr died, she surprised everyone by insisting that she would run the spirit grocery with her sister, who had also been widowed recently. As a child, Declan loved watching the brewery men roll barrel after barrel past Mamó down to the cellar, her delicate face glowing with attention. She knew each of the men by name and remembered their eldest boys, but she never lost count of the barrels or the bottles of spirits that they brought.

His uncle's hold on the reins was so light that the mare seemed to be directing herself. What did Connemara look like in the light of the moon? Declan reckoned he'd never be able to explain this to his friends in Dublin. Not that they'd be interested. Houses and haystacks were interchangeable in the silver light, and shadows of hawthorns and rowans were grotesque. The silence was broken only by the occasional dog barking. Sometimes the road brought them closer to the sea and they could hear the waves.

The Boyles' pub had been called the Two Widows since the time that Séamus died, but really it was the one widow who ran it. More than the church, the pub was at the centre of life in Ardnabrayba, and Mamó was at the centre of the pub. It was a concert room every Friday, when musicians would come from neighbouring townlands to play into the small hours. It was a funeral parlour where corpses were brought to be washed and laid out before removal to the church. It was where the parish priest came to have a word with Mamó when he couldn't get his way by other means. And it was a kind of court of law whose sessions worked out innocence and guilt in the eyes of the families of Ardnabrayba, more accurate and more binding than the District Court (which had used the Two Widows for hearings until the courthouse in Casla had been built).

It was also a place that continued to surprise Declan into adulthood. He'd see a few old men talking in a corner and from a distance reckon them pure products of the west – fishermen and farmers, who'd battled the native Irish elements for their entire lives, all that *Man of Aran* stuff that Americans loved, and some Irish also. Approaching closer, he often found that the flow of their speech in Irish was punctuated by jocular references to Flatbush and Edgware Road. They were true cosmopolitans.

He'd heard that Mamó had visited Mount Merrion when he was born, the year after her husband died, but he himself had never seen her out of Ardnabrayba. He could imagine neither the village without her nor her without the village. If he were to see her walking down a Dublin street, he wouldn't have recognized her; if the Two Widows were levelled, the village would be dragged after it in a slipstream of rubble and glass.

Declan spent six days of the week helping Uncle Joe with the farm, and three nights behind the bar helping Mamó. His uncle had cattle and sheep, as well as some of the best crop fields in an area that was generally poor in that respect. There was a constant struggle with the rocks, which were churned up year after year by the earth and had to be removed and carted away. Declan for the most part worked with the livestock, driving them through the lanes to graze and back, and clearing out the byres each day. He stayed with his grandmother, but had his tea at his uncle's. Often, in his mind, he would trace the journey back to Dublin: the night-trip on the cart, the train through the midlands and past Ballyfermot into the station, the car from Kingsbridge, lifting the luggage from the car to the front door of the house on Mount Merrion Avenue. Although he knew each link in the chain of events that transported him from one place to another, he still couldn't join Ardnabrayba to his life in Dublin – Deerpark College and then UCD, its buildings scattered through the city's Georgian terraces and squares. How could one small country hold such different places?

It was usually around four in the morning when his uncle would pull the cart up outside the Two Widows. The hall light was always on, and in the doorway his grandmother was always waiting.

§

St Dermot's Ward was, as far as he could make out, identical to St Ailbhe's, St Malachy's, St Brigid's, St Ita's, and so on, except that some were for men and some for women. The number of beds was the same, as was the arrangement of bathing and treatment rooms. At the head of each ward was the nurses' station, with a small office beyond for the head nurse. He tried to recollect details from the lives of these particular saints, a subject in which he'd been examined during his third year at Deerpark, but nothing came to him. The only trace of their early Christian travails and glories was a picture above the entrance of each ward, each seemingly executed by the same artist.

Sister Colette avoided his eye as much as was politely possible. Vanity, however, was apparent when she walked down the centre of the ward, her white habit swiftly rearranging its folds about her striding body, here and there brushing against the enamelled legs of the beds. In a place where all other movements were brusque and functional, the gracefulness of the motion did not escape Declan. Did she think she was showing the patients what devotion to Christ was? Did she think they would learn something by watching her humble yet decisive steps? She kept her head inclined slightly downwards, perhaps to offset the pride welling in her chest. Such a performance would have been impossible in a small house in Glencolmcille; it required a larger stage, better lighting, a more educated audience. It required this building where he now lay.

Declan found himself wondering if her parents had encouraged her vocation, or if she'd made the choice on her own, perhaps over their objections. The path he'd chosen for himself, and would embark upon in September, was one that his own father had tried to discourage – a fact that bred in him a mixture of misgiving and defiant pride. He had, he knew, taken his father by surprise.

Deerpark College, like all the other respectable schools in south Dublin, had a rugby team. They practised three days a week and played a match against another school every other Saturday. The boys' fathers attended on Saturdays wearing sheepskin jackets and tweed flat caps, which marked a difference from the stiff wool suits of the working week. Daimlers, Mercedes, Jaguars and some smaller Fords were parked along the school's avenues. Barristers who'd flayed each other in courts of law the day before made small talk. Surgeons who'd spent the week gazing at the unspeaking innards of respectable citizens now looked up to consider the faces of their patients' friends, brothers and cousins. Businessmen who seemed prosperous to the uninitiated kept up the pretence with volleys of jokes and banter. The priests moved around directing the boys towards dressing rooms, resolving kit issues, chivvying the substitutes.

It had the feeling of antique ritual, even though Deerpark had been founded only a few decades before. The brown-grey photographs of the first principal and the four other teachers, hanging in the school corridor, could have been taken in 1831 and not 1931, as far as Declan was concerned. It felt as though teenage boys had fought each other savagely on this grass for centuries, roared at by the upstanding burghers on the sidelines. Declan had been an indifferent player on an indifferent Deerpark team, but it was generally understood that these matches were part of the preparation for adult life in south County Dublin.

It was only now, lying at his leisure in the county hospital, that Declan saw the significance of a conversation he'd had with his father after one such match. Deerpark had been thumped, as usual, by Blackrock College – for which James Boyle had played on the Senior Cup team in his own day. Declan knew that he had nothing of his father's flair for rugby, but they were both usually able to deal

17

with it in a humorous way. There were no jokes for a while after this match, however, because it had cost the visiting team so little exertion. Declan felt as though he'd let his father down.

They drove out of the school grounds into Clonskeagh, and coasted along the Dodder for a while before turning left onto Sandford Road, rather than home to Mount Merrion. Declan knew this meant they were going to Searson's. It was a detour, but James Boyle had gone to school with one of the Searson boys, and preferred their cellars to what was on offer in the off-licences closer to home.

'How are things going at school?' his father asked after a few minutes of silence.

'Very well, Dad.'

'Still set for law?'

Declan looked at his father, who faced the road ahead. He had no expression.

'Yes.'

They came to the canal and turned left. James Boyle seemed at ease in the silence.

'Do you know what I did after UCD?' his father asked eventually.

'You went to King's Inns.'

'I didn't. I worked on the barges for a year.' The car was stopped, waiting for a horse-drawn cart to manoeuvre out of a laneway. Boyle was looking to his right. 'On the Grand Canal,' he added, nodding his head in the direction of the waterway.

'You never told me that before. Why did you do that?'

'I didn't want to study law in the first place. My father insisted, just as he insisted I attend Blackrock College. At that time, all I wanted to do was stay on the farm. But my father said he'd had enough of first-born sons staying on farms. He was an ambitious man. A hard man.'

Declan saw that his father's face itself had hardened.

'He'd have done anything to get back from Philadelphia and buy the business in Ardnabrayba. He wanted to return from the States as a success.'

Declan studied the water in the canal. Gold leaves gathered

around the locks like ledges you might walk across. What would it be like to step off the bank onto such a surface? You would see the fallen foliage tilt slightly then launch away from your foot as you went down. One moment you would be admiring the beautiful shapes of the leaves and the facets of water, and the next you would be panicking and fighting for air. He wanted to find other things to study – the grassy banks, the bare trees, the buildings across the way – in order to postpone looking at his father.

The saloon car idled as the rag-and-bone man once again led the two horses back, and then forward again, in an attempt to get the heavily loaded cart around a pile of rubble that builders had left on the corner. The horses were unhappy and reared their heads in protest, made nervous perhaps by the cars, still a rare enough thing in the late 1940s. The cart, like the man, seemed from another century, roughly used, the bolts rusting, the timber battered and worn. The man had apparently filled the cart with wrought iron from where the builders had been working. Black metal curlicues and floral patterns were piled awkwardly at the back. Every time the horses juddered, the whole crazy structure shifted dangerously.

'It's difficult to describe what Ireland was like back then just after the Civil War,' James Boyle said. 'It was all upside down. My father . . . he thought I was going ahead for the Bar examinations and it wasn't for a few months that he discovered what had actually happened. My year before the mast. Hardly the high seas. But the canals allowed me a breather to step back from everything.'

Declan had never heard his father talk in this way. It seemed almost as if he were conversing quietly with himself.

'Though I knew I wouldn't be working the barges for ever, I didn't know what I would do. I gave myself twelve months to decide. In the end,' he sighed, 'I could think of nothing and I signed up for King's Inns.'

Declan let out a long breath, realizing at that moment that he'd been holding it in the expectation of some revelation.

'Does that mean you never liked the law?'

'Oh, I liked it well enough. And still do. But I never went at it with the same passion that I saw in some colleagues.' He turned to look at Declan. 'So, my man. There you are. The life and times of James Boyle, Senior Counsel. I have succeeded in making the tedious interlude of the horse and cart even more tedious.'

Declan didn't respond. They both knew that there'd been nothing tedious about the last five minutes. He was confused by his father's languorous tone, so different from his customary jovial brusqueness. Was he dreaming of other paths his life might have taken, away from his career, his house, away from his wife, his son, his daughters?

'And he's off at last!' James Boyle pointed to the rag-and-bone man on his cart, who was now moving off at a fair clip along the canal. 'No flies on him. I'll only be a tick in Searson's.'

§

By Saturday, Declan had become so used to the hospital's daily rhythms that he was starting to feel unmoored from his previous life and future plans. The particularities of the weeks he'd spent with his grandmother and uncle receded quickly, dissolving into the many summers he'd spent in Ardnabrayba as a child. University and the examinations felt like the memories of a fictional character. Despite himself, he discovered he was dozing a lot during the day, and he savoured the moments before he surfaced fully into consciousness. His temperature hadn't gone over a hundred degrees, but even small exertions made him sweat. He could hear the nurses moving about the ward, talking to the patients. He could hear the distant sound of construction work going on outside. He could hear the birds singing also. He could hear Arthur shifting awkwardly in the rigid sheets. As these sounds washed up against the edges of his consciousness, he felt cradled by the whole building, as though it were a liner buffeted by waves.

He had no visitors. His grandmother could have made the trip only with great difficulty, and his parents were busy in Dublin (though he had received a letter from his mother). The man who had undergone the appendectomy had been discharged. The intrigues with Arthur had settled down into English lessons, as it turned out that the boy was anxious to learn more. They kept up their joke about Sister Colette, trying to remember the most ridiculous surnames they'd heard, as explanation for her silence on the subject.

She woke him at some stage on Saturday afternoon, wanting to take his temperature. 'Ninety-nine point six,' she said, and noted the number on the clipboard.

'What does it amount to?' Declan asked.

'I don't understand, Mr Boyle.'

'Is it bad or good, the fact my temperature hasn't changed?'

'It's not for me to say. Dr O'Dwyer will tell you that when he does his rounds.'

Declan found out later that day that it was in fact bad, and the doctor suggested that Declan might not be leaving at the end of August, as he'd presumed.

'But a temperature like that isn't serious, and I just feel a little tired.'

The doctor told him to wait a minute and went back to the nurses' station. He returned with a large, flat brown paper bag from which he removed an X-ray.

'This is your good self,' the doctor said with a smile, 'though only your mother might recognize you. I don't normally show the X-rays to the patients, but you're an educated man. You see that large clouding there?'

It was about the size of a hand. Declan nodded.

'That's what we call pulmonary consolidation, and it's what makes it difficult for you to breathe when you exert yourself even slightly. You need complete rest for several weeks to come. This is the latest image we have; the one from when you were admitted was much worse. Frankly, I'm surprised you were able to walk from the door of the hospital to here. You must have a sturdy constitution.'

'Not sturdy enough to keep this thing away, obviously.'

'It has nothing to do with that. The upshot is that we want to keep an eye on you for a while longer. If you had TB we'd pack you off to a sanatorium. But you'll be fine here for the moment. You can see there's no rush to fill the beds.' The doctor gestured at the near-empty ward behind them.

'I'm supposed to start in the Department of Finance on the 1st of September.'

The doctor looked up from his notes. 'Indeed. Well, Mr Boyle, I'm still not certain. We'll see in the next week.' The doctor then turned to Arthur. 'And what about this young man? I think we'll be letting you home soon. Lucky you came in to us when you did.'

§

From the chapel across the muddy yard, Declan heard the nuns singing a hymn that he didn't know. The Irish words and simple melody made him think it was quite old. There was no ornament in either, but none was required as the air and images carried enough beauty in themselves. Yet the singers didn't seem to know it that well, as they continually stopped and began again, which allowed Declan to catch the first verse.

> Ag Críost an síol, ag Críost an fómhar;
> i n-iothlainn Dé go dtugtar sinn.

The hospital was surrounded by tillage farms, and most of the harvest was already in. Declan saw that in one of the fields the farmer and his labourers had begun baling the hay and carting it off. He supposed they would drag the plough across the land soon. It was possible that this farmer had sold several of his fields so the county could build the hospital. The farmland was better than in Ardnabrayba, with larger fields and fewer rocks. This farmer had cattle also, visible in the distance. The scene could have been from a few hundred years ago, except that it was framed by the industrial precision of the hospital window. How did it look to the farmer? What did he think of the hospital's bright angles, its panels of glass, the sweep of concrete road leading up to the main entrance? How was Declan's head framed in that view?

The nuns continued to sing how Christ's is the harvest, the image floating sweetly through the sharp lines of the hospital itself. That man's work outside – that was how they thought of Christ and themselves. All their works and days gathered into Christ's arms. All the farmer's works and days as well. All Declan's. He was sure that was true.

The obscenity which the farmer roared at one of his labourers at that moment did not spoil Declan's contemplation, rather it brought a smile to his face. The nuns had begun the hymn again, from the beginning. The labourer came running back towards the farmer with a fork in his hand, and the farmer gave him instructions, vehemently pointing in another direction. The labourer countered. The farmer concluded. Their transaction also was gathered into that fate. *Do dhá láimh, a Chríost, anall tharainn.* That was the business of things. And their beauty.

§

He nearly hadn't met her. This thought kept coming back to him as he lay in the hospital bed, waiting for his economics books to arrive. He had nearly decided to go to the library. They'd been filing up the steps of the theatre after a lecture when Liam Creighton had caught his arm.

'You're coming with me.'

'Where?' Declan asked.

'To the Grand Central. I know it's not the Shelbourne. But I want to see a certain party that I call Funny Face, and she'll feel a lot more comfortable if it's not just a tête-à-tête. You, the lion of the debating chamber, the valiant warrior against cynicism in all its forms, shall be my chaperone. Come on.'

Creighton whistled 'Chattanooga Choo Choo' as he tried to get past the other students shuffling their way out into the large Edwardian hall.

'I have to get some books from the library, Creighton, and then I thought I might read them.'

'Oh, for God's sake, Boyle, how many books will fit in your head? It is my considered opinion that you have a sufficiency there already.

Certainly more than enough to get your Civil Service exams, where, to judge by our elders, it's more of an advantage to have read nothing at all. *Quod erat demonstrandum*: that is the irrefutable argument for your accompanying me to the Grand Central.'

Declan enjoyed the way they conversed: he always adopted a high patrician tone, and Creighton switched between patrician and plain countryman in response.

'Your logic escapes me,' Declan said. 'But all right then. I'm to be shown a new café in my city by a Mayo bogman. How any girl would agree to meet you mystifies me. Perhaps she's from Mayo also, Creighton, and you'll be talking of the pig fair at Belmullet?'

'That's the spirit, Boyle. You're a brick.'

'Where is the Grand Central in any case?' Declan asked.

'Down on Wicklow Street. You Blackrock Brahmins really should consider a guided tour of the city at some stage. You'd enjoy the place so much, if you only let yourselves see it. Oh, the delights I could show you. I bet you couldn't even find Phibsboro if you tried.'

'Creighton, where would I be without you? Deep in my orthodox slumbers. Who is this girl anyway?'

'All in good time, my man, all in good time,' he said as they stepped into the street. There was a band of gold sunlight along the top floors of the facing buildings, burnishing their Georgian brickwork, and the windows threw down surreal reflections on the wet pavement at their feet. Above, to the east, they could see the receding rainstorm.

As they turned left out of Kildare Street, opposite the long stretch of Trinity, Liam turned to Declan, pointing to the university's tall railings. 'Are they to keep the Protestants in, or us lot out?'

Declan had heard the line before and didn't gratify Liam with a laugh. Instead, he said to his friend, 'By the way, Creighton, would you like to come to our bosky family seat on Mount Merrion for a party that my parents are throwing next week?' Liam had not been to Declan's house before, and they were both aware that the invitation marked a step forward in their friendship. For this reason, they retreated to a bantering tone.

'Is it the back entrance I'll be using, sor?' Liam asked.

'No. My father says that the back door is for government minis-ters. Or at least, he says that's the only way they'll get into his house.'

Liam smiled at this, and changed his tone. 'I'd be delighted.'

They entered the Grand Central Café, and after a bit of looking around Liam waved across the expansive room at two girls, and received a nod in exchange.

'Oho, we're in trouble, we are,' Liam said, and looked at his watch and drew in his breath. 'Well, yes. I said I'd be here a little earlier.'

'You mean *you're* in trouble. I deserve to be praised for playing the cicerone, while you . . .' Declan didn't have time to complete the sentence as they were at the table. The girls rose.

'The cicerone while Mr Creighton what?' one of the girls asked.

Declan found himself being interrogated by a tall, athletic girl with a long, well-proportioned face. She was looking at him with amusement. Liam introduced them, and Winifred McKenna in her turn introduced the two men to her friend, Sinéad Grogan.

'We went to Roebuck together, but have lived to tell the story. Haven't we, Sinéad?'

'And this is the afterlife, Freddy,' Sinéad said.

'You don't look like a ghost to me, Miss Grogan, in any case,' Declan said.

She stared straight at him, and smiled. 'Have you had much ex-perience with ghosts, Mr Boyle?'

'Well, I'm attending UCD with Liam and we harbour suspicions about whether some of the lecturers are clinically alive. And yet they seem not to have the vigour that one usually associates with ghosts – movement, howling noises and the like.'

'I think we must have some lecturers in common.'

'What do you study, Miss Grogan?'

'French and Spanish.'

Liam was gesturing for them all to sit down, and Winifred declared, 'No more of this "Miss" and "Mr"! We're not our parents after all. Let's be daring and modern today.' Everyone smiled. She then turned to Declan, repeating her question: 'The cicerone while Liam what, Declan?'

'While Liam enjoys the charming conversation of the brilliant and beautiful maidens of UCD Arts.'

'You've passed.' Winifred smiled at him, then turned back to Liam.

'Winifred mentioned that Mr Creighton, I mean Liam, says you're from Connemara,' Sinéad said to Declan.

'Well, my father is. From Ardnabrayba. Do you know it?'

'I'm afraid I don't. But I'm going to Connemara next summer for the first time in my life. Spiddal, if you please. My parents want me to stay with my aunt, but are a little nervous that all the good work of Roebuck will be undone.'

'I don't understand.'

'They think I might pick up a country accent.' She pronounced the last words with a comic brogue.

Declan laughed. 'It's a Gaeltacht area, so there's an even bigger danger you'll come back speaking Irish.'

'Oh, my mother would hate that altogether. That's what I'll do, so.'

'Your mother's not much of a patriot.'

'Oh, she is, only her *patria* is the Principality of Foxrock. Allegiance to other dominions, realms or polities is punishable by death.'

Declan laughed at that. 'And what about you, Sinéad? Where do your allegiances lie?'

'My fealty is not clear. I'm awfully tempted to become a turncoat. I've a feeling I might be Irish.'

'What is the punishment?'

'Oh, Roebuck strikes you off their books. Moreover, you can never have cream tea in the Shelbourne. The Royal Dublin Society blackballs you, and the worst cut of all is that you stand no chance of admission to the Foxrock Ladies' Choral Society.'

Although they were seated, he judged she was almost as tall as him. She was wearing a two-piece fine woollen suit. Its scrupulous folds and pleats drew in tightly around her waist. On her lapel was a cameo brooch which depicted the head of a woman, her locks swirling in all directions untrammelled. Her own hair was russet-coloured, lightly curled. Her brown eyes were not large, and sharpened with delight when she smiled. As she deployed her ironies, her face was animated histrionically, and yet she observed his face carefully, not oblivious of her audience.

'What will you do after university, Declan?' she asked.

'I'll be doing the Civil Service examinations.'

'Really? I'm surprised. Well, not surprised, I hardly know you. Are you interested in the diplomatic service?'

'In fact, no. If I'm lucky, I'll be working for the Department of Finance.'

Declan noted that Sinéad did not make any of the usual smart retorts to this information, but rather studied him more closely.

'And yourself?'

'I . . . well . . . I don't know.'

'What do you like doing best?' Declan tried, with this question, to return to a tone of raillery, but he saw that he'd hit a spot outside that arena. 'I'm sorry if the question was . . .' Declan didn't want to say 'improper', as it wasn't.

'No, your question was fair. It'll sound strange I know, but I enjoyed myself best when I worked for three summers in the accounts department of my father's business.'

'It doesn't sound strange at all,' Declan said. But it did sound strange, and intrigued him. 'What did you do there?'

'I learned the double-entry system and how to structure a balance sheet, if you'll believe that.' She spoke deliberately and seriously.

'I will indeed.' Declan observed her, disoriented slightly and attracted by the way that shades of emotion played over her face. He couldn't unpuzzle her present tone. He sensed that something more was at stake than balance sheets and the double-entry system, but its exact contours were unclear. And now seconds of silence were passing between them.

'What's going on over there, Boyle?' Liam asked, opening the conversation to the four of them. Declan brought himself to face his friend.

'The Foxrock Ladies' Choral Society,' he answered, as Sinéad sat back and took a sip of her tea. 'Sinéad was explaining that she runs the risk of not gaining admission to that august group.'

'Is that why you're so sad?' Liam asked Sinéad.

Sinéad rallied. 'Well, wouldn't you be sad? You still have a chance, Liam, but I have burned my bridges.'

'Oh, I wouldn't be up to you Southsiders. A simple country lad like me.'

'We try to bring you along, Liam,' Declan said.

Afterwards, Declan and Liam made their way back along Nassau Street. 'Boyle, she's taken, I'm afraid,' Creighton said. 'Some black-guard from Science and Engineering.' Declan smiled back, not bothering to deny the inference.

§

Dr O'Dwyer told him that although the X-rays were improving, he couldn't release him before mid-September at the earliest. He advised Declan to let the Department know, and he would of course be happy to write a brief report to that effect.

Despite this news, Declan now felt able to turn to the economics books his father had sent him. Arthur had been discharged, and Declan found he now conversed little with other patients. Reading the books, he was struck by how few equations there were in comparison to the textbooks he was used to. He found he was able to read them, not perhaps at the speed of a novel, but quickly never-theless. Unlike novels, it seemed to him, they dealt with reality, with actual lives and incomes, which added up to the product of the country. When he thought of his own country – the disconnection between the city and the country, the demands of farmers, the young men and women in a slow march to the boat every week – he couldn't work out how anything might be done with it. The shock of macroeconomics came from pushing aside all the clutter of the byres, the fairy-forts, the distracting demagoguery in the news-papers; at last he could see the country for what it was and what it could be. Declan was excited to encounter a version of Ireland stripped of the usual winsome stories, animosities and traditions.

He imagined fields being cleared outside Galway, concrete being poured into foundations, creating jobs with decent wages that would stop the droves taking the boat, and let them bring up their families where they were born and where their people were from. The rocky land had failed to give the people a livelihood, but industry could do it.

The Civil Service was not the only way of changing the country, but he knew he didn't have the stomach for politics. The evenings he had spent in the university debating society had shown him that he couldn't hold theories in his head and dodge an attack at the same time. One part always suffered, and it was usually his fence-manship, leaving him embarrassed in front of his peers. 'But my point is that if my colleague took the time to consider the complexity of the . . .' Before Declan had time to finish his sentence, his unlearned colleague had already dispatched him: 'Mr Boyle asks me to take my time, but we have no time left. I don't think I am alone in feeling that Mr Boyle's *point* is so *fine* as to be immaterial . . .' In the laughter that followed, as it echoed around the chamber, off the fogged panes, the shoulder-high gloss paint of the walls, the wooden benches, the heavy cast iron of the radiators, the cheap suits of the students, their animated faces, their bodies like parliamentarians twisted in different directions by the different arguments, Declan agreed with the man who had outwitted him. The fineness of the point made it literally immaterial. This was one of the first lessons.

An orderly was making steady progress down the ward, cleaning the floor. She moved silently and efficiently, never lifting her eyes from her work. Her hair was tied back and there were threads of grey through its brown. Declan had noticed her on several occasions in the ward, but couldn't say if it was the woman he'd seen on his first day in the hospital. Some days another woman cleaned the floor, and it had taken Declan some time before he realized that the ward had two cleaners and not one. They looked alike and their movements were identical: they dipped the mop in the bucket, they turned it slightly, they paused a beat, then pressed it down against the spherical wringer before pushing it out in long sweeps behind, with each sweep taking a step back. It seemed that no idiosyncrasy

29

could enter even this most menial and unnoticed chore. Did such a self-erasure make the women happy? Were they fulfilled by their work? Declan presumed that, unable to become nuns, they'd dedicated themselves to helping the order. Each time the women cleaned the floor near his bed he thanked them politely. They never spoke in reply or looked up. The mop's rhythm seemed to be moving the body, not vice versa.

He saw Sister Colette watching the woman with him from two beds down. Oblivious to his own observation, her eyes followed the movements of the orderly. Her face, usually disciplined, betrayed a trace of disgust. If the orderly knew she was being observed by both Sister Colette and Declan she did not manifest the knowledge in any way, but continued her work with the same rhythm. Declan studied the nun's face. No, he was not mistaken: Sister Colette found this orderly in some way abhorrent. He couldn't imagine why and he knew it was pointless to ask. Sister Colette then realized that she herself was the object of study and walked briskly down to the office across the shining glossy band drawn by the orderly's regular strokes. The orderly stopped, lifted the mop out of her way and resumed work once she'd passed. She did not lift her eyes.

§

One afternoon, Declan woke to find his grandmother sitting by his bed. She was studying a missal-sized notebook, which he recognized as the one she kept in her apron pocket at the Two Widows. It was some time before she realized he had woken. Indeed, Declan wondered for a moment if she was there beside him at all. Her grey hair and stout figure neatly enclosed by her Sunday coat stood out against the tall white walls and sheet glass of the ward. Declan could see where the left pocket seam had been carefully repaired and the colour of the heavy wool about the shoulders was a shade lighter than the rest. He wondered how old the coat was and where it had been bought. Before he had a chance to pursue the thought, his grandmother closed the pocketbook and looked up.

'There you are!' she announced to him.

'It's so good of you to come, Mamó. I didn't expect it,' Declan said, smiling.

She nodded in humorous acknowledgement. 'I had some business in the vicinity . . .'

Declan knew she had no business in the vicinity and probably had gone to a good deal of trouble to arrange a lift in a car.

'Now, tell me how you are doing,' she demanded.

'Well enough.'

'Your mother has my heart scalded with letters asking how you are. And why wouldn't you be tip-top, I'd like to know. A fine strapping fellow like yourself.'

Declan smiled again.

'I even received a letter from your father,' she said with droll emphasis.

Declan was surprised. He imagined that news of his illness and hospitalization had not overly bothered James Boyle after it was clear his son was not in danger. Declan could see his father's life in Dublin now from a distance, as though framed by the hospital window. He could see the large house, with its grave, elegant façade, set back from the road behind iron railings congealed with black paint, and the bottle-green postbox to the right, with the letters ER embossed on it – Eduardus Rex – suggesting empires and dominions that had since come under its sway; he could see the trees surrounding the house, the roads that ranged between Dublin Bay and the mountains behind. This was James Boyle's world, and now Declan could see the limits to it. He had a sudden sharp intuition of the magnitude of what he had told his father the previous December.

It had come upon him over the months of September and October: he simply couldn't practise law. He had moved towards the resolution in a kind of bloody-minded confusion, reasons and justifications littered about his feet, but nothing clarified into simple statements before the day that he stood before his father in the living room and made his case.

It was after lunch, last December, when he'd gone to his bedroom to apply himself once more to Buckland on Roman law; the tome lay waiting open on his desk. The tall casement overlooked the back garden. At the end of the lawn stood a chestnut and an ash, custodians whose bare branches failed to cover the sight of thirty new semi-detached houses arranged in a cul-de-sac. The builders had cleared away the trees that had stood there before, and most of the new householders had planted saplings in the small plots which they no doubt called gardens. Although they were nominally neigh-bours, his family knew no one on the cul-de-sac. Most of the new arrivals were a half-generation younger than his parents.

The Boyles' friends in the neighbourhood – the Devlins, the Bagots, the Aylwards – lived, like the Boyles, in spacious Victorian and Edwardian houses. The Bagots' Alsatian, Marco, could now be heard barking forlornly, the only sound in the cold December afternoon. Polly Bagot was his mother's closest friend; they had both attended a finishing school in Dijon, and one of the reasons Catherine Boyle had been enthusiastic about purchasing the house on Mount Merrion Avenue was the proximity to Polly, whose family had lived there for two generations. That friendship had been a gateway for the Boyles, introducing them to many neighbours with similar pedigrees, and accelerating their absorption into the neighbourhood, despite the unusual provenance of James Boyle.

Unable to focus on Buckland, Declan observed the window frame, its sturdily chiselled wood covered with at least five coats of thick gloss paint, one for each decade. It always jammed halfway up. Frustrated by the fact that he couldn't open the window fully on summer days and nights, Declan had, at the age of fifteen or six-teen, tried to smooth one side of the casement, but succeeded only in driving an ugly groove into the frame, still visible though painted over.

He pushed back suddenly from the desk and stood up. The move-ment was so quick and forceful that the chair behind him tilted a moment on its back legs. He closed Buckland and turned his back on the window, making for the door. On the landing, he heard the front door open and close – his mother going out to the garden to check on the flower beds that flanked the short drive, or Mella returning a book or a record to Delia Aylward. At the banisters, he felt a slice of the December cold that had entered the house on the back draught. The fanlight showed a pewter sky and brought diffuse weak light into the hall, making it impossible to discern the pattern in the wood-block floor.

He heard Frances cough in her room. The most bookish of the family, she'd been uncomplainingly bed-ridden for the last week with influenza. It would not have crossed his mind to discuss his decision with her, or with Mella – they were his little sisters, after all, who looked up to him. He didn't want to seem to dither. He wanted to stride at least as purposefully as their father.

It sometimes felt to Declan as though he had lived in the house for his entire life. But the family had come here when he was three, and a vague memory of the chaos and mess of that arrival would revisit him occasionally. Now, for the first time in almost two decades, he had the identical feeling – as though the house were temporary and his family's arrangement of furniture, drapes and ornaments was not the solid world he had grown up in, but rather a fragile arrangement that the faintest breeze could sweep away. Involuntarily, he put his hand on the newel to steady himself. But even that bastion of Edwardian sturdiness felt like a shadow of its former substance.

As he opened the door to the front room, a wave of applause erupted from the wireless beside the armchair in which his father was seated, and eddied about the room. It was the Sunday lecture that James Boyle liked to listen to alone after lunch, broadcast live from the Royal Dublin Society. The presenter announced a commercial break. Having seen Declan in the doorway, his father reached out to turn off the machine, and sat forward slightly in the chair.

'Declan, come in.' Then, 'Take a cup and saucer there and have some tea with me.'

James Boyle smiled at his son when they were both seated and had tea. He still had on the trousers of the suit he'd worn to Mass in the morning, as well as the same stiff shirt and tie, but a brown cardigan had replaced the jacket.

Declan lifted the cup to his lips and sipped the liquid, then returned the cup to the saucer and placed them on the nearby table. He took a long breath. He knew his father would be unhappy with what he was about to report. He'd heard him say that the Civil Service was just a finishing school for the likes of Synge Street. 'The Brothers have knocked the rough edges off them, and now those boys'll get the nuance they need.' Declan had given his father no indication of the turmoil he'd been feeling as his intention had hardened over the past few months.

From the bay window facing the avenue, you could just about imagine yourself to be an aristocrat of a bygone age, though the road outside had become busier in the last few years – now you might see a car every five minutes. Declan had rehearsed his first sentence several times, intending to begin with some brief general remarks about how the country had been changing in the preceding decade, but all that fled from his mind as he found his father's eyes and inhaled.

'I'm afraid I have some bad news.'

His father sat forward, with concern. 'I trust all is well at school . . .'

'Oh, yes. That's all going fine.'

His father subsided slightly in relief, but as another realization came upon him he sat forward. 'And there is no other . . . embarrassment?'

Declan sensed the nature of his concern and stopped his smile in time. 'No, nothing like that.'

'Then what?'

Declan stated his intentions briefly and firmly. He could hear all the usual sounds of the house about them, and from the corner of his eye see the trees in the drive swaying in the wind, as they had always done for as long as he could remember.

'A civil servant? After all your work in the last three years you want to be a civil servant? An *Irish* civil servant to boot. With the pension. Surely you're joking.'

'I'm afraid not, Dad,' Declan answered, worried that his voice would betray his nervousness. He began his explanation, employing phrases such as *public service, economic expansion, the role of the*

34

state, and referring to the good work that his father's friend Niall Falkner was engaged in at the Department of Finance.

'Falkner, is it? He's the one who got you fired up on this? How many other civil servants have you *met*?'

Declan shook his head and shrugged his shoulders lightly.

'Well, you'll get the land of your life if you think they're all like Niall Falkner, with an LSE doctorate in their back pockets. Most of them don't even know what the LSE is. And public service? As you know well, I have served as a TD, and I saw soon enough that you couldn't do a damn thing with the country without the gombeen men and the gob . . .' Boyle stopped himself and took a breath. 'Don't you want to do something a bit more ambitious than push paper around a government office for the rest of your life? Declan, please think about this.'

'I *have* thought about it, and I've made my decision.' Declan tried to put as much conviction in his voice as he could muster. His father's imploring expression changed to one of anger.

'People only go into the Civil Service for the safe job. But you *have* security,' Boyle gestured towards the well-appointed living room. The Jellett painting, which Declan had never liked, was in his line of vision. There was a high-stacked fire in the grate, loud and hot.

'You can do anything with the law, Declan. Once you're up and running as a barrister you can devote all your time to all kinds of idealistic work, as long as you don't mind starving occasionally. Wouldn't that be a better way of going about it?'

For the first time, Declan felt the man's force fully concentrated upon him. He understood now how his father could command a jury to decide one way or another. He knew little of this side of James Boyle, having been raised with indulgence and love, but today they were involved in a man's business. The realization drew something from Declan that he hadn't known was there.

'Look at what this country is like, Dad. And people like you are supposed to care. I want to train in economics, which I'll do after I get into the Department. I'll do a Master's at my own expense . . .'

'Suddenly you'll pay for everything!' The shot was so far below his father's dignity that Declan was pulled up short. His father's face was red and he was breathing quickly. It crossed Declan's mind that he might, in grand Victorian style, be cut out of the will. The preposterousness almost made him laugh. Suddenly he felt free, secure in the knowledge that if his father did indeed do something so archaic, he would not mind.

But his father said nothing. James Boyle got up from his chair and left the room. It was approaching cocktail hour, when Mr and Mrs Boyle sat and drank gin and lime juice alone in the front room, so Declan knew that the conversation would have ended soon in any case. He sat there alone looking out the window, half expecting something to have altered in the view. Instead his eyes met the same trees and driveway as ever, unchanged.

§

He woke to find himself embarrassed. A full moon poured light generously on the floor of the ward and everything was still, but Declan's head was full of hurried movements of flesh and a lingering pleasure in his loins. Clouds sailed swiftly across the face of the moon, changing the illumination, and as the gratification and relief of his dream's climax receded, guilt took their place. For a few minutes he refused to consciously identify the flesh he had joined with, and then powerlessly gave himself over to the contemplation of Sinéad's body, wishing he could enter his dream again, draw her towards himself and feel the answer in her body.

With disappointment he looked around at the other patients, all asleep. Where was she now? She had said she was in Spiddal this summer. In the same county. Not twenty miles from where he lay now in the middle of the night, taut with longing.

After a while he lost consciousness, turning his body fitfully between the sheets, only partly satisfied.

§

During the week following the interview with his father, the Boyles were busy with preparations for their annual Christmas party. When the day arrived, Declan got up and, instead of cycling in to university, stayed at home to help his mother and sisters with the preparations. His first job after breakfast was to go down to Blackrock village to collect the flowers. It was a sunny morning. Mount Merrion Avenue was about a mile long, and perfectly straight. It was also wider than other roads in the area, like the approach to an aristocratic mansion of great proportions. But when you looked up to the top of the road there was no building commensurate with the avenue, just a rather small manor house. Further off the avenue, buffered by old oaks spread out over a few acres, were one or two even bigger houses, like the Blackhalls', which had tall stone pillars on either side of the entrance and a curving drive.

When he came back, he heard his mother's voice from the landing: 'There you are, Declan. What took you?' And then to the Searson's man, 'Can you put that in the living room, please? Inside the door.' And then to Declan again, 'Leave those in the hall, Declan, and come up and help your sisters.'

His mother was outlined for a moment against the high window on the landing and then was gone. She would not come to a halt until the party was over, in the small hours of the next day. Her voice filled the house. Declan put the flowers down on the hall table and went up to find his mother. He found her in his parents' bedroom, moving frantically around in search of something. Mella was standing in the middle of the room holding a box of decorations with a long-suffering expression on her face. She sighed loudly when she saw Declan, who smiled back at her. His mother turned around and saw what had passed between her children.

'Do you see her, Declan? My own little girl, and she's standing there now indulging me. The cheek of her.' Mella smiled falsely. It was an old game between mother and daughter. 'It will be the happiest day of your father's life when you walk up the aisle, you know that, don't you?'

'Yes, Mother.'

'And mine too.'

'I know, Mother.'

'All right, all right, you've heard enough, I can see. You can put that box downstairs, Mella. And Declan, I need you to make sure the candles are done and that the glasses that Searson's brought are all clean.'

His father came home early from work that day, and the first guests arrived just after seven. Mella and Frances had the job of greeting them at the doorway, and the housekeeper's niece, who was helping out for the evening, took the coats and hats. Declan's heart sank a bit at the sight of Edmund Aldiss arriving with his wife, their faces flushed from the cold outside. Aldiss was a literary man who'd gone to school with James Boyle but looked ten years his senior. His face was pale and swollen, tinting to an unhealthy green and red around his eye sockets. The eyes themselves moved quickly around the hall and seemed small in Aldiss's face. He spoke volubly to Declan's sisters, while his wife murmured her greetings and thanks monosyllabically.

'Ah, the student prince!' Aldiss declared as he strode forward to shake Declan's hand, leaving his wife to trail silently after him. 'I hear that *la dolce vita* is now coming to a close and that you'll be pitching your honed legal mind into the Civil Service of our fine republic. What?' Aldiss snorted his amusement at Declan and scanned the guests in the living room over the younger man's shoulder. He released a long whistle.

'Oh, bedad, this is going to be a fine party. I can see that now. The quality's already here.' Aldiss nodded in the direction of two dark-suited figures talking together near the bay window. Declan didn't turn to where Aldiss indicated, but instead looked over the other's shoulder at his wife.

'Mrs Aldiss, how nice to see you again. Can I offer you a drink?' Aldiss's wife uttered a couple of words, but so quietly that Declan couldn't make them out.

'She'll have a cup of tea is what,' said Edmund Aldiss. Mrs Aldiss smiled in agreement.

'And Mr Aldiss, what can I get you?' James Boyle's friendship with this man puzzled Declan. Aldiss scraped out a living writing penny-dreadfuls and hackwork for the *Press*, and this had twisted him gradually but inexorably into the specimen that stood in their front room that evening.

'I'll have a glass of that claret over there. Nineteen forty-seven. Only the best for the Boyles, I can see.'

'We also have whiskey,' Declan remarked, keeping his face as impassive as he could. Aldiss registered the shot, but refused to return it.

'Ah no, Master Boyle. I haven't tried this vintage yet,' he said as he took a glass from a waiter. He emptied half of it at once. 'Hmm. Will you look at Mulcahy and Cosgrave over there. The vanquished heroes. Oh, I'd say they sorely miss their ministerial cars. Didn't they love the glamour of it? The only thing that kept their government together was Fianna Fáil. They hated each other, but they all hated Fianna Fáil even more. And now look who's in the saddle.' Aldiss guffawed and looked around again. 'No Labour people here, I see. Unless they're below stairs. A Fine Gael house through and through. Good man, good man . . .' His voice trailed off as he slapped Declan on the shoulder and waded into the room, making straight for the two former cabinet members. Their bodies perceptibly sagged at his approach, and they drew apart from each other slightly, each wondering who would be left to talk to the new arrival.

Suddenly his mother's voice was in his ear. 'Your father can't extricate himself from Monsignor Byrne. There's Eugene Shortall just arrived with his niece. He's recently been seconded by Barclays to Dublin and his wife is ill. That's her sister's daughter. They're the Grogans, from Foxrock.' Declan looked towards the hall, where he saw a short, stocky man with a ruddy face taking off his mackintosh and hat. Behind him stood his niece: Sinéad Grogan, whose face had floated through his head since they'd met at the Grand Central.

'Mr Shortall, I am Catherine Boyle. You and your niece are very welcome to our home. I'm sorry your wife was taken ill. Please come in. This is my son, Declan. And you, my dear,' she said, turning to the young woman, 'your mother and I have many friends in common. It is a pleasure to make your acquaintance at last.'

He marvelled at his mother. She was able to infuse these phrases of politeness with a warmth of feeling that made the new arrivals look at her more carefully and relax ever so slightly.

'Mrs Boyle, thank you for your warm Dublin welcome,' Shortall said in a smooth English accent. Declan shook hands with Shortall, as his niece was giving instructions to the girl about her umbrella and scarf.

'Sinéad, it's a pleasure to meet you again,' he said, reaching out his hand. His mother turned to him questioningly, and he explained, 'Sinéad and I met through mutual friends last week in the Grand Central.'

To give herself time to assess this information, she said, 'Oh, the Grand Central. That's the new place.'

'I'm surprised you know it, Mother.'

'In any case, come in, come in,' his mother said, 'and meet our friends. Declan, I'm sure Mr Murphy would be very pleased to make the acquaintance of Mr Shortall and Miss Grogan.' Declan guided them across the room to Mr Murphy and made introductions. As the two men worked to find common ground, the younger man and woman took a small step backwards.

'I'm very happy to see you again, Sinéad,' Declan said.

'And I you, Declan.'

'I'd no idea you were coming tonight.'

'It's a pleasure to be here.'

They were throwing ropes across a river, neither reaching the further shore. Where had the fun gone?

'I hear you know Burke in Science and Engineering.' Declan had taken the trouble to find out the name of her boyfriend.

She looked surprised. 'Why, yes. Do you know him?'

'Not in so many words, but his sister knows mine. And I believe we have some friends in common.'

'Why, that's . . .' But Sinéad didn't know what that was. She was looking at Declan, considering, when Liam Creighton appeared at his side.

'Ah, Creighton. Welcome. I'm so glad you could come. You remember Sinéad Grogan of course.'

Liam greeted Sinéad, then took an appraising look around the room. 'So this is how the Brahmins entertain themselves, Boyle. I'm impressed.'

Declan drew himself up, intending to respond with some suitable repartee, but felt oddly inhibited by Sinéad's presence, and said nothing.

'That's Niall Falkner and his wife,' said Liam to Sinéad, pointing across the room. 'He's the youngest Secretary in all the ministries. Causing quite a stir.'

'Which department is he in, Liam?' Sinéad's interest was of the politest kind, but Liam failed to notice, and launched into an expert rendition of the tale of Falkner's rise to glory in the Department of Finance.

Declan glanced across the room at Falkner; his bland exterior suggested nothing of a flashing intelligence. But the fact remained that Falkner had been elevated to Secretary of the Department of Finance before he turned forty, and had got the government behind his plan to modernize the economy. Sinéad Grogan was saying that she should go to her uncle, who'd now been disengaged by Mr Murphy. Declan and Liam shook hands with her and turned to the buffet laid along the dining-room table. They took plates, and Liam sank a large spoon into the jellied salmon salad. Declan loaded his plate with pressed beef and creamed potatoes.

'Can I ask about the rice concoction?' said Liam.

'That is a pilau,' replied Declan. 'I know, Creighton. Far from it we were reared. But it's actually quite good.'

'Well, I'll stick to the salmon,' said Liam, as he lifted a forkful to his mouth. A blob of jelly fell off and lodged itself on his lapel. 'And it seems to be sticking to me.'

'Liam, tell me. What's this Burke fellow like? Do you think he's serious about Sinéad Grogan?'

'I wouldn't know much about it. Funny Face says he's a bit of a fool and that she'll do everything in her power to further your suit.'

'Oh, for Jesus' sake, Creighton. You didn't tell her?'

'Why wouldn't I?'

Indeed, why wouldn't he? On balance, Declan was glad that the information might find its way to Sinéad.

There was also braised goose, a crown roast of lamb, savoury pastries and a lentil loaf. Declan saw that Sinéad and her uncle had ended up in the queue beside Aldiss, and none of the three appeared particularly happy about it. His mother was moving smoothly from guest to guest, keeping a close eye on wine levels and stalled conversations. James Boyle merely positioned himself beside the fire for the evening and let his guests come to him.

'What do you think, Declan?' His mother had glided to his side. 'Mella seems to be absorbed by John Fitzsimons. Do you know him?'

'I'm afraid not. He's older than me and went to Blackrock.'

'Mr Shortall seems pleasant enough.'

Declan looked at his mother, knowing that Mr Shortall was of no interest to her. 'Mr Murphy seemed to enjoy his conversation with him. I even overheard them make plans to meet in the New Year.'

'Well, that's a success then. What about his niece?'

'Creighton overheard a line last week and now calls the likes of Sinéad Grogan "convent girls with *Ulysses* in their handbags". I don't know where he got it from.'

'It seems to me there are not many of the likes of Miss Grogan, Declan. In any case, your father told me to tell you to go over to him. He's talking to Niall Falkner at the moment.' Declan and his father hadn't spoken to each other since their Sunday-afternoon disagreement over Declan's career. What was the purpose of this now?

'Ah, Declan,' his father hailed him. Declan shook hands with Niall Falkner. 'I was just rebuking Niall for leading you astray into the Civil Service.' Falkner was in between the father and son generationally, and he didn't quite know how to go at Declan. Once more, Declan found himself the prisoner of his own polite sentences, and Falkner, unlike Sinéad, did nothing to help him out.

'I hope you'll like the Department,' he said. 'I'm sure the examinations will be no obstacle to James Boyle's son. But tell me, Declan, why aren't you going to pursue the law?'

Declan flashed a look at his father, who was smiling gratefully at Falkner.

'Yes, why is that, Declan?' said James Boyle. 'I've told Niall that I don't agree with it.'

All the fine talk suddenly seemed of little substance. And yet wasn't such a moment as this a decisive one? If he couldn't make himself clear to Niall Falkner, then what was the point?

'Because I think things are changing . . .'

Before he could finish, Falkner interrupted. 'You mean, in the country?' he asked incredulously.

'No, not yet in the country. I mean in the people who will be able to change the country.'

Falkner's stance relaxed a little as he began to catch Declan's drift.

'I feel somewhat embarrassed in saying this in front of you, but since my father wishes to hear it from me . . . If there's no one to explain economics to the politicians, then there's no hope for the country. Someone has got to make them understand, and the people best placed are advisors in the Civil Service. Men such as yourself, well, you have the ear of the minister who signs the documents. That means something.'

'You overestimate our influence, Declan,' Falkner said.

'But who else is there?'

Falkner merely nodded in agreement. There was a silence before James Boyle spoke. 'Are you going to stay there, Niall? Would you not be tempted by a professorship, perhaps in America? Surely that would provide more scope for your powers.'

At that moment a fourth man approached the group – a Mr Maguire, who worked for Aer Lingus – and the question went unanswered. Eventually Falkner and Maguire drifted away. Declan wasn't sure if he had failed or succeeded.

The main dishes and salads had been cleared away, and the waiter was replenishing glasses. Declan saw his mother take Sinéad Grogan by the elbow in order to show her the Jellett painting, most likely telling the complex story of its acquisition. His mother's gestures were flowing and elegant. Sinéad stood to attention, carefully following each of the older woman's movements, her own hands clasped together behind her back. Occasionally she smiled and nodded.

The aged figure of Mr Mulcahy, who had recently resigned as leader of the opposition, was crossing the living room, saying his farewells, scattering good cheer and jokes in his wake. When he eventually reached Declan at the door of the living room, he looked exhausted.

'I'll get your coat, sir.'

Declan escorted Mulcahy to the front door and watched him walk out the gates, his black leather shoes crunching on the gravel. It was cold and windy, drizzle whirling down out of the night. The avenue was quiet. Nearly eleven o'clock. Gusts whipped through the trees, dragging the branches back and forth with violence. Declan savoured the contrast, while thinking over his brief exchange with Falkner.

A young man walked past the gate soundlessly, a knapsack on his back. Declan heard the party he'd left behind, the voices loud and joined together into an undulating roar. He stepped back inside and closed the door. Turning in the hall, he faced Sinéad Grogan as she came down the staircase, her hand lightly brushing the banisters.

'What a beautiful house this is,' she said.

'Thank you. My mother has done a lot with it.'

'You can see her care and taste everywhere.'

The realization came upon him then: Sinéad was beautiful. Why hadn't he seen that when they'd first met in the Grand Central? Perhaps he'd been too intent on keeping up with her, so impressed had he been by the way she seemed to hold all of south Dublin in the palm of her hand, regarding it ironically. And now this: she was inarguably beautiful. What could he do about it?

Primarily, he would have liked to kiss her. The fact bore in upon him with crushing force. That very force propelled his foot forward. It was a force that moved within him, but one that he couldn't recognize as part of himself. She didn't step back, but held her ground, observing him curiously.

'I . . .' Declan didn't know what to say next. What could he do about it? The girl was going out with someone else, and here he was like a fool about to force a kiss on her when she was a guest in their home. He felt loosened from the bonds that had held him in place – surprised, firstly, that he was able to confront the full force of his father for the first time in his life and not falter, and, secondly, that he was even entertaining the idea of kissing this girl standing in his hallway. He looked at her again. She hadn't flinched.

What was she thinking? He tried to read her expression, but found it inscrutable. She was not unhappy to be the object of his attention. She did not find the situation awkward. But neither did she encourage him. Suddenly – or what seemed sudden to Declan, as he concentrated upon her – she raised her hand and smoothed a lock of hair back from her temple, curling it around her ear. She parted her lips as though about to say something, but then didn't. The noise of conversation from the next room seemed to surge even more loudly at the moment when Sinéad forbore to talk. Her lips remained slightly parted. She stood there, not with her hands behind her back, as she had when talking to her mother, but with one by her side and the other resting on her neck.

Then they were both awakened by the sound of a glass being tapped – his father about to make a speech. They smiled at each other, and Declan raised his arm to direct Sinéad back into the front room.

§

Towards the end of August, Dr O'Dwyer seemed happier with Declan's condition. His temperature had returned to normal, and he'd begun taking longer walks in the hospital grounds. On one afternoon he'd decided to walk the mile and a half into the town, but he'd been exhausted and covered in sweat on his return.

'That's fairly normal,' the doctor told him. 'Pneumonia takes a terrible toll on the human constitution. I'd advise that you return to Dublin and postpone beginning your job till the third week in September.'

On the last day in August, Declan slept after lunch, and when he woke he saw a young woman, not a nurse, entering the nurses' station at the top of the ward. From the back she seemed smartly dressed. Sister Imelda came to speak to her, and the two women then went out the door, the nun leading. It was Sinéad. She must have come from Spiddal. But how did she know he was here? There was an ironic tilt to her smile as she caught Declan's eye, whereas Sister Imelda's own expression made it clear that her good opinion of Declan did not stretch to any of his lady visitors.

She led Sinéad down the middle of the ward, past the beds lined up like pews. As they neared him, Sister Imelda asked Sinéad a question which Declan couldn't catch, but he heard Sinéad reply, her body bridling slightly: 'Of course I do.'

Sister Imelda superfluously announced to Declan that he had a visitor, 'a Miss Grogan'. Sinéad stood at the foot of his bed looking at him as the head nurse retreated to the office. She had an amused expression on her face as if to ask, 'What kind of country is this at all?'

2
Confinement

1968

It is not really an exaggeration, Sinéad had read, to say that peace and happiness begin, geographically, where garlic is used in cooking. She'd have to remember the exact wording of the quotation when the moment came to place the casserole on the table that evening in front of the guests.

Greek food, the first time she'd encountered it, had been a shock. They were holidaying on the islands, the year before Owen was born. Like most of their friends they normally took their holidays in Ireland, two weeks or so at the better resorts in Galway or Sligo, but that year they had splashed out for a change. When a plate of dolmades was placed in front of them for the first time, she nearly began unwrapping them with her cutlery; just in time she saw others in the taverna cut them in two and pop whole halves in their mouths. Laughing, she and Declan followed suit. Even a simple salad of feta and tomatoes with olive oil and basil seemed a small revolution. When they returned to Ireland, Declan bought her Elizabeth David's *A Book of Mediterranean Food*. There was the challenge in mastering unfamiliar techniques, and a greater difficulty in purchasing the ingredients necessary for the recipes. The only place in her neighbourhood where she could buy olive oil was the pharmacy, where it was sold as a moisturizer. It was the same colour as the 3-In-One oil in Declan's tool kit and had a similar aroma.

Eventually she found Alfieri's, off Camden Street in town. It was a bit of a trek from Dundrum in the car, but she made it regularly to stock up on Mediterranean specialities, and worked her way through Elizabeth David. Five years on, the pages were stained with oil and the binding was beginning to give up. Guests would compliment her on the exciting dishes that she carried steaming from the kitchen, with their strange flavours and aromas, but some of the recipes were simply too peculiar, and the expertise that Sinéad was gaining seemed somehow unfeminine, an accomplishment not unlike carpentry, an activity that one expected other people, on lower levels, to carry out for one – or, at a push, one's husband on a Saturday afternoon for his amusement.

Declan had bought the Wolseley Hornet for himself so that he could avoid the bus, but it soon became clear that Sinéad had greater need for it, what with ferrying Owen around Dundrum and the shopping to be done. It had also become clear that Sinéad was a natural driver, much better than Declan, and they didn't quite know how to deal with this fact. Mastery of a car seemed such a masculine attribute. At this stage, she obviously got more practice driving the Hornet, but that was not it. The car responded to her in a way that it did not respond to him. Once, when she was dropping Mrs Boyle home after one of her occasional midweek visits, her mother-in-law commented on the ease with which Sinéad negotiated the road up past Roebuck School, around the park and down the long length of Mount Merrion Avenue. As always with Mrs Boyle, Sinéad found it difficult to tell whether she was being complimented or diplomatically ticked off.

Like few other grocers, Alfieri's was open on Saturday mornings, and so Sinéad was able to buy ingredients there before dropping into the off-licence on her way home. With four guests that evening, she wasn't shopping in large quantities. She needed the Chianti that Searson's didn't stock, Italian cured ham, more olive oil, and perhaps some cheeses to finish off the meal. She parked the car in front of the shop, so that Mr Alfieri didn't have far to bring the groceries when she was finished. Seven months pregnant, she was in no state to carry them herself.

The day was truly beautiful, and the forecast was good for this evening: they could open the French doors to the back garden. She manoeuvred herself with difficulty into the driver's seat. Driving up Camden Street, she considered the logistics of the dinner. Declan would help out, and she called him her *sous-chef*; they had even bought an apron for Owen, and she jokingly referred to him as her *chef de partie*.

There were a few bookies with the paint peeling off their wooden shingles, a launderette that had recently squeezed in to service the flat-dwellers, an ironmonger's whose brawny owner lounged in the doorway, on the corner of Harrington Street a TD's clinic, and of course lots of pubs. The Bleeding Horse. O'Donoghue's. Cassidy's. Ryan's. Jack the Nailer's.

The arms of the housewives on the footpaths were made rigid by the shopping bags hooked on their hands, their perms protected from the wind by tightly knotted headscarves. Their expressions were stern, as though prepared for the worst.

A pawnshop. A Bovril sign painted on the first-floor gable of a building. A garage with leaping, life-sized jaguars in aluminium, and outside it a milk cart full of empty bottles, its two shafts leaning on the ground, the horse probably grazing on the patch of grass near the dairy. She knew there were workshops around here that serviced the rag trade on South William Street. What must it be like for the women working in those places, the long hours and the conditions? At least those women had one another, a kind of company.

There was the cinema, the Theatre de Luxe, which didn't look too luxurious. The poster outside was for *Valley of the Dolls*. She might be able to persuade Declan to go. Further up the street was Goravan's department store, the railings pulled across the entrance. There was Albert Lindy, Jeweller, where Declan and she had nearly bought her wedding ring. How gentle Mr Lindy was, how delicately he took her hand to slide a ring onto her finger; but none was quite right, and Sinéad was sorry to disappoint him. Here and there on the footpaths were women selling fruit and vegetables from carts. Unlike the department stores, they were open for business on Saturday, and probably Sunday too, though Sinéad never had any reason to come down Camden Street on Sunday.

Sunlight filled the car, glinting off the borders of the wood on the dashboard, as she guided the Hornet over Portobello Bridge. In Searson's she handed Mr Maunsten, the manager, the names of the wines that Declan had drawn up at home. Mr Maunsten nodded seriously, acknowledging the judicious choices of the other, absent man, her husband, before slotting the bottles into a cardboard box. 'There you are, Mrs B.' She would not have Mr Maunsten's approval, and possibly not even his service (the job would have been delegated to one of the younger sales assistants), if he hadn't known Declan, and his father before him.

She didn't linger in Searson's, breezing out as Mr Maunsten instructed her to pass on his regards to her husband (she was always careful not to). A young lad carried the box to the car, and she was happy to be in the sunlight again, driving along the Lower Rathmines Road, past Lee's department store, past Slattery's. The shopping was done, and for now there was just the rhythm of clutch, gear change and accelerator.

A lot of the girls who came up from the country to work as secretaries, nurses and shop assistants lived in flats in this area. In twos and threes they rented small rooms in the redbrick terraces. Sinéad had never met any of the secretaries from the Department, only talking briefly with them on the phone from time to time. But they exerted a fascination, these women her husband encountered every day at work.

Waiting for Declan once in the Horseshoe Bar of the Shelbourne, she'd overheard a conversation between one of these girls and her older sweetheart. He called her 'amigo', and she, more tenderly, called him Dermot, or Cormac, or John. He promised her things, and the girl was excited at the prospect. He complained of his wife, and she consoled him. Would she like another Bacardi? She would. Would she like to go with him for a weekend to Paris? She might. Did she understand his achievements at work? She certainly did. Sinéad could hear her making soft noises of praise, smoothing his plumage.

She daren't turn around to see their faces, half afraid she'd recognize the man – one of her father's younger friends, perhaps, or a neighbour from Foxrock. There was no fear of recognizing the woman: all these fast little pieces were only five minutes off the train, these Bridgets and Kathleens. They had no family in Dublin, no fathers, uncles, Mothers Superior or teachers to keep a watchful eye on their antics. When she saw them on the street she noticed how they had a bit more on show than she did, how their colours didn't quite go together, how they always chose the wrong scarf, how there was often a run in their tights, how they laughed as if they were having so much fun. But when they looked at her, there was resentment and dismissal in their eyes. They resented her because she had her markets made – it was clear, even if you couldn't see her ring finger, that she was a married woman – and thus had done what they hoped to do in the city: find a man who'd look after them, a cut above the oafs they knew in the townlands. And at the same time they dismissed her, because they didn't want that just yet, didn't want to be embalmed in respectability too soon, especially not when they were having such a good time in Dublin. Her fun was clearly over, but theirs was just beginning.

§

It was not until the awful early fog of new motherhood had dispersed that Sinéad started to understand that something was wrong. She longed for company during the slow suburban days, preferably that of another woman who had also had a child and had some idea of the feelings coursing through her body. She ached to pour out her thoughts and have somebody receive them and help her make sense of them.

The bubbling water in the central heating, the call of birds outside and a very occasional car or delivery van moving through the estate: this was what passed for silence in suburbia. These were the sounds that came forth when there was no one else there to divert your attention.

Busy with Owen, bending over to change his nappy or to clean his face, she was distracted from the roaring silence. There must have been other women like her in similar houses all across the estate, but she knew none of them and couldn't very well walk up to their door and invite herself in for consolation. The minute Owen went to sleep and she sat down in the armchair with a cup of tea and some biscuits, the silence enveloped her again, as though it'd been waiting there all that time to claim her again for its own.

Once she'd tried to explain this to her cousin in Spiddal who'd also recently become a mother, but she'd stopped halfway as the incomprehension spread across the girl's face. Her cousin mentioned the aunts, sisters and neighbours who'd been able to help out and look after her child for an hour here or two hours there, and she actually went so far as to complain she never had a moment for herself to sit down in an armchair, drink a cup of tea and simply just think quietly. It was as though the builders, in constructing the new estate, had created a new type of loneliness that her cousin knew nothing of, and which was Sinéad's to taste for the first time.

When Owen started going to playschool she had even more time on her hands, and her growing desperation bred wilder and wilder ideas. She serially dismissed them all, until she came upon one that gave her pause: what if she could help some local businesses in Dundrum with their accounts? As she'd told Declan the day they first met, she'd spent three summers helping with the books at her father's fruit and veg wholesale business.

Walking past Uncle Tom's Cabin, the local pub, she would imagine what it would be like to work there, coming in, say, once a week to administer pay day and tot up the deductions. Perhaps they would let her use a back room, a table, a slim box of carbon paper, a comptometer like the one she'd once used at Grogan's Mart and Market. She'd never met the publican: would he be red-cheeked and rotund, happy to employ a little local wifey for half the price of a regular accountant? Or pale and nervous, constantly looking over her shoulder to check her arithmetic? The loud barmen would come in and out, respectful but bantering. There would be a cleaning lady whose docket she'd also have to prepare. There would be activity, and at the centre of that activity, keeping it all ticking over, she would be sitting, happy.

Declan would be puzzled. He would ask her why she'd want to do something like that. They didn't have a huge amount of money, but there was enough, and in any case wasn't her place at home looking after Owen? As she ran and reran the conversation in her

54

head, her reply would be that it was merely a diversion for her, a bit of challenge to break the monotony. What monotony? he'd ask. The monotony of being stuck in this suburban silence all day long. But a woman, working in a pub? A woman couldn't go into a pub on her own. But she wouldn't be *in* the pub, as a customer. She'd be in some back room, doing the books.

Eventually Sinéad decided that it would be best not to discuss it with Declan until there was proof that the whole thing wasn't just some hare-brained scheme. She chose a quiet day – a Monday – and walked into the pub's dark cave, with its reassuring smell of old tobacco and old beer. The barman was sitting at the bar, reading the newspapers and smoking a cigarette. When he turned around and saw her, he first smiled and then checked the smile, as he realized, before she said anything, that she wasn't that type and she wasn't going to have a drink. He was in his early twenties and wore a tight black waistcoat over his poorly bleached white shirt.

'Can I help you, ma'am?' he lazily enquired, having lost interest in her already as a prospective source of scandal or fun.

It was somehow wrong. This wasn't the sort of man she'd imagined coming to knock on the back-room door, joking respectfully with her. There was a slow insolence in the boy's delivery that was surprising. She bristled in response, and in delivering her next question she heard – blasted hell – her mother's tones creeping into her voice.

'Could I speak to the proprietor?' She hated the sound of her voice, because it wasn't hers any longer.

'Not here today, ma'am,' he said, already hefting himself back on the bar stool and turning his head down to the sports page open on the counter.

Sinéad stood there for a second or two, considering her options. Would she insist that this pup tell her the owner's name and when he would be available to consider the applicant of a lady-housewife accountant?

Who was she fooling? She walked out the door and never went back.

In the days that followed, depression settled on her as it had never before. She was nobody, a nonentity, a blank that depended on a husband for colour, shape and status. She didn't want a career; Declan's work, and Owen, would always come first. She simply wanted to do something.

Her next plan grew gradually. She knew her father's business was expanding. Her father and his bookkeeper, Mrs Dolores English, a widow from Dolphin's Barn, considered her capable. She wouldn't be asking for a full-time position, only to work one day a week, on Fridays perhaps, to help with the pay cheques. He wouldn't be able to refuse his own daughter, and Declan would be happy to have a bit of extra money coming in. It wouldn't be as if Malachy Grogan were employing a married woman full time; she'd just be helping out. After a while, Mrs English might let her take on more.

The following Monday, she arranged things so that she would drive into town with Declan; Owen had gone to his 'Merrion granny', as he referred to her, on Friday and would be returning that evening. They sped along Dundrum Road, leaving Glenshane Estate behind as the Hornet conducted them into the noisy, smoke-filled centre of the city.

She dropped Declan at the quays, where the buses reached their terminus, and drove over O'Connell Bridge and then left towards Smithfield. When she reached the office, she found Mrs English wasn't there – bringing one of her children to the doctor, her father told her, after he'd come out of his office.

'You're a sight for sore eyes. In your fine get-up.' He stood back to look at her clothes and nodded in approval. She glowed in his gaze.

'I'm here with a business proposition, Daddy.'

'Well, doesn't that beat all! Is it more back-pay you're coming for? I've spent it all, I tell you. Come on in and sit down. I'll brew us up a cup of tea, if I can find out where Mrs English keeps the sugar and milk.'

'In the press over there to the left.'

'You remember everything! We've missed you round here, I'll tell you that.'

She couldn't have engineered a better lead-in. So when he handed her the tea, she began explaining her idea to him. As the outlines of the plan came into focus, his expression changed from happy indul-gence to troubled consideration. But she ploughed on, convinced that once he got over the strangeness of the idea, he'd see its sense. When she paused, he looked up from his desk at her.

'But, Nadie, you're a married woman . . .' He was the only per-son who called her by this nickname and it made her feel like a little girl once more.

'But that's just it, Daddy, I wouldn't be a full-time employee, I'd just be helping out. You said yourself you've missed having me round here . . .'

'And so I have!' he protested hotly.

'And you know I can do the work. It's not only the sugar and milk I remember . . .'

'But, Nadie, why on earth would you want to, with Owen to look after and a dinner to cook for Declan?'

'But of course I'd do all that too . . .'

'And wouldn't that be enough for you? Enough for any woman? Look at poor Mrs English, coming in here every day when she'd much prefer to be at home with the nippers. Isn't it the dream of every woman to have a husband as fine as yours, and a grand little lad to boot? And won't there be more on the way? Just look at your sister . . .'

'But I can do the job, I really can.' Her voice was no longer steady. Her father was up off his chair and round to her, taking her shoul-ders in his hands. That broke her, and she cried.

He stroked her hair, repeating over and over again, 'Ah, love, it'll be all right.'

§

Then she was pregnant again. She realized this on a cold, depressing December day. Just home from dropping Owen off at Mrs Dixie's, she'd run quickly upstairs to the bathroom. While sitting on the toilet she looked at the facing shelves, where she saw a soft purple cylinder of cotton wool, like a Swiss roll packed tightly, a bottle of Parstelin, and the small cloth towels, folded and ready. This week, she thought to herself. No, wait. Her mind went back through November and she realized that she'd miscounted. It should have been last week. With a growing dread, she realized that it should have been as long as ten days ago. No, it couldn't be. But it was. She got up, flushed the toilet and looked at herself in the mirror. She removed her top and reached her hands behind her back to unclasp her bra. Was it getting tighter already? Released, her breasts seemed unwieldy. She smoothed out the dark skirt that hid her lower half so well while making it compact and attractive. She put her top back on and went down the stairs to the kitchen, feeling with each step the flop of her free breasts, and hating them for it.

On the wall she looked at the picture of Declan and herself, cut from the *Irish Press*, taken six years ago as they were going to a dinner dance. They'd been uncertain whether it was a good idea to frame it in the first place, and then they'd been uncertain about where to hang it. They were not vain enough to put it in the living room, but neither were they modest enough not to display it, and so it was here in the kitchen. Minor celebrity status had descended upon them in the weeks after the photograph was published. Their smiling, youthful confidence caught something of the mood among their set in Dublin. Declan held Sinéad by the elbow, guiding her up the steps of the Gresham Hotel as she held the train of her ballgown so as not to trip on it. The flashbulb dazzled her eyes and she caught only the briefest glimpse of the shabby suit of the middle-aged photographer.

Some days she was proud of the photograph, but increasingly it oppressed her: the elegance of her dress and the sculpted shape of her hair seemed to mock the mess that she was now, standing in her own kitchen, all set up – a good husband, a beautiful boy, a nice house in a nice area and nothing in the world to do. Declan, on the other hand, was the same in the photograph as he was on each and every day: modest yet determined, intelligent playfulness in his eyes, his dress suit only a slight modulation away from the suit he wore into work. It was unfair, but she couldn't say how. Where would one point the finger? Wasn't she being childish in any case for wanting to point the finger? There was no reason on earth for her not to be as happy as that woman in the photograph, and if she wasn't, there was no one to blame but herself.

Outside the kitchen window, the scraggly forms of the rose bushes and the patchy lawn ragged with weeds mocked her. The clothesline stretched down the back wall, shirts and underclothes swaying slightly in the breeze. The innocence and intimacy of them. Declan's body came before her eyes and once again she was unable to connect their loving with the rest of their lives. They seemed like different people during those moments in the dark of their bed, always at night, always in silence.

She placed her hand on her abdomen and left it there for a minute. The silence, waiting here for her when she returned home, closed around again. A few doors away, a car pulled out of a drive. The second hand on the clock moved and seemed to take much longer than usual to move again.

When she went to collect Owen from Mrs Dixie's, she took a peek through the living-room window before ringing the bell. Her son was standing apart from the other children, laying out building blocks in a large pattern on the floor. His absorption was complete as he adjusted and readjusted the various parts of the abstract design. Another child asked him a question, and he looked up as though surprised to be there. At that moment, he caught sight of Sinéad in the window and his features brightened. She felt a strong movement in her chest, as though there was a conduit from her solar plexus to his, now charged with current. He came over to the window, tapping on the glass gently to see if she would do the same. Rather than answer his tap, she mimicked a spider darting up from the frame to attack his hand, and he, with a delighted shock, snapped his hand back as though he'd received a tiny bite.

All the way home, Owen chatted away. But as Sinéad pulled the car into the drive, she could no longer be sure that she'd be able to maintain the jaunty tone that he required of her. She was balancing precariously, and it would take little to push her over. Fits of crying engulfed her for no reason, mostly when she was alone. It was like being possessed: a force took hold of her guts and seemed to shake her. The sobbing could last for as long as half an hour, and she was exhausted afterwards.

Owen crawled into the front seat of the car across the gearstick and handbrake.

She discovered that she was crying when he asked her why.

He took her head in both of his hands and moved it gently from side to side, telling her not to worry. She'd had a bad dream, he said.

§

Now, on this sunny Saturday, her mood lighter than it had been in some time and the Hornet full of food and wine, she pulled up to the kerb two or three turns away from their own road in Glenshane Estate. It was about 11.30, and the houses on this road were identical to her own. A bit further down, some boys were playing football; two or three girls were talking together near a wall, huddled around a small object they held between them.

Sinéad reached over to the glove compartment and took out a pair of scissors. She got out of the car and walked across the road to a garden wall. There was no one to be seen moving in the windows of the house. A large bush hung over the wall; it obviously pre-dated the house, and by some fluke the builders had not destroyed it.

It was rosemary, and Sinéad loved its pungent fragrance. It seemed to penetrate further than any other herb – more than sage, more than mint. All she needed was a fair-sized sprig, which would leave no marks whatsoever on a sturdy bush like this. She was uneasy about what she was about to do, but it would be ridiculous to go up to the front door and ask for some rosemary; the people probably didn't even know that they had such a herb in their front garden. If caught, she'd have been embarrassed. But she couldn't do without its flavour in the dish for the evening. She took out her scissors and snipped a sprig, turned on her heel and walked briskly back to the car.

When she turned into her drive, she saw Declan and Owen in the front garden, raking leaves.

'Will you look at all the work this little man has done?' Declan said.

'Oh,' Owen said, and drew the back of his hand across his brow in imitation of something he'd seen his father do. 'I am . . . exhausted.' He barely knew what the phrase meant, but he knew the right time to use it.

Declan spent Saturdays with Owen, doing men's things such as visiting the ironmonger's. Today the boy was wearing the bright red gansey he favoured when doing messy, mannish jobs. He looked back at his father for confirmation of the good work he'd done, and Declan rubbed the top of his head encouragingly. Only then did he run towards his mother and throw his arms about her legs, burying his face in her lap. Her mood had lost some of the buoyancy she'd enjoyed in the car, but then she also felt a shift in her chest as she opened herself to the need of this small being, clinging to her, still not ready for full membership in the world of men.

She hunkered down and took his face in her hands: 'Aren't you the great man, helping your father like that?' The boy nodded, avoiding her eye.

'Do you both want to come in and I'll make you a sandwich? What about cheese and English mustard? That'll tickle your nose. You must be starving. Here, Owen, can you take this piece of rosemary carefully into the kitchen so that none of its leaves fall off? There's a good boy!'

'It smells nice.'

'It does, doesn't it? I got it from an old man, who might or might not have been a wizard, and he said that if I put it in our food, we'll be able to remember everything. "Rosemary for remembrance" is what he whispered in my ear.'

§

In the time when they first came together, Declan's face seemed to be everywhere. After each of their rendezvous his voice would linger in her head for a day, sometimes two, before they met again. Then came the surprise of his actual voice, its timbres and its turns slightly different from what she'd imagined, and this deepened her delight and drew her further into the labyrinth of his ideas and his feelings. Her old life was disappearing at a breathtaking speed. The scuffs on the skirting boards, the dowdiness of the curtains, the smallness of her father's achievement in business compared to the visions that Declan had conveyed to her, the diminishment of her mother's control over her: all of this became more apparent.

The first thing she'd noticed about him when they met at the Grand Central was his hands, slightly larger than those of other men, the veins making their way across the bony ridges from his wrists to his fingers. They had strength in them (which she later found out came from farm work each summer in Ardnabrayba), and he drew them up and moved them in precise emphasis of a point. Here and there the cuticles were a little raw, but the nails were smooth and healthy.

When they were courting, Sinéad would often cycle from Foxrock down the leafy roads through Stillorgan, past Oatlands, and swerve the bike widely around the turn for Mount Merrion Avenue. There were few cars on the road then, and she sometimes free-wheeled down its centre, as though aiming for the patch of Dublin Bay at the vanishing point in front of her. There was a beautiful sense of the whole still world turning fluid with the speed. It was hard to stop at Declan's house halfway down on the left, because the avenue took another tempting dip just after, before flattening out for the final run to the sea. Once or twice, she miscalculated the angle and came dangerously close to the granite pillar of the Boyles' gate, the bike nearly going from under her. That was fun, although Mrs Boyle didn't seem to view the matter in that light on the occasion when she was coming out the front door to meet Sinéad skidding to a giddy stop on the gravel of their drive, flushed and smiling.

It had been a slow start with Declan. She'd taken the initiative, after she'd broken up with James Creed Burke. A letter had arrived from Freddy in which among other things she mentioned that Liam's friend, Declan, who she might happen to remember, was in the county hospital not too far from Spiddal. Getting permission for the trip from her aunt had involved only the whitest of lies, changing Declan to 'Deirdre' Boyle, an old school chum from Roebuck hospitalized with a respiratory infection, and deserving of the fifteen-mile bicycle ride. And so when she arrived at the Boyles' Christmas party for the second time, at the end of that year, she was not accompanied by her uncle, but stood before Mrs Boyle at the front door in a different role. Her future mother-in-law expressed her customary warmth and gave no indication that she was sizing Sinéad up.

Sinéad still had a year and a half to go at university, and she'd arranged to spend the spring term in Bordeaux, staying with a respectable family, to study French intensively. This was a frustrating hiatus, just at the time she and Declan were getting going. In her letters she regaled him with stories of misunderstandings and new revelations, and received in return witty accounts of his beginnings in the Department of Finance. He had a gift for caricature, and the target most often to hand was his immediate superior, Mr Jarlath Leonard. Such passages often gave way to more serious considerations of economics and the state of the country. Even in the first flush of love, Sinéad struggled to focus on those paragraphs. But every day, her mind moved with him: down Mount Merrion Avenue to Blackrock Station, along the bay, past Booterstown, Sandymount, Sydney Parade, and arriving at Pearse Station, where he disembarked and walked up to the Department offices.

After she returned to Ireland, he brought her occasionally to a better restaurant, and this seemed suddenly adult and unstudent-like. The deference of the waiters, the older clientele, the expense of the dishes and wine, intimidated her slightly, as though she had encroached on her mother's territory.

A few months from her finals they were sitting in Jammet's, the finest of all Dublin restaurants. She whispered to him for the first fifteen minutes, afraid that some gaucherie would spill from her mouth and disturb the propriety of the place. Declan was amused, and whispered with her. When their waiter arrived, she sat up straight in her chair and put on her convent-girl smile. But the man, in his forties, was not in the least forbidding and joined in their conspiracy, suggesting in an undertone that they avoid the fish on that particular day.

This, along with the first glass of wine she gulped, helped considerably, and she found herself listening to Declan with indignant outrage as he told her of his frustrations in the Department. In the debating society at UCD, he said somewhat bitterly, they'd thought that if they showed the merest interest they would be handed the gears of change. But he'd yet to catch even a glimpse of those gears; they were hidden somewhere in the distance behind the regulations, procedures and professional deference to mediocrities like Mr Jarlath Leonard.

Sinéad saw the matter clearly: this man whom she loved for his intelligence, his wit and his occasional reckless idealism was being stifled by people too benighted to acknowledge him. They were all afraid of his energy. As far as she was concerned, she said, their only job was to get out of his way.

He was about to speak, but then he noticed the shift in her attention.

'What?' he asked, smiling.

She laughed. 'Nothing, nothing. It just struck me as strange that we should be talking about all this during a romantic candlelit dinner at Jammet's.'

'It's not exactly appropriate, is it?'

'No, I think you're wrong. It's actually completely appropriate. I've never been able to work out what proper romantic talk was anyway. After all, what can you say about moonlight and roses except they're very nice? What are you left to talk about then if not Mr Jarlath Leonard?'

Declan laughed out loud, happy, as Sinéad could see, to be led out of his labyrinth into the sunlight to play. They paused for a moment.

'Would you like to talk with me about this kind of thing for the next few decades or so?' He had taken a small, hard, dark velvet box out of his pocket and laid it on the table, obviously having forgotten to open it, so intently was he looking at her. Sinéad noticed that the table of four next to them had stopped talking and were trying and failing not to stare at them. She felt as though she were on her bike going down the middle of Mount Merrion Avenue, the cold wind burning her cheeks and making tears well under her eyelids. She returned his gaze, and it was as if her speed had suddenly increased tenfold. She reached her hand across the table to his, which still held the small box. She wanted to say something funny, but all she could say was yes.

After Jammet's they walked the quiet length of Grafton Street up to the Green, arm in arm, stopping to look into the shop windows of Switzer's and Brown Thomas. She loved the city at this time of night, and would often walk her bike the distance between here and Donnybrook to experience it all the more intensely. Her mother questioned the propriety of a respectable young woman out alone in the night, but no one ever accosted her.

Her happiness was huge, and not because she now had her markets made, not because of the ring that he'd placed on her finger less than an hour ago. She was too interested in Declan to bother thinking about what it would be like to be a housewife and perhaps a mother. That was the kind of thing that her mother thought about, first and foremost, and it would have felt to Sinéad like a betrayal of Declan to deliberate upon the consequences of her love for him in such a way. The city was theirs to walk through together, and it seemed that it would always be thus. The heaviest and most awkward objects could be lifted up and spun through the air.

'So what do we do next?' Sinéad asked playfully.

'I didn't really think of that,' Declan said, surprised. 'I spend all my days planning matters of state, and I couldn't think beyond the ring and getting the right table in Jammet's. What do people usually do?'

Sinéad didn't smile, but put on a serious face and said, 'As senior consultant to the Jerquers Office at the Department of Finance, I must instruct you to purchase a house with adjacent lawns, in a salubrious part of Dublin city; arrange for the delivery of three to four children; and generally set your affairs and assets in order to the satisfaction of your future wife, Mrs Declan Boyle.'

He brought them to a halt at the corner of Stephen's Green, drew her close to him and kissed her. She struggled to get away, protesting, 'As senior consultant to the Jerquers Office, I must protest at your handling of . . .' And then she gave in, because, ultimately, it was more fun that way.

They began walking again, and Declan said, 'Well, I admit I did think of it a little.'

Sensing his drift towards seriousness, Sinéad folded her arm around his more tightly, bringing herself flush against his chest, enjoying the proximity of his body.

'I don't think I have enough money yet to buy a house,' he said.

'Oh, thank God for that.'

'Why?'

'We've spent all our lives in houses. Let's have fun in a flat for a while instead.'

'Really? Do you mean that? I thought you might be disappointed.'

'What a load of old dope,' Sinéad said. She'd heard the phrase a few weeks ago, and she'd been charmed by its spirit of carefree dismissal.

'Well, we'll have to get a house sometime, but even in three or four years we wouldn't have enough to buy something in Foxrock . . .'

'Well, thank God for that again. Were you planning to make a respectable south Dublin matron of me so soon? You might as well shove me straight into Deansgrange Cemetery now, if you think that's what I want. I couldn't care less about all that codswallop.'

'I was thinking about Churchtown or Dundrum – somewhere around there.'

'Oh, Mother would *hate* Dundrum,' Sinéad said gleefully.

'What's your mother got to do with it?'

'You're right. My mother has absolutely nothing to do with it.'

'You know also that we'll probably never be able to afford a house as big as ours on Mount Merrion Avenue? Even if all goes well in the Department. You won't mind that?'

'Mind that? How could you even ask? I know what your work means to you, and I want to support you in every way I can. That's what will make me happy. I couldn't give an iota for a big house and a big car. Just because I went to Roebuck doesn't mean that I'm mad for money. It'll be like a big adventure. Imagine, they probably haven't even built the house yet that we'll live in. There's probably just trees and old bushes there, and a bit of old mud.' She was almost out of breath and saw from Declan's face that she had hit home with this, that he liked the idea of the house yet to be built, the experiment in the offing, drawing them into the future.

'You say things I couldn't have imagined and always wanted to hear,' he said.

They walked in silence for a few minutes past Loreto College and onto Leeson Street, then south-eastwards out of the city, through the mild night.

§

After lunch, Declan and Owen went back out to the garden, full of big talk of all the things they had to do. Sinéad cleared the dishes away and washed up. The plan was to pop down to the school hall in Dundrum village to say hello to her sister Fiona, who was taking part in a flower show. That would take only half an hour, leaving her plenty of time to prepare the dinner.

She parked near the village. The aromas of the world came towards her when she opened the door, a little more sharply, a little better defined than even five minutes before, when she had pulled away from her own kerb. There was the smell of rotting wood, emphasized by the light shower of rain earlier in the morning, mixed in, she supposed, with the smell of the leaves. Someone had cut the grass. The exhaust from the car also seemed to linger for a while longer than usual. She liked the fragrance of the leather seating inside it so much, but now as she stood on the path the prospect of getting back into it twenty minutes later was slightly nauseating.

The fragrance that billowed towards her from every corner of the flower-filled hall was shocking. Women were here and there attending like bees to particular blossoms. They talked to each other peripherally, nodding in agreement or low laughter, without removing their eyes from their work. Their summer dresses rippled across their legs, the fabric stretched tighter around their breasts and the gradual spread of their hips. Her sister, whom she could see now in the second row, partly obscured by an explosion of lilies and palm leaves, had also taken on substance. Although younger than Sinéad, Fiona had married three years before her, and was now pregnant with what she called 'my fourth and final'.

The lady ministering to the outsized lilies and palm leaves smiled tartly at the sisters, and Fiona exhaled forcefully. The woman then made for another part of the hall, with scissors in one hand and cropped stems in the other.

'The competition,' said Fiona.

'I hope she's not a sore loser,' said Sinéad. 'I wouldn't like a tussle with her.'

Fiona laughed. 'Oh, I'll be grand.'

'Well, my money's on you!' Sinéad said.

'Can you stay for the announcement?'

'I'm afraid I have to go back and make the dinner. We have people coming around this evening. Will you telephone me and let me know?'

Her sister equably said she would. Then, after a while, she remarked, 'Mother says you haven't been to see her in a long time.'

'Really? Did you go to Knocksinna this week?' Sinéad asked.

'Like every other week,' Fiona answered, reproach in her tone.

In a world without their mother, Sinéad and Fiona would have been uncomplicatedly close friends. Belinda Grogan often treated Fiona like a dolt, but what rankled with Sinéad was Fiona's inextinguishable desire to please their mother, and her seeming belief that their lives were not valid except by reference to her.

Fiona now bent down to pick up the cut stems and stray petals that had landed on the damp floor. She gathered them neatly together and placed them in a spare brown paper bag, taking care to roll the mouth closed and pack it like a thick baton. She then held this in one hand, not wanting to leave Sinéad to put it in the rubbish and not wanting to put it on the floor, lest it be considered slovenly.

They stood in the middle of the school hall in silence for a while. Other ladies were still arriving, their arms full of blooms and greenery, a child occasionally trailing behind carrying other paraphernalia of their suburban art. There were loud greetings. Perms and earrings were patted into place. Funniest of all were the two husbands standing apart, waiting for their wives to give them something, or relieve them of something, or merely instruct them to leave – at a loss, shifting from foot to foot, trying to look at ease but knowing that they stood in one of the few spaces in which they had no power whatsoever over their wives.

'Dymphna's getting married and she wants to have the breakfast at the Royal Marine like you,' Fiona said. 'They're buying a house in Sutton.'

'That's lovely.'

Fiona smiled and agreed that it was. Then she lifted her eyes from the flowers and looked at her sister. 'But it wasn't so lovely that she had to pop over to London for you-know-what in December.'

'You're joking.'

'Nope! Deadly serious.'

'Dymphna? You'd think butter wouldn't melt in her mouth.'

Fiona laughed. 'Well, Bernard must have melted it for her, then.'

Sinéad instinctively rubbed her hand over her abdomen. Fiona registered the movement, but continued: 'She went to Dr Goodbody on Fitzwilliam Square. Dymphna says he's better, much more sensitive . . . well, to women.'

Sinéad flushed. In their final year at Roebuck School, they'd been addressed by a priest on the subject of 'women's matters'. For the most part, he'd explained that their duty was to become loving wives and loving mothers ('To fifty little bishops,' Freddy had whispered in her ear). When he concluded with dire warnings about the 'boat to England', most of the girls didn't know what he meant. Was it because England was Protestant? Again, Freddy provided a gloss: 'Because in Dublin they stick a coat-hanger up your fanny, but in England they do the job properly.' Sinéad blushed to the roots of her hair, but couldn't suppress a giggle.

'Dr Goodbody arranges little trips to London for wives who don't want to go through with it.' Fiona paused and looked around the hall. 'She had to get a certificate from the psychiatrist, in London of course, to say her mental health was endangered. She'd that by lunchtime, and was finished in the clinic by four o'clock in the afternoon. She was back in Dublin the next day, with some fancy shopping bags under her arm and a loving smile for her husband, "honeymoon fresh", as they say.'

Fiona put the finishing touch to her arrangement, sighed and smoothed her hands over her hips.

'There we are now. What do you think?' she said.

'It's beautiful.'

'It is, isn't it? Better than her ladyship's . . .' Fiona threw her eyes over her shoulder, gesturing to the lilies and palm leaves behind them.

Now Sinéad laughed. 'Yes, it's better than her ladyship's.'

'Two months left then,' Fiona said, nodding at Sinéad's belly.

'Yes,' she sighed.

'And you're going to stay in Dundrum?'

Their parents had visited that Easter, and Belinda Grogan had said how wonderful it was that they were able to fit everything into such a small space, how inventively the kitchen was arranged given its size, and how she herself would be at a complete loss faced with such challenges.

Sinéad stiffened. 'Oh yes, we still have plenty of room. Who's judging the competition anyway?'

Fiona nodded to where the priest was talking to three of the ladies, telling what appeared to be a funny story, as laughter broke in soft volleys and travelled towards them over the sea of petals. The blackness of his soutane amidst the blazing colours seemed ascetically appropriate, but his face shone with enjoyment of the ladies' appreciation.

'Father Duffy is the chairman.'

'Well, you'd better go over there and butter him up a bit.'

'Oh Lord, the butter.' Fiona laughed. 'But you're right, I'll go over. Thanks for coming.'

They kissed each other once on the cheek, warily, but not without affection.

§

She'd cook the Italian lamb stew first and then work on the starter and dessert while it bubbled on the hob. Declan would open the claret later, and it was his job also to set the table. All the windows were open and she could hear her two men trundling leaves and branches down the back garden in a wheelbarrow. Then she smelled the sweet fragrance of a bonfire. Declan usually lit them only in the autumn, but Owen had obviously persuaded him to do it for the thrill. The bonfire aroma mixed pleasingly with that of the simmering lamb and rosemary. Crème caramel for dessert; this was next up, and the acrid smell of burnt sugar filled the kitchen. Declan would peel the potatoes later, while Owen had his bath. The stew was really a winter dish, but she loved the profligate amount of Chianti the recipe demanded, as well as the four solid cloves of garlic, and of course the rosemary. She prepared a salad as a starter, which was a little unusual. But that was part of the fun of the thing – the looks that would travel around the table.

Declan came in for a cup of tea, but since most of her work was done, she managed to talk him into a gimlet.

'With the muck on me?' he asked.

'With the muck on you, yes. You just sit there and I'll rustle it up.'

'Well,' he said, looking around the kitchen and smiling, 'you're an extremely resourceful lady.'

She let her hand run along his upper arm as she went to the refrigerator.

The gimlets were a custom they'd adopted from his parents. Their icebox wasn't big enough to freeze the glasses, but at least the gin fitted snugly into it. This was perhaps the moment in the day that Sinéad enjoyed most of all. The awful emptiness of the house was now filled by her two men, one playing out in the garden, the other sitting here beside her, telling her about the great world. This must be it: this must be what she was supposed to do with her life.

71

'What about this man Robert who's coming this evening?' she asked. 'You didn't say much about him. He's in tractors?'

'Robert Poschik. He's over for a few weeks to supervise service and spare parts for the tractors the East Germans are exporting to Ireland, and his wife is with him – for a bit of a holiday, I suppose. Robert didn't say it outright, but I think they had to leave their kids behind so they wouldn't get notions about staying in Ireland. In any case, he's an extremely affable man. He's been my main contact when I've gone over there to reassure the communists that all of their dealings with the importer have the blessing of the Irish state. It turns out I'll be going over again in August, just before the baby's due.'

Sinéad murmured in acknowledgement. This wasn't the first time he'd explained to her why the exporting of tractors from East Germany to Ireland required the frequent presence in East Germany of an Irish civil servant, and no doubt it wouldn't be the last.

'Has Liam met Robert?' Liam Creighton and his wife were to be their other guests for dinner.

'No. He hasn't had anything to do with the whole business. This is purely social.'

Liam had been stoically in love with her old friend Freddy until he met Helen Farragher, a gym mistress at Loreto Dalkey. They enjoyed strenuous holidays together – hill-walking and biking, mainly, and once they'd tried downhill skiing on Goldeck.

Sinéad and Declan remained in the kitchen with their gimlets for another quarter of an hour, and then Declan called Owen in so they could get cleaned up. Father and son tramped up the stairs, and she heard the boy begin to tell Declan about his plans to grow up, wear his father's suit and, if he didn't mind, marry Sinéad.

'You've got it all worked out, haven't you, my little man!' declared Declan.

'Yes, I have. But I can also marry Mrs Dixie, so don't worry if you want to keep Mummy.'

'I think that'd be better, as I don't want to let your mother go so soon. I don't know what I'd do without her.'

Sinéad, standing in the kitchen, found she needed to hear this, even though she knew it was said in jest. It would be nice to think it was true, that his grand adventures in the world were dependent on her.

There was some Rose's cordial left, and she fixed herself another gimlet, to drink while she finished cooking. By six o'clock everything was prepared and the counters scrubbed. She sat down at the table and looked around her. She had done it. Then, out of nowhere, the dreadful realizations arrived, as though for the first time. She had kept them at bay since the afternoon, but now they shoved their way towards her mercilessly: she had to get through a dinner party, and in two months' time she would have a baby.

§

First to arrive were the Creightons.

'Sinéad. Very good to see you.'

'Liam. Helen. And lovely to see you too. Come in, come in.'

'Declan. Perhaps I can trust you with that.'

'Helen. Liam. Why, thank you!'

The Poschiks arrived soon after.

'Come in. You're very welcome to our home. It's so nice to meet you after hearing all that Declan told me. You've been so hospitable to him on all his visits. It's a pleasure to be able to welcome you here.'

'Thank you, Mrs Boyle . . .'

'Please call me Sinéad. And you must be Eva.'

'Yes, I am Eva. Only little English. I'm sorry.'

'Well, your English is better than my German. I tried to learn with Declan at the start, but he left me far behind. These are our friends Helen and Liam. This is Eva and Robert Poschik. Declan will get you something to drink. I have to pop into the kitchen.'

§

Sinéad closed the kitchen door behind her and leaned back against it. She exhaled as quietly as she could. This was only the first ten minutes.

§

When she returned to the front room, Sinéad found them still standing and talking. They were a small group, and despite the awful feeling in her chest, despite the weight of the child in her belly, despite the aches in her breasts as they tugged against her bra, Sinéad recognized the hum in the room as the sound of people getting on well with each other. That was a relief.

To Robert, Liam said playfully, 'We hear a lot about communism in your part of the world, but that doesn't stop you making good tractors or selling them to us. Perhaps you're good capitalists after all.'

Poschik smiled. It was obviously not the first time that he had heard this argument. 'Why should communism stop us from making good tractors? On the contrary, it helps us to make better ones. We are not distracted by capitalist competition, and so we can devote our energies to perfecting the product.' The idea was obviously new to Creighton, and he was briefly balked.

Where had Poschik learned to speak English so well? Was that a hint of an American accent, at odds with the decorous, European manner of his expression? His wife, who had hardly any English, had obviously decided that she would survive the evening by fixing a smile on her face. The combination of colours in her outfit was unfortunate – black mixed with the wrong brown – and her shoes (were they really dark purple?) bespoke a moment of desperation in their hotel room earlier in the evening.

Eva Poschik felt Sinéad's eyes on her and appeared to think she should make some further effort to communicate. But even simple conversation was a gargantuan task, and she stalled as though standing at the foot of a large mountain.

'Your picture. On wall.' She pointed to a small painting. 'Beautiful.'

'Why, thank you, Eva. We bought it in Greece.' Sinéad wasn't sure if Eva had understood, but before she had a chance to explain, Robert said some words to her in German. It struck Sinéad that Eva might have dreaded this dinner party even more than she herself had earlier in the evening. Perhaps. But Sinéad couldn't see around Eva's smile.

'Where did you learn to speak English so well, Robert?'

'It was pure chance. It was after the war, when I was in Bamberg. Our country was desperate for soldiers as the enemies were closing in and were drafting boys like me. But it's a long, boring story . . .'

'No. I'd very much like to hear it,' Sinéad said.

'Really? The war gave us so many stories, and mine is not a particularly gripping one.'

'But,' countered Sinéad, 'we have no stories of the war in Ireland.'

'Well, I was fifteen when I was sent with the train away from Görlitz with fifty other boys from the area, some of them younger than me. We were going to fight. I remember the mothers crying on the platform. They thought they would never see their sons again. The Russians were coming from one side and the Americans from the other. But before they could put me in a uniform and give me a gun, the Americans liberated us all, and since I wasn't a soldier I avoided the *Rheinwiesenlager*, as they were called. Meadow camps for the prisoners of war. But I could not get home and I had nowhere to sleep and nothing to eat. After about three days I am beginning to think it would be good to be a prisoner of war. I had to go to dustbins for my meals, but nobody was throwing food out the way they do now, and anyway hundreds of people like me had the same idea.'

His speech in parts had a predictable clipped Germanic delivery, but with certain words or phrases an American modulation flowed in, moving the words faster and more naturally.

'On the third day I decide to walk to Görlitz and take my chances in the countryside. But I wanted to see if I could persuade one or two of my friends from home to join me on the journey. I knew where they were usually to be found – an old warehouse that had been bombed two years before. I wandered all over it, calling and calling, but there was no answer. As I was leaving I heard a faint cry, and I eventually came across an American soldier who'd broken his leg and couldn't move. I found out later that he'd been on a night patrol and had entered the warehouse to see if anyone was there. But he slipped, breaking his leg and also jamming his rifle, so he couldn't fire a shot to alert his fellow soldiers.'

Robert Poschik paused and took a sip of his wine. None of his listeners said anything. They were all waiting for him to continue. The warmth of the evening could be felt in the dining room through the French doors, and they could hear the sounds of birdsong, and older children in other houses still playing in the bright evening. Sinéad could also hear the faintest sounds of tiny insects flying in and around them, drawn by the lights.

'I had nothing against the Amis . . .' He saw the Irish people's incomprehension. 'I mean the Americans. My family were socialists and had suffered under the Nazis, but I couldn't explain that to him, and the soldier pulled his knife when he saw that I wasn't one of his comrades. I saw there was no point in trying to persuade him that I meant no harm, so I ran as fast as I could to where I knew the Americans were billeted. I explained to one of them in German what had happened. Five of them came with me, carrying a stretcher. They'd been looking for him since he'd failed to return at dawn, and were very grateful. I spent the next few months as a kind of – how do you say it? – factotum. That was the word. One of the Americans had just heard the word from some British soldiers and thought it very funny. Soon they just called me Totem. But all this is of no interest to you. I'm sorry for talking for so long. I am very rude.'

It seemed to Sinéad that Declan hadn't heard the story before, and was fascinated like everyone else. Poschik was about seven or eight years older than them, but more than that separated his life from theirs. He had charmed them all by the way he'd told the story, presenting to them a younger version of himself lost in the world and yet still resourceful. But they maintained a little reserve. Was it that he was a German, a man who had nearly joined the Nazi army himself? Or was it that he was a communist? An American or an Englishman they could assimilate; even a Frenchman or an Italian. Robert Poschik was something different on many counts.

Finally Liam spoke. 'We can't begin to imagine what it must have been like. We haven't had war in this country for fifty years.'

'For which you are lucky,' responded Robert.

Liam paused. 'But what about all that business with the Jews? What do Germans think of that now?'

The question's hostile implication hung in the air for a second or two. Liam flushed slightly with the awareness of his having gone too far, but couldn't retract it now.

'You are right to ask. When I returned to Görlitz after university, I found that all the neighbours who had turned into Nazis when I was a small boy had now turned back into normal neighbours again, and couldn't exactly remember where they had been for the few years of the war. Or the ones who could not transform themselves back so easily cried that they were only doing their jobs, only doing what they had been told to do. Of course no one would forgive them that, as the rest preferred the attention to be focused on a select few. But our socialist republic has worked hard on this problem, much harder, I might add, than our neighbours to the west. My brother Mato was particularly zealous in this work during the late 1940s.'

Owen, in his pyjamas, quietly pushed open the door of the front room. The hall behind him was dark, and he appeared frightened of the lights and the tones of adult talk. He had tried to knot one of Declan's ties around the collar of his pyjamas, a parody of a man, his timid eyes fixed on his mother. Declan went over to him and picked him up, orchestrating the brief ceremony of goodnight. Sinéad withdrew to the kitchen.

'And what has the little lady rustled up for us in the kitchen, I wonder?' Liam asked. Sinéad placed a large casserole on the table and returned to the kitchen to get the potatoes and carrots. When she came back, she lifted the lid of the casserole and the strong aromas of garlic and rosemary, along with the sweetness of the wine, filled the small dining room. Liam had intended the question to be

jovial, conveying that he bore Poschik no ill will and did not intend
to press him regarding the Jews. But the patronizing tone irked
Sinéad. Helen said, 'Oh, Liam, Sinéad leaves us all in the ha'penny
place when it comes to cooking.'

Sinéad was about to deliver the line about garlic and happiness
that she had read in the cookbook, but at that moment she saw
Robert's and Liam's faces. The aroma from the casserole dish had
reached them, and the first contact, before pretence set in, told all:
they didn't like it, and it must be the garlic. Well, they would have to
eat it anyway, these men who preferred boiled unseasoned meats,
bland staples, wan vegetables. East Germany must be like Ireland in
this matter, Sinéad thought.

The food was shared out, plates passed first to the ladies, then
heftier portions for the men.

'Oh, and I have your book for you, Sinéad,' Helen declared. 'It
was awfully good.'

'Do you mean that rubbish you were telling me about the other
day?' Liam cut in. 'I wouldn't have thought you'd be interested in
that stuff, Sinéad.'

'Oh, Liam, don't be such a dry old stick. Even Declan enjoyed it.'

'You didn't read it, Declan, did you?'

Declan laughed. 'Does that scandalize you, Liam? It wasn't
Dickens, but it wasn't so awful.'

'How do you know it's bloody rubbish anyway, Liam, if you
haven't read it?' Sinéad could feel the earlier gimlets and two glasses
of wine giving a slightly bitter edge to her tone. 'Do you have
magical powers that you can just put your hand on books and dis-
cover what's inside them? We didn't know your abilities stretched
to literary criticism.'

Creighton, to her surprise and relief, laughed.

'But the girl was such a silly goose, with all her notions,' said
Helen. 'I wasn't surprised that she died in the end, without a husband and her boy grown up over in Canada.'

Declan had got up to refill glasses. Sinéad considered putting her
hand over her glass, but then let him fill it again.

'You know they burned the book in some of the villages,' Helen remarked significantly. No one responded, and no one knew where to take the issue. Declan was smiling to himself.

Robert Poschik stepped in. 'Excuse me for asking, but why would a book be banned here? I thought that was the speciality of my country.' Sinéad saw Declan look up at this. Was he surprised to hear Poschik lightly criticizing his own government?

Helen cleared her throat and looked around the table before saying in a voice just a hint higher than its usual level, 'Because of the sex.' There was a pause, and everyone turned towards her.

'Was the sex very . . . strange?' Robert enquired.

All the Irish people exploded in laughter, relieved to have the tension broken at last. From the look in Poschik's eye, Sinéad was unsure that he was quite as ingenuous as his question implied. Perhaps he was trying to help them, and perhaps they needed help.

'No,' Sinéad said, 'it was just because there *was* sex.' They laughed again, not as loudly as the first time, and Poschik joined in as well, his laughter fading out into a rapid translation of the exchange for his wife, who, after a pause, smiled herself. Sinéad wondered what minor statements Poschik had inserted in the translation to explain the strangeness of their hosts. If there had been any mischief in his commentary, it was not visible in the couple's faces.

Helen looked up at Sinéad as she started clearing away the dishes. 'You were going to tell me about Owen's school.'

'I'll just put these in the kitchen. But Declan, perhaps you could tell them?'

'We're going to send him to Deerpark.'

'And pardon me, Liam,' said Poschik, 'did you and Declan both go to the same school? Declan mentioned that schools are important here.'

'No, I'm from the west of the country, Robert. But what do you think, Declan?' Creighton said. 'Does it make a damn of a difference which school they go to?'

'Probably not.' Declan got up to help Sinéad clear the dishes, which she merely took from his hands, leaving him with no option but to sit down again.

'Well, sometimes it's good for connections, in politics and all that sort of thing,' Liam said. 'But I have to say that Rockwell has been little help to me in that direction.'

'Why not?' asked Poschik.

'Well, a crowd from across the river has the whole thing stitched up.'

'What Liam means,' Declan explained, 'is that across the river you'll find the working-class districts of the city – we drove through them on our way from the airport – and the men who are in power now, well, a number of them came from that part of Dublin.'

'You mean your Minister for Finance, Declan? I have heard from the people at our embassy that he isn't very working class. In fact, they were disappointed in his lack of pride in his origins.'

'That's the man,' Liam agreed. 'He'll be running things in no time. We all thought we'd be running things, didn't we, Declan? That's what they made us think at Deerpark and Rockwell. But it didn't work out like that. Those lads were faster out of the box and didn't care as much about the niceties.' Liam turned to Poschik again. 'But tell me, Robert, what else do they say at the embassy?'

Poschik realized that he had said a little too much and retreated swiftly. 'That he is very capable, very hard-working, and they agree with you – that he'll go very far.'

'So your people keep a close eye on things, do they?' Creighton enquired.

'Oh, I don't know much about that, but I imagine it's just the usual political reporting, information they get from the newspapers, and so on,' Poschik responded.

'Nothing cloak-and-dagger then?'

Poschik laughed. 'I'll have to ask them at the embassy. They'll like that very much! I'll be seeing them next week. With all due respect, I don't think Ireland is at the centre of their espionage operation. We wouldn't get very far with you anyway, as you seem to be enjoying capitalism so much.'

Sinéad brought in the crème caramel, and there was relief in Creighton's face when he looked down and saw a foodstuff he recognized. Helen's eyes ranged over the ornaments and a few shelves of books in the room, searching for something that would steer the conversation in a different direction. Her eye fell on the picture of Sinéad with Owen the day after he was born, taken by Declan in the maternity hospital. Owen's body, cradled in her arms, was at the centre of the photograph, his mother's face turned down towards him – her ear, the foreshortened shape of her left cheek, the corner of a smile just visible.

'But you must be so excited, Sinéad! When's the baby due?'

Sinéad inhaled and shifted slightly in her chair. Her back pained her. She was grateful for any opportunity to get up and go to the kitchen – as a break from the conversation, but also to stretch. The men turned to her, acknowledging the precedence of this subject over their own.

'Two months to go now,' answered Sinéad, looking across the dinner table at Helen. There was silence as the guests left Sinéad a chance to continue. But she didn't.

'So, in August!' Helen tried to sound enthusiastic, but she was at a loss about how to go on.

Eva leaned over to Robert and said something to him in a low voice, and he nodded twice in comprehension.

'My wife says that you have . . . blossomed in pregnancy.'

How does she know what I looked like before? Sinéad thought querulously. What a stupid thing to say. Blossomed. What a stupid, stupid thing to say.

§

Sinéad was taken into Mount Carmel Maternity Hospital in mid-August, having begun to feel pains that were definitely not contractions. It turned out to be nothing, but they kept her in for observation as she was so close to her term. Beneath her window the Dodder ran through the leafy valley of Churchtown, and she could hear the occasional car race down Taney Road on the other side. One friend of hers said that she could tell by the shape of Sinéad's bump that it would be a boy. At this stage, Sinéad joked, it was more likely to be an elephant.

Declan had left for Germany earlier in the month, as planned, swearing to her that he would be back by the 21st. But that hadn't happened and instead she'd received a telegram on the 22nd from Berlin, telling her he loved her and that he was sorry to be late but he had to go to Yugoslavia. He would definitely be back by the 26th.

What was he doing in Yugoslavia? What was going on? Why had he abandoned her?

His parents and hers were sharing the responsibility of looking after Owen, and on the two occasions the boy visited her his reports suggested that it was a wonder he wasn't ill from all the sweets. He looked happy, and Sinéad answered all his questions about the brother or sister who would soon be arriving.

After two more days had passed with no sign of labour commencing, her obstetrician, Dr Marcus, began to mention alternative procedures and even the possibility of a Caesarean section. Sinéad wondered if the child wasn't waiting for Declan to return home, but then dismissed the idea as ridiculous.

Clare, the woman in the next bed, was from Kilkenny and had moved to Dublin three years ago. She told Sinéad that only a week after she'd arrived she'd met a man who worked in the bank and now she was here with his child. Both she and Sinéad were nervous about the labour that lay ahead of them, and they offered assurance to each other that everything would be OK. Without knowing exactly why, Sinéad found herself crying one day as she talked to Clare. With much effort, Clare got out of her bed and came and sat on Sinéad's, taking her hand in her own. Until it happened, Sinéad had not been conscious of her need to be consoled.

They listened to the sounds of bustle out in the corridor.

'Any news from your husband?'

Sinéad sighed and looked out the window. 'He said the 26th. That's in two days. I've started to think that this baby won't come out until he gets back. It's stupid, I know, but I can't get it out of my head.'

'It's not stupid at all,' Clare said. 'I know he'll be back in time. Don't worry.'

Whole hours would pass in conversation with Clare, and it helped Sinéad forget about the coming labour and Declan's absence. After a week of talking, looking out the window in silence at the end of the summer, of the routines of the hospital and the occasional visits of her family and some friends, she had drifted into a kind of dream state, at times unable to say which day of the week it was.

Dr Marcus came in on the evening of the 25th to say that she should eat no dinner because they were going to give her a Caesarean in the morning. For the first time since she'd been admitted, she slept without interruption, as though no energy was left to her to be nervous. Then the ceiling was moving and she was waving goodbye to Clare, who raised her crossed fingers as they wheeled Sinéad's bed into the operating theatre. He hadn't arrived.

The anaesthetist was talking to her. She was answering his questions, but gradually began to feel that they made no sense at all, and she was worried that perhaps he was a lunatic. She thought she heard one of the nurses say, 'Your husband is waiting outside,' but they were fooling her, or she was fooling herself. 'No, he's not,' she managed, enunciating the words clearly, but it was as though her mouth was full of marbles, bubbles, candyfloss, or clouds reeled down out of the sky and released into her head. Blue skies. Silence.

After what seemed like a few minutes, the process reversed: the silence gave way to blue skies, blue skies to clouds, and so on till the marbles changed to blue circles against a white background that rippled in front of her eyes. Her gaze followed a line of small buttons like stepping stones curiously up in the air, until she met the eyes of her husband looking intently down upon her. She felt his hand caressing her temple, and she turned her head so that it pressed even closer against his palm. She tried to raise her head, but she felt pain as though someone was driving a knife into her stomach, or rather, in one swift movement drawing a knife across from hip to hip. The pain was so intense that she couldn't see for a second or so. 'Stay there, my love, don't move.'

'My baby? Where is he?' It was only as she spoke the words that she realized she'd been hoping for a boy all along.

'She's right here. Hold on a minute, I'll bring her over.' Declan's face was replaced by the ceiling, but he returned in a moment, cradling a baby in his arms. She felt the tears coming to her eyes. She looked at the small face of her daughter, who was frowning at the room she'd been brought into. Declan was smiling in a way she'd seen only twice before. First, when they were walking up Stephen's Green and he had said to her – his exact words, she had never forgotten them, she had fed on them ever since – 'You say things I couldn't have imagined and always wanted to hear.' And second, when she had handed Owen to him in the hallway of their new house and he had said, so wrongly as it turned out, that everything was perfect.

'I've so much to tell you,' he said. 'I'm resigning from the Civil Service. We're going to build a factory, in Ardnabrayba. I didn't want to worry you, but now I know it's all going to work out. Everything will be all right. For you. For Owen. And for . . .'

'Iseult. Her name is Iseult.'

Declan looked at their daughter's face and then back at Sinéad.

'Iseult,' she said.

3
Industry and Commerce

1968

As he drove home, the news kept breaking over him: he'd been passed over for Assistant Principal Officer. 'Not this time round, Mr Boyle,' they'd said. In confirmation, the rain lashed the windscreen of the Wolseley Hornet. Already he was lagging behind Niall Falkner's career path. That man had made Principal Officer at the age of thirty-one. Declan, at thirty-two, was only an Administrative Officer, two grades behind.

It was unfair: he'd shown some initiative, and now he was being punished for it. Three years ago, he'd heard from a businessman he knew that an Irish company was keen to import tractors from East Germany; as good as Massey Fergusons, apparently, and cheaper too, provided the Irish taxman and the GDR authorities did the sensible thing. The main sticking point, Declan determined after making a few phone calls, was that the East Germans were not comfortable dealing directly with a capitalist company, and had demanded the presence of a state officer as guarantor for all agreements with importers. Declan proposed to his superiors that he could act in this capacity, and they agreed. After a couple of years and a few trips to the GDR, some literal-minded person pointed out that the Department of Finance was not really the place for the work Declan was doing – it was more a matter for Industry and Commerce. By this time, the Germans had come to trust Declan, and were charmed by his increasing grasp of their language; they did not want anyone else. So he moved departments. At first he was happy about this, but quickly he realized that he would have to prove himself over again with his new superiors. And so these men spoke blandly to him of 'certain ambiguities in your position' by way of explaining his non-promotion.

Glenshane Estate was not looking its best. What he had once thought of as an adventure in modern living now seemed grim and trivial, a warren of roads lined with little boxes full of uninteresting people. Next door were the Griffiths; he was a construction engineer who spent most of his weekends on his knees in the garden mud dedicated to the cultivation of rare roses. On the other side were the Walshes; he was a bank manager and obsessional home-improver who, when everything else had been shined, sanded, lacquered and mown, would set about painting the exterior of his house again, the paint barely dry from the last time. The wives, to his perception, were merely compendia of headscarves, smiles and cheery waves. Declan tried to avoid conversation with the men, ducking back into the house or out the front gate to the shops, often leaving them to shout across his garden at each other about brands of lawnmower, rose cultivars, undercoats, insulation and the Virginia creepers that would one day hold whole houses in their grasp.

At least he had the car this evening. He pulled into the drive, turned off the engine, and put one hand on his briefcase and the other on the door handle. A pause and then a dash, slamming the car door closed behind him, leaving it unlocked. The porch kept the rain off him while he went through his keys. In the door, briefcase down, wool coat off. 'I'm home,' he called. There was no answer. The silence of the house felt strange. The heating was off. The rooms were in darkness of various depths. Then he remembered: Sinéad was in hospital for tests to do with the pregnancy, and Owen was staying with his parents.

After he'd made a cup of tea, he sat down at the kitchen table with the newspaper, but he couldn't concentrate. Usually when he came home there was the noise of Sinéad in the kitchen preparing dinner, and Owen perhaps in the front room playing, then scrambling up from his knees to run towards him. The teacup was empty. The newspaper lay before him unread. In the refrigerator, he now recalled, there were bacon and eggs. He'd been supposed to pick up a loaf on the way home, but hadn't. Perhaps there'd be a crust at the back of the bread bin. Rain was still coming down outside. He should turn on the heater in the living room, so he could read there after his food. He should put the radio on for company. He should clatter the frying pan across the hobs.

Instead he moved quietly and respectfully through the silence of the kitchen and the house. This was Sinéad's place, this was where she spent each day. But it must be different for her, busy with the washing of clothes, the ferrying of Owen, the cleaning of floors, the preparation of food. Whereas he had a long evening ahead – two evenings, in fact – with nothing but his disappointment.

§

He moped for a while, and then started working on an idea that had been troubling him for a while: why should Ireland, still a heavily agricultural nation, import its tractors? Could a foreign manufacturer be convinced to set up a factory here? Or could an indigenous firm be given the support it would need?

By August, as he prepared for his trip to Görlitz, he had talked to the relevant people in the departments and state agencies, and received a mostly encouraging response. If the right people and the right amount of private capital could be brought to bear, the Irish state could probably be convinced to step in and provide the necessary assistance. With such thoughts in his head, the coming trip to the GDR – for the purpose of finalizing contracts and agreeing numbers for export to Ireland over the next two years – seemed a dull prospect.

His first trip to the factory in Görlitz, three years before, had not been the slightest bit dull: it had been a shock. His train had stalled, not for the first time, outside a town the size of Limerick, and for fifteen minutes he found himself observing builders at work on a high-rise apartment block. They'd completed about six floors of the concrete structure; at the unfinished height two or three were moving around, but the rest of them were standing around a brazier, drinking beer and smoking. An even stranger sight was the mountain of window frames stacked badly at the foot of the building and sinking into the mud, much of the wood warped already, made worthless by the oversight. It depressed him more than he could explain: the waste, the carelessness, the apathy that seeped out of the scene, like the rust stains down the concrete walls.

The Agro-Trak delegation who met him at the station in Leipzig were full of cheerful stories of the great progress being made on all fronts in socialist Germany. But the lethargy that Declan had seen in the faces of the builders on his way there remained with him for the entire car journey to Görlitz, which offered similar glimpses of exhaustion. He was surprised, then, when it turned out that the factory was run with capitalist efficiency. It wasn't until later, when he'd grasped the figures behind the whole venture and got to know the place better, that he understood that socialist utopias also needed hard cash, and that was the purpose of Agro-Trak in the midst of East Germany's desolation.

On most of his trips to Görlitz, Declan had accompanied the chief executive of the Irish firm that imported and distributed the Agro-Trak tractors. This time his travelling companion was to be the number two, Seán Guilfoyle. Raised on a small farm outside Limerick, he was two years Declan's junior, and Declan found him livelier company than his boss. At the last general election, Declan knew, Guilfoyle's brother Mick had been elected a TD for Galway North West, having moved to that part of the country as a young schoolteacher. Declan was curious about Mick Guilfoyle, who was seen as a rising star in his party, and all the more so because his constituency included Ardnabrayba.

On the train from Berlin to Görlitz, Seán filled Declan in on the rise of his illustrious brother. He had become well known in his area through the GAA club – he played and coached – and the party asked him to run for the county council. To his own surprise, he'd taken to politics, excelling above all as a canvasser – tirelessly charming, involved in every detail of community projects. While serving as a councillor he built a network of friends, some not even in the party, who supported him in his efforts to improve the locality. They'd meet on Friday evenings at the local GAA clubhouse, sharing a frustration with the government's neglect of the area. At the next general election, Mick humbly accepted the fifth place on the party ticket. Addressing his *cumann*, he said he'd do his very best – as befitted the fifth candidate on the ticket – to support the other candidates, putting all his network of canvassers behind them.

'But Mick is a cute hoor,' Guilfoyle said to Declan. 'He told me that on the same evening he went to meet his mates at the Clubhouse and told them what had happened. They congratulated him and slapped him on the back and bought him pints, but he left his pint untouched on the table. Then he stood up and told the other lads to come into the back room. They didn't know what was up, as they followed him in. When the door was closed, he asked them to sit down and handed each of them a typed sheet, which listed the canvassing areas of the constituency, with their names under different headings. He told them that he'd no intention of canvassing for that old fucker Badge O'Brien and his lackey Vincent Martin. "They've held on to those seats since the dark ages," says he, "and they've done nothing for this place except feather the nests under their arses. We won't get Badge this time, but his amazing dancing bear is finished. Bye bye, Mr Martin. We're going to canvass their areas, but not for them – for ourselves. It'll be too late before they realize."

'That's what he told them. I'll tell you how it went: Badge barged his way into the Clubhouse after the election results came in, roaring, "Where's that fucking bastard Guilfoyle? I'll have him strung up by his balls. Where is he, the fucker?" But, like I said, Mick is a cute hoor. He was ready for Badge. He came out – and I saw this myself because I went down for the count and the celebrations afterwards – innocent as the lamb. He had a pint in Badge's hand before the old fool could say another word. And he was telling Badge that he'd do anything for the party, give up his seat if the party asked him, anything, because no one man is more important than it.

'Then he persuaded Badge that this wasn't a good place to work it out and asked him to come into the back room where they could talk privately. He gestured to me and two others to come in with them, and we all sat down around the table. I think Badge still didn't trust himself to raise the pint to his lips – he was still shaking with anger. When the door was closed, Mick turned to Badge and he says, "Now listen, you old prick. If you ever talk like that to me again, it's you who'll be strung up by the balls, not me. You're finished now, Martin's gone, and I don't know if you noticed a few of your people out there in the Clubhouse tonight. That's because they know which way the wind's blowing and that you're finished. They're over here talking to me now and we're all good friends." You know Badge O'Brien, don't you, Declan, from Ardnabrayba?'

'Yes. My grandmother never thought much of him. He was also on the finance committee, and I had some dealings with him.' Declan recalled how the politician had openly dozed through hearings, rousing himself only when there was something that affected the small patch of the country that had elected him. He made no secret of the fact that the rest of Ireland could go to hell, as far as he was concerned. Some of Declan's colleagues had joked about it afterwards, but Declan found he had no reserves of humour. He couldn't rise above it: the fact that, as a civil servant, he existed to serve the will of such men. It stung his vanity more than he liked.

'So if you know Badge, you can imagine the face on him when he heard Mick talk like that. Not even the Taoiseach or a minister had ever talked to him like that. He was like Mount fucking Etna about to explode. But Mick didn't give him a chance, and he started in on him again, but this time in a nice soft voice: "Now listen, I'm sorry. I lost my temper. Nothing's going to change here for you. Nobody's going to touch your seat. And no one's going to ask questions either about where all the money's been going."

'Badge looked even more as if he were going to explode, but Mick held his eye in a way I'd never seen him do before. And I think it was that, more than anything, Mick said, that made Badge realize that he was talking to his new boss. The speed of the thing was something to witness. It couldn't have taken more than two or three seconds, but Badge was up, smiling and shaking hands with Mick, saying things like, "No hard feelings," "You won your seat fair and square" and "Let me buy *you* a drink, Mick."

'Not even the top brass in the party could work out what had happened, but after a while they found themselves addressing their questions about the constituency to Mick, not Badge, even though Mick was always very careful to defer in public to Badge and his "wisdom of the elder statesman". I heard Badge hated that one most of all, as he was a vain man and kept a little lady in fine style off Shop Street.'

Declan's view was that the likes of Mick Guilfoyle were among the problems that had to be extirpated before any progress could be made in Ireland. But the ferocity of the story told by Seán – a lover of classical music, and a man who understood economics – was unlike anything Declan had ever encountered in his work, and he was fascinated.

They were met at the train station by a young Agro-Trak manager and driven to their hotel in the town centre. In the evening they met Robert Poschik and another engineer, Bernd Vogel, for a drink. Vogel was in his twenties, and as the son of a senior civil servant he'd been permitted to study engineering at the University of Cardiff. He relaxed with Declan, knowing that his superior's discretion could be trusted. This was a dynamic that Declan had noticed in his dealings with GDR officials: they always toed the party line at an official level, but then in private wished him to know that they were men of the world who, unlike their fellow citizens, could appreciate the fruits of the West.

The next morning they went to the factory, about twenty kilometres from the town, and concluded the necessary business. Robert had invited them to spend Monday night in Hermsdorf, the village where his brother Mato was mayor. Their government handlers had approved this, both because of Mato's credentials as former partisan (he'd sabotaged German communications and supply lines between Berlin and Prague, as well as torching two munitions factories in Dresden) and because of his present position as mayor. It was also deemed appropriate that the Irish visitors experience the beauties of the East German countryside and the happiness of the German Democratic people. Thankfully, the handlers didn't feel obliged to accompany Declan and Guilfoyle, so confident were they in the reliability of the Poschik family.

Robert drove them down in the afternoon. He asked after Sinéad and Owen, commiserating with Declan on the sleepless nights that lay ahead. He himself, in contrast, was off with his family to Yugoslavia later in the week. Along with three other engineers and their families, the Poschiks had been given a holiday at Split in reward for all the fine work they had done in exporting tractors to Ireland. 'Only for the faithful!' Robert said, and winked ironically.

'What do you mean?' Declan asked.

'For the party faithful. We are all good communists, so they trust us not to go scurrying over the border into Italy. Still, there is a little risk involved. They love so much the hard cash we make that keeps the socialist experiment going and they love us so much that they want to keep us close. But they have to give us some fun too. They have to give us a little pat on the head, so our neighbours can envy us our luxury holidays.'

'You don't seem happy about it.' Guilfoyle was asleep in the back, and they were speaking German.

'A feeling like this takes a long time to grow in a man. And also, for a pleasant change, we are travelling today without our friends from the Ministry. I'm thirty-nine years of age. I've seen this country improve under socialism, but what's happening now is wrong. In the 1950s, we all believed, we all pitched in to help build everything. But now . . . Well, it doesn't seem like socialism any more. And even this contract – you know how it works. I don't wish to go to Yugoslavia with my family just so my neighbours can envy me, but if I don't go it will seem suspicious and they will begin to think I'm not to be trusted completely.'

'If there were any way I could help . . .'

Robert looked over at Declan, who held his eye for a second.

'Ah, Declan. You are kind to even think of it. But no, it can't be done. It would be very easy for me to go to Ireland on a business trip and simply not return. It would even be easy for Eva and myself to do that. But they'd never let us over there as a family. Oh, my credentials are very good, but there remains a shadow of doubt. Perhaps because I'm Sorbian, from Lusatia, not fully German. I don't really know in the end. No one is trusted now.'

Was this just talk? Declan sized up his friend. 'You know . . .' he began slowly, 'the main reason we can't set up something like Agro-Trak in Ireland is that we don't have engineers with the right experience. The way things are going now, the money could be raised . . .'

Robert nodded. After a pause, he said, 'I'd leave immediately if I could take my children. I know some people who left both their wives and their children behind. In one case it was clear that if he'd stayed he wouldn't have lasted long anyway. I don't particularly like the system I work for any more, but I want to do my best to ensure that my children won't be perverted by it.' He then changed tone abruptly. 'In any case, I don't think there's really any way you can help me in this, except to be a good guest this evening and drink all the slivovitz that Mato pours you.'

It was not a very humorous remark, but after the tension of the conversation they both laughed, and woke Seán Guilfoyle.

Robert steered the car under the arch of a gate and into a spacious square farmyard, surrounded by two barns and two buildings with living quarters and storage. The farm had been restituted to the family in 1947, Robert had said, and under Mato, who had successfully lobbied for its exclusion from the collectivization process in the early 1950s, it had prospered. Because of the fine weather they would eat outside in the evening, and already farmhands were bringing out trestles, chairs and lanterns.

A large pot of goulash was placed at the top of the table and dished out to the ten people by Mato's wife. Then a girl brought out two steaming plates of dumplings from the house. Dunkel beer was served in heavy, ornate steins. There was little talk. Not having had time to change, Declan felt strange to be sitting in a farmyard in his suit.

After the women had cleared the dishes and left the men to their drinking, Mato pushed his chair back from the table, stretched out his legs and put his hands behind his head.

'So, Declan, what is the news of the great world?'

'You're asking the wrong man, Mato. We Irish don't know much about what's going on in the world. We're tucked away out of sight.'

'But you belong to a different world from us. People come and go, unlike here. Tell me, what do Irish people think of us?'

'To be honest, for many people you're part of the great godless empire of Russia.'

'But I am a Christian, though I do not shout that from the roof-tops.'

'My grand-aunt is still shocked that I come over here, and she asks me if you're normal. I think deep down she's convinced you all have devil's horns on your heads.'

'Oh, but we're normal. There are births, weddings and funerals like everywhere else. We would like a little change now and then, a little more freedom perhaps, like they have in Prague. But we are told that that is not a good idea. Who knows but we might run a bit too wild?' Mato paused. 'Robert tells me that your wife will soon give birth.'

'Yes,' Declan said. 'It should be next week. I return to Ireland on Wednesday and I hope to see my new child by Friday.'

'Well, let us drink to its safe arrival! We do not have any French wines, but this,' Mato said, holding up the clear spirit, 'is ours, and it is good also. The health of your child!' Guilfoyle also raised his glass, though he didn't know for what, as the others were speaking in German, Mato having no English.

'How long has your family lived here, Mato?' Declan asked.

Mato looked around. 'These were all built in the middle of the last century, so they're not so old. But my father's people go back much longer in this village. Sometimes we belonged to one country, sometimes to another. We were not always part of Germany, and German's not even my native language. We really have more in common with the Slavic tribes across the border than with these Hermanns and Fritzes with their blood and iron. And of course we were pitched off it by the Nazis.'

'When did that happen?'

Robert took his cigarettes off the table and said quietly that he was going for a brief stroll, asking Guilfoyle if he'd like to join him, which he did.

'My brother doesn't like to remember it,' Mato explained, when Robert was out of earshot.

'I'm sorry if I—'

'Please don't be sorry. In any case, it is a story that I'm proud to tell. The Nazis knew my parents were socialists, but they had left them alone for a long time, I suppose because they had better things to do. But one day, without any warning, a car drove up with a young officer – probably not more than twenty-two or twenty-three – and three soldiers. My father came out of the farmhouse and stood on the doorstep watching them getting out of the car. It was almost comical: the officer's door jammed, and he became angry, blaming his subordinates. I saw it all because I was over there in the barn. When he got out, the officer told my father that he and his family had one week to vacate this property. My father didn't move and he didn't say a word in reply. This angered the officer further and he shouted in his face – had he heard, or perhaps he was deaf as well as stupid? My father waited for him to finish the insult, and even left it hanging there in the air for a second or two, just to let the officer know what he thought of him. Then, deliberately and calmly, he spat in the officer's face.

'The soldiers drew back in shock and the officer himself couldn't believe what had happened. Then, as though caught by spasm, he began struggling with his holster to get his pistol out. But, like the door of the car, it seemed to be stuck, which made the young fascist even angrier. My father remained standing there, watching him without a flicker of expression. He didn't even move when the officer fired a shot at his head. The bullet went past my father's ear into the lintel over there. He merely continued watching the man.'

Mato sighed and looked down at the table. Declan nearly asked him what happened next, but stopped himself in time. Mato looked up. 'He didn't miss with his second shot, and my father collapsed, dead before he hit the ground. We were carted off that evening, and didn't see the place again till 1946.'

'I'm sorry.'

'There is really nothing to be sorry for. I'm proud of my father, and, as I said, I'm proud to be able to tell the story, in the same place it happened. The Nazis are gone, but we are still here. That is something.'

The story shifted something in Declan, much as had the story that Robert told at their house in Glenshane Estate earlier in the summer. These were lives so far beyond the scope of his experience. The strength of the man must have been something. Mato had obviously inherited that, but Robert too seemed capable of determination and action, despite his urbane façade.

They returned to Görlitz early in the morning. Robert and his family had to pack for Yugoslavia; Declan and Guilfoyle had to catch their train to Berlin, where they were to dine at the Irish Embassy that evening. East Berlin was a retirement posting for Maurice Henchy; he had only one year left before he returned to the family smallholding in north Cork to spend his days fishing and talking with the locals in the pub. His career had been as illustrious as was possible in the Department, crowned by postings to – as he said with a twinkle in his eye – 'the Court of St James' and to Washington.

Guilfoyle had been buoyant about the prospect of that dinner, telling Declan that the embassy was officially the territory of the Republic of Ireland, and thus they might get some decent food and drink there. He was crestfallen when he saw the waiter pouring the same dunkel he'd been served in Görlitz, and listened to the ambassador extolling the superiority of German beers over Irish. Guilfoyle whispered a request to the servant for 'whiskey, the good stuff'. There were other guests – some from the Ministry, one university couple, and an Irishman whose name no one could quite catch.

After they'd finished dessert, there was a ring at the door and the first secretary entered the dining room with a strained look on his face. Begging the indulgence of the ambassador's guests, Henchy asked whether they would excuse him for just two minutes. The Ministry guests all looked down at their plates, as though they knew what the news was. The university couple and the three Irishmen looked around the table for information. None was forthcoming.

Henchy came back about twenty minutes later and said little for the rest of the evening. Declan had learned that embassy dinners ticked like clockwork: coffee and just one *digestif* served ten minutes after dessert when the guests had moved to the couches and arm-chairs for more relaxed conversation; then, twenty minutes after that, the guests would look at their watches with a mournful expression and apologize for having to leave such a wonderful gathering. The waves goodbye and heartfelt promises to return the hospitality confused Declan at first, but then he realized that this was the way one country doffed its cap to another, expressing its goodwill. After two or three more such dinners he realized that sometimes, very occasionally, there was personal liking between these people, so well camouflaged beneath the professional goodwill that it had taken him time to recognize it.

As the German guests were putting on their coats, Henchy touched Declan on the elbow and said that he would be happy if he and Guilfoyle could remain for some minutes. When he saw that one of the German civil servants had overheard him, he said more loudly, 'For more Agro-Trak business before these gentlemen depart for Dublin in the morning, and perhaps for a drop of the special whiskey that we are legally forbidden to serve to non-Irish guests.' The Germans didn't smile at the sally, but only nodded and said goodbye.

When the three Irishmen sat down in the quieter room, it turned out not to have been a joke: they were served whiskey, and it was the special stuff. After it had been poured, the servant withdrew, closing the doors behind him.

'I'm sorry for all this cloak-and-daggery, gentlemen,' Henchy said quietly. 'But Michael has just told me that things are on the move in this part of the world tonight. You've heard, no doubt, what's been going on in Czechoslovakia. Well, the Russkies don't like it, and tanks are on the way there from the other Warsaw Pact countries to put a stop to it. I don't think it will affect your flight tomorrow morning, but if there should be disruptions at the airport – I wouldn't put it past them to commandeer a few planes to fly in some of their back-room boys in comfort – you should come straight back to the embassy, and we'll fix you up.'

Declan and Guilfoyle thanked him, and twenty minutes later they got into the embassy car to be driven back to the hotel.

'We're getting out of here just in time,' Guilfoyle said. 'If the flight had been a day later, we might've been stuck here for another week.' He paused and continued: 'And you must be worried about your wife.'

Declan said nothing, and the two men parted outside Guilfoyle's door. After his colleague went into his room, Declan padded down the corridor and stood in front of the correct room number for a full minute before reaching for his key. The hotel was silent. A car horn trumpeted on the street below and woke him from his reverie. He went into the room and sat on the bed fully clothed for several further minutes. Then, mechanically, he undressed, brushed his teeth, turned off the light and opened the window. He did not get under the covers, but lay on the bedspread in his pyjamas, thinking about tanks, about Robert and his family in Yugoslavia. Perhaps this was the end of Ireland's business with Agro-Trak. There could well be a clamp-down that would restrict trade for years to come.

A mosquito orbited the air above his face, approaching and then drawing off. Then nothing for a while and Declan began to doze, imagining the headlines in the days to come and, beyond it all, Sinéad in Dublin, anxious to have him back, barely able to walk with the weight of the child.

He woke minutes later, a slight itch on his left ear where the mosquito had got him. Turning on all the lights, he got up from bed and scanned the walls and ceiling, hoping to locate the insect. But it was no good, and he slouched back to bed. He slept fitfully, harassed by the mosquito, and tanks rolled through his brief dreams. He dreamed too of his second child swimming out of Sinéad into the light of an operating theatre; and of Sinéad, without child now, springing off a diving board and descending the long way into his hotel room, beside him in bed shivering, and he placing his hands around her face, smoothing back her wet hair.

Then he saw Robert and the other engineers and their families getting on a plane and flying out of Yugoslavia to Dublin. All twenty of them would camp in the house on Mount Merrion Avenue. His mother would provide them with tea and sandwiches for the years to follow. They would build a tractor factory in the back garden.

Now he was awake. He turned on the light and saw the mosquito on the wall beside the bedstead. He slammed it flat with his palm.

He rose and bathed, the late-summer morning still dark. He had made a decision; now he had to work out the details. He had always thought that the likes of Guilfoyle and his brother were the people who made decisions like this, and his job was merely to stay in the background, providing expert advice, smoothing things over, nudging them forward, without any profit or glory for himself. Now, without any premeditation, it seemed to him that there was no reason he couldn't make a bold decision of his own.

Yugoslavia was famous for being the softest of the communist regimes in Central Europe, not even a member of the Warsaw Pact, and flexible in its relations with the West. Relations with Ireland were cordial enough, and it was conveniently close to Italy. He would get them out – the Poschiks and the other engineers and their families. He would get them all out, he'd resign from the Civil Service, he'd line up state backing and start seeking private capital for a tractor factory in Ireland.

As this sequence of actions fell into place in front of him, he felt a kind of mastery. It was as though levers had suddenly been thrust into his hands and he was capable of directing large loads through the air – girders, slabs of concrete, people – without hesitation or, what surprised him more, fear.

He might be able to count on Henchy to arrange entry visas for Ireland, if he explained the matter in detail. The difficulty would be exit visas from Yugoslavia for a group of almost twenty people. But this was where the tanks came in: with everyone's attention directed towards Czechoslovakia, it would be an excellent opportunity to offer a bribe – Robert had explained how flexible communist bureaucrats could be in the right circumstances. Declan would have to work out the correct size of the bribe, and then where to get it in dollars. Tomorrow it might be possible to get to West Berlin, and fly from there to Yugoslavia. His father could wire him the money if he called him this morning. Ireland was an hour behind . . .

He could probably get the cash, he could probably get the tickets, he could possibly get the visas. But would Poschik do it? And if he persuaded Robert, would the others follow? Their conversation on Monday in the car on the way to Hermsdorf suggested that Robert could be persuaded. He'd expressed his disillusionment with this country, but could that be turned to what his country would interpret as betrayal? Well, he would find out soon.

Over breakfast he explained everything to Seán Guilfoyle. The other man was outraged and resistant at first, listing all the things that could go wrong. But Declan pressed home the rewards of the risk. Seán could come aboard as his number two. And of course the factory would have to be in his brother's constituency – 'and why not near Ardnabrayba, which would mean further state money because of the Irish-language angle'. As he began to perceive the outline of the venture, Guilfoyle saw the prize waiting for them at the end, and he warmed to the risk of it.

Declan dialled his parents' number. It wasn't yet seven in Ireland, and James Boyle was probably reaching for his dressing gown, switching on lights as he made his way downstairs through the house, its old beams and plaster still retaining the cold of the night. Eventually he answered. Declan requested more money than he thought he would need, and told his father that he'd explain everything when he came home. James Boyle grunted his agreement, noting the details. His mother would be wondering if it was Mount Carmel calling about Sinéad.

He then sent a telegram to Sinéad. His father had said that she was doing fine and that he'd pass on Declan's love. Even if this whole business went well he'd be at least five days late, and could miss the arrival of his child. This was a painful thought. Liam Creighton thought there wasn't much point in pacing up and down in the hospital corridor – much better to go off to the pub, or just work – but Declan had needed to be outside the door when Owen was arriving. Throughout the whole pregnancy their words had had to cover ever greater distances. Why? Shouldn't the prospect of the child bring a husband and wife even closer together? But it was probably nothing. It would all come right after the birth. He was tempted to forget the whole thing and take his plane back as originally planned. Perhaps Guilfoyle could pull the gambit off alone.

But he wouldn't. He realized that only he could persuade Robert Poschik.

Declan and Guilfoyle made their way to the embassy, where Henchy warmed immediately to the scheme, saying that it would be fun to get up to some high jinks again after the thorough boredom of the East Berlin posting. His advice was to get transit visas through Austria, and spin a story about a change in travel connections because of the tanks in Czechoslovakia. Then they'd be able to fly directly from Vienna to Dublin on an Aer Lingus flight. He would arrange things at Dublin Airport, and he agreed that it was a good time to bribe a bureaucrat for the visas in Yugoslavia.

The car pulled away from the kerb at the embassy into the scant traffic of East Berlin. The morning was hot. He was excited in a way he had never felt before, and this made him feel guilty. Sinéad could even be in labour by now, while he and Guilfoyle sat in the comfortable embassy car, cosseted, protected, special envoys who were waved through Checkpoint Charlie once their papers were glanced at.

What would Sinéad think? This would change everything. If the factory was located in Ardnabrayba, they'd have to move there. Or could he commute? Question after question came towards him, and he had answers to only some of them.

The airport was mainly used by the US military, but one or two commercial airlines also flew in, and they were able to book a connecting flight through Vienna. The wired money was waiting at the Western Union office. Their plane taxied past large military carriers marked USAF, perhaps twenty or thirty of them, each resplendent in the sunlight. Maintenance personnel slouched along the runway, and one or two crews were loading up, chatting as though on an airbase in Montana or Delaware.

During the flight to Split, Declan realized he didn't know which hotel the Poschiks were staying in. There'd been so many other things to organize in Berlin that he'd hardly thought about this detail, just as he'd hardly thought about how he'd begin the conversation with Robert. Now he was in Yugoslavia, he realized his stupidity. It was a big seaside resort; people came from Czechoslovakia, Poland, Hungary and the GDR to enjoy the Mediterranean waves. They couldn't go around to every hotel asking for the Poschiks without attracting unwelcome attention.

By the time they landed, it was too late at night to try to solve that problem. The two men had enough of a job arranging accommodation for themselves. Eventually they were able to find a room with a double bed in a pension off the main street of the town, and had to assure the woman who ran it that their intentions were of the best kind; the negotiations were clinched by the twenty-dollar bill Declan placed on top of the dinars they'd offered her. The money disappeared off the counter quickly, and they were shown to a room on the first floor.

Next day, they were the first down to breakfast. After some small talk with the landlady, Declan asked if there were any particular hotels that East Germans stayed in. She told him there were two, beside each other, about two hundred metres down the main street. When they finished breakfast, Declan said to Guilfoyle that it'd probably be best if he dealt with Poschik alone, as they had been good friends for a few years. Guilfoyle saw the sense in this and took himself off to explore the town. Watching the other man depart, Declan felt nervous for the first time as he faced the utter unlikelihood of his plan succeeding. He should have been in Mount Carmel Maternity Hospital with his wife, not in a Yugoslavian seaside resort about to ruin the life of another man and his family, as well as his own.

But as he made his way down the street towards the hotels where the East Germans stayed, it was Owen he thought of most. He was caught off balance by the strength of the feeling. If this whole thing worked, it would be a story to tell him in ten years or so.

He didn't even have to enquire at reception if he had the right hotel. As he stood in the lobby of the first one he'd walked into, he could see Robert, Eva and their three children walking back from the buffet to their table, plates in their hands. When Robert

recognized Declan's face, he stalled in shock for a second. Eva
noticed her husband's expression; then her eyes followed his out
to the lobby. Robert said something to Eva, and they all put their
plates down on the table. Eva and the children seated themselves,
and Robert walked across the expanse of hotel carpet to Declan.
His apprehensiveness was betrayed by his laugh, which was louder
than usual, almost jovial.

'Good morning, Declan! If you'll excuse me saying it, you're the
last person I expected to see here. Was there perhaps a contract I
forgot to sign? I can't imagine there was, nor that you would come
out here with it.'

'No, no contract. But things are on the move.'

Robert, still puzzled, gestured to a couple of chairs. The men sat
and Declan began to explain the plan he had concocted. Although
Robert hadn't been in Split long, he had managed to get a tan
already and he appeared more relaxed than he had earlier in the
week. He didn't interrupt, but now and then looked past Declan to
his family eating breakfast in the dining room. He was sitting back
in his chair, his posture relaxed in contrast with Declan's, as though
he were merely deciding when to go for a swim later in the day.
Declan knew even as he spoke that Robert was aware of every
implication of what was being proposed. In fact, he was probably
aware of more implications than Declan had even considered. The
more Declan talked, the more preposterous the plan sounded.
Eventually he came to a halt.

'You've planned this carefully,' Robert said. He told Eva and the
children to go ahead to the beach, and over the course of two hours
he carefully interrogated Declan about how they would get to
Ireland and what would happen there. There was no disguising the
fact that, although Declan's contacts had made favourable noises
about state support for a tractor factory, there was no guarantee
that the necessary capital could be raised. For a long time it was
unclear which way the decision would go. Eventually, Robert told
him he couldn't be sure of the reliability of two of the other engineers, but he was confident that Bernd Vogel would say yes
immediately. Robert also said that he had half a suspicion that one

of the other two had cordial relations with the Ministry of State Security, which Declan knew to be called the Stasi.

'If we are to do as you suggest, Declan, then it would be best if all four families proceeded to Vienna together. Then we can say farewell to our friends in the safety of Austria, rather than here.' Robert paused, not for the first time, as his mind picked over the plan. 'The others will also be wondering why we have to return so early, having just begun our holiday.'

'What will you say?' asked Declan.

Robert thought for a moment. 'I will say we have been called back and that we have no choice in the matter. I will present myself as suspicious of *their* motives and reasons for wanting to stay. That sort of thing always works best.' He fell silent again. 'It would not be easy for my family . . .'

'But we'd do everything in our power to help Eva and the children settle in. My own wife . . .'

'Oh, yes, thank you for that. But I meant my family in Hermsdorf, and Eva's.'

Declan hadn't considered this aspect. 'I see. I can understand.' He felt his entire body deflate.

Robert uncrossed his legs and sat forward in his chair for the first time. He asked a passing waiter, in German, for two glasses of chilled slivovitz.

'No, Declan, I don't mean by this that we're not going. We are. There will only be one such opportunity, and I can no longer stomach the idea of my children growing up in such . . . hypocrisy. My parents are gone. Mato will survive, as he always does. And he will also understand. Eva's parents, well, they are old and hopefully will not be harassed too much by the police.'

The slivovitz arrived, though Declan didn't register it until his friend lifted it up and smiled.

§

Declan and Guilfoyle flew to Vienna, and Guilfoyle flew straight on to Dublin to prepare for the families' arrival. The plan was that after crossing the border at Maribor, the Poschiks and Vogels would take the turn for Vienna at Graz, while the other two cars continued north-westward to Bavaria. And, very simply, after all the planning and balancing of risk, that would be that. Declan, with twenty-four hours to kill, tried to call his house in Dundrum, but there was no reply. Then he tried his parents, and again there was no reply.

With no way to communicate with the Germans, Declan had to wait at the airport terminal from around midday and hope for the best. If they didn't make the afternoon flight to Dublin, there was a flight to London that evening – which would mean a layover, with a flight early the next day. As the hours passed and the Dublin flight departed, Declan began to think that the whole thing had failed. He managed to get through to Guilfoyle in Dublin, who told him that Henchy had arranged for a welcome party on arrival. Declan left Guilfoyle in no doubt that everything was going according to plan, only that they would arrive the next day.

He read the reports about the invasion of Czechoslovakia. There was a picture of tanks pushing through crowds of protesters on one of Prague's main thoroughfares. There were also unconfirmed stories of fatalities.

And then they were there. The two cars had pulled up right where he'd imagined they would, and Robert waved at him through the glass. Declan jumped up, hurried outside, shook the men's hands triumphantly, kissed the wives on the cheek and presented the children with chocolate bars that had wilted slightly in the heat. While the children attacked the bars, the engineers made rueful comments about having to abandon their cars for ever. Declan promised them Daimlers, Lagondas and Jaguars in their stead, as the wives looked on sceptically.

Two hours later they were queuing in the searing heat of the tarmac, waiting to be allowed to board the plane. Eva Poschik bent down to her children and forcefully smacked the eldest, Janek, across the face. Declan could see the mark on his cheek, but the child took the punishment bravely. The girl, Pavlusha, was smoothing the hair on her doll's head. The youngest, Kasimir, at two years of age, was observing how Janek dealt with the slap. Instead of short trousers he was wearing swimming trunks. Declan hadn't changed his shirt in three days, his suit was stained on the lapel and his silk tie at the end of its tether.

Feeling responsible for everyone's happiness, he hunkered down to Kasimir and told him that there were no snakes in Ireland. A man had come and chased them all into the sea. The boy's eyes widened, though he said nothing. And best of all, Declan continued, the sea is all around the country.

'Like in Split?' asked Janek.

'Like in Split. Maybe not so warm, but still we all go swimming there.'

Kasimir seemed troubled. 'Snakes in sea.'

Declan got it. 'You mean all the snakes are still waiting in the sea. That's rather clever of you, but they're long gone, I promise.'

Declan stood up again and looked over the heads of the other passengers. Only a few hundred miles away, rocks were flying through the air to land loudly on tank armour. People were streaming through streets, seeking confrontation or fleeing it. Someone, no doubt, was being shot and left on a pavement for a few hours, as in Hungary over ten years before. And here he was with two families, stranded on a vast expanse of concrete in the middle of Europe, vulnerable and nervous, wondering if they would be allowed up into the air and to sail over the clouds to a quieter island. Kasimir's sun hat was whipped off by a gust of wind and went tumbling away at great speed. The boy began to cry, and Declan looked around to see the other children were close to tears also, having picked up their parents' nervousness and suddenly realized their precarious position. The adults' faces had stiffened and they didn't try to console their boys and girls. Declan was at a loss. The air hostess descended the steps and instructed them to board the plane immediately.

§

In Dublin, Guilfoyle took over and had the Poschiks and Vogels settled in a guesthouse. Declan made straight for Dundrum in a taxi. When he found no one at home he panicked and called his parents.

They told him that Sinéad was having a Caesarean that day. He ran out to the drive and started the Hornet.

Glancing at his dishevelled suit and soiled shirt, the nurse at reception directed him to the second floor. There he was told that Sinéad had just been taken into the operating theatre. He pleaded with the nurse to let him inside, but all she would promise was to let Sinéad know that he was waiting in the corridor. Shortly afterwards the nurse came back out to say that she'd informed his wife of his presence just before she went under. Soon another nurse came out of the theatre and left the door ajar for a few seconds. He saw Sinéad's body lying on the gurney, her belly huge, her head turned to one side, her eyes closed. Then the door was brusquely shut.

He stood there for about twenty minutes before he thought of going to the waiting room, where he found his mother and Belinda Grogan. His mother embraced him with relief and he shook hands with his mother-in-law. They told him what had happened and how Sinéad had been concerned that he wouldn't make it back in time. They were anxious to know where he'd been and why. But they didn't get a chance to find out: the nurse called him to say everything had gone well. Sinéad was still unconscious, but if Mr Boyle would like to follow her . . .

She brought him to a small room adjacent to the operating theatre and bent down to take his child out of a crib. 'Your daughter, Mr Boyle.' His daughter. As the nurse withdrew her fingers from under the head and back, and she nestled fully in the crook of Declan's arm, it came home to him with full force: there was another woman in his life, when he still hadn't got used to the fact of Sinéad.

The following weeks were the busiest of Declan's life. He took some days off, but spent most of the time on the phone. Mick Guilfoyle TD rang to warmly congratulate Declan on the birth of his daughter. He also said he thought the factory was a great idea, and he fully agreed with Declan that it should be built in the vicinity of Ardnabrayba. That area needed it, he said. Declan found the man likeable, and couldn't square the voice on the line with the ruthless character of Seán Guilfoyle's story.

He handed in his notice the same day he returned to work. Nothing was certain yet – neither the private capital nor the state support was in hand – but he knew he could not pursue the venture properly while working as a civil servant. Having made extensive notes for his report on his trip to Germany, he had the document typed up by lunchtime.

§

Towards the end of September, Declan drove down to Ardnabrayba with Robert Poschik to meet the Guilfoyle brothers. Mick went back there late on Wednesday every week so he could spend his Thursdays canvassing. Over dinner at the Clubhouse, he told them that he did this whether it was an election year or not. 'Once the punters get a sniff of Dublin Jackeen off you, you're finished.' Declan found himself agreeing with Mick Guilfoyle more frequently than he would have expected, and when the talk turned to Ardnabrayba he was impressed by the TD's knowledge of the families in the village, including his own. Mick said he was never able to get Declan's grandmother on his side, but she'd once been helpful to him in the matter of a dance hall which the parish priest was dead set against.

The main task, Mick said, was to get a decent road linking Ardnabrayba to the Galway road – and he reckoned he'd have it built within two years. Mick then switched into Irish as though he were just changing subjects. 'So you must have Irish so.'

'I wouldn't get far with German round these parts.'

Mick Guilfoyle laughed. 'I know your father's with Fine Gael. Ah sure, that's not to be helped. There are some fine people in that party as well.'

If Declan was puzzled as to how he should respond to this charm, then it was also clear that Mick Guilfoyle was puzzled by Declan. He must have struck the politician as a dry stick. Not man enough. But then again, Declan reminded himself that he'd pulled off a stunt to be proud of, far away from Ireland, whereas this politician was still uneasy about travelling up to Dublin. Guilfoyle wouldn't get any crack out of him, but he'd get a factory instead, and that would do the politician no harm at all.

When Declan walked through the door of the Two Widows, Mamó was there to greet him, though she'd little to do with the running of the place now, delegating most of the work to Dara, her grandson. Declan's uncle Joe still ran the farm outside the town, and the proposed site for the factory was a big rocky field that belonged to him. The day was overcast, but they could make out the grey forms of the Mweelrea Mountains in the distance. Rippling curtains of rain were dragged across the land to the west, leaving them, Declan reckoned, at least two hours before it reached Ardnabrayba.

Declan considered the landscape in front of them. He loved it, and now he would destroy it. That he'd known such happiness in pre-industrial Ardnabrayba was irrelevant. The village couldn't survive in the form he had kept in his memory; it needed machinery making ugly noises, even if that meant displacing the birdsong which they now heard in the meadow.

There was a substantial logistical problem to be solved. Declan had to take a call the following afternoon from Steinman Brothers Cohn in New York, who were considering a visit in order to decide if they would invest in the venture. James Boyle's father had worked with a man in New York whose son had become a partner in the firm. His name was Conor Larkin, and his call had to get through. This might not be easy in Ardnabrayba. Declan considered going in to Galway, but in the end he gave Larkin the Ardnabrayba number of his grandmother. She told him they had a party line and were dependent on the goodwill of the telephonist in the next village, where there was a small exchange in the post office. He had to go there and find the woman and agree with her that she would keep the line open between two and four in the afternoon.

When he arrived in the car he'd borrowed from his uncle, he found a handwritten sign on the post-office door which said 'Back in an hour', even though the posted opening hours claimed it was open. He went into the adjacent pub to ask what the chances were the postmistress would be back today. The publican pointed to the figure of a woman sitting by the window with a half-drunk glass of Guinness, apparently engrossed in the day's crossword. When Declan asked if he could disturb her for a short moment, she didn't appear put out. He introduced himself and she seemed to know about him. Why of course she'd be delighted to help him in the matter.

She was here on state time. He looked out on the street: there was little happening. 'Can I get you another?' he asked her. She dispatched the last of her stout, daintily touched her fingers to her lips and said that would be very kind of him.

At two o'clock the following afternoon, he positioned himself in his grandmother's spirit grocery. The shop had been closed temporarily. All was quiet.

The phone rang. He picked it up and he heard the postmistress say, 'Putting you through now, Mr Larkin.'

'Thank you,' Declan heard an American voice say.

'Hello, Mr Larkin?' Declan asked.

'Conor, it's Conor. And Declan! Very good to talk to you! Your secretary is very pleasant. She has the gift of the gab, like all us Irish.' Declan laughed, and didn't put Larkin right on either count.

'I haven't been to the old country since my father brought me as a boy. I'd like any excuse, I can tell you. But I've got to sell it to the board.'

Declan looked at the heavy rotary dial of the phone and cleared his throat. What he would say next was important, but *how* he said it might be even more important. This man Larkin was sitting in a well-appointed office in Manhattan and his secretary was a real secretary, not a postmistress. Declan couldn't begin to explain where he was and what was around him; the New York banker wouldn't be able to understand.

At that moment there was a *tap-tap* at the window and Declan looked up. A man was trying to get into the shop, clearly frustrated because he could see someone was inside who wouldn't open up for him. This must be the only person in the village who didn't know that Declan was taking an important call today.

The tapping continued. Declan realized that he had to speak as though he were already installed in a large office on the tenth floor of a modern building in Dublin. There was a pretty secretary. There were about fifty people working for him on the two floors below. If he wanted to make it happen, he had to sound as though it had happened already.

He took a breath and began. In the months that followed, he would remember little of what he said or how he said it. He would only recall that he stared the whole time at the infuriated face of the old man at the window who refused to stop tapping. The man tried the door and then returned to the window. *Tap-tap*. Pause. *Tap-tap-tap*. Declan didn't recognize the man. Perhaps he wasn't from the village. After a while, his grandmother went to the window upstairs and shouted down at the man, who stepped back from the shop window to look up. He roared something back. She roared again. He shook his fist. The upstairs window was loudly shut. The man glared into the pub again and then disappeared.

The phone call was finishing. Larkin was confident he'd be coming over with another partner next month. Declan might explain about the postmistress after Mamó had put a pint in Larkin's hand on a Friday evening when the fiddle players were taking a break and the pub was full of people, heat and fun. Then again, he might just leave it as it was.

4

The Royal Marine

1974–5

In the mornings the road was just a snaking band of dull tarmac leading down from their bungalow on the side of Doolagar Mountain to the village. But in the afternoons, when the sun had hauled itself from one side of the sky to the other, and the clouds with any luck had lifted, it shone like revelation, smooth silver grains mixed with gold, as it twisted between fields, stone walls, and the odd rowan tree listing to one side. Between two further mountains, in the distance, a shining wedge of the Atlantic was visible, and Sinéad often stood at the front door of the house in the porch, in an effort to absorb as much of this illumination as possible. But it never sufficed.

On winter mornings she would lie alone on the couch in the living room. How was it that there was no one to talk to; that even the smallest decisions baffled her; that she wished to eat nothing; that she never slept – or when she did, that she had only the most awful dreams; that she was, without doubt, the most worthless wretch in the world?

By four each morning she was wide awake and looking forward to the dawn. That would solve most problems. When it finally arrived and the family woke up, she'd prepare breakfast for them, riding an exhilarating wave of happiness. Declan would take the children off to school in the car. Then, slowly and remorselessly, parts of the bright world would disappear in blackness. A shadow behind the door would edge more largely into the room, the darker lines in the drapery's folds would thicken, and then the process accelerated as large regions of sky and land vanished, sucked clean of all colour and shape from behind. Even the band of sunlight that stretched some mornings from the window to the vinyl kitchen floor, catching a few legs of chairs, and to which Sinéad held on to as though it could save her, even that would blink out of existence, leaving her paralysed with fear, often shivering.

The problem, as she told herself over and over again, was in her head, which meant it couldn't be so hard to fix. The tops of the two yew trees they'd planted in front of the bungalow were tussled by the wind, and although the wind was usually fairly fierce, it seemed like slow motion. Everything was slow motion. When she got up from the couch and walked to the toilet or kitchen, it was like swimming through treacle. When she ran the tap into the kettle, each rounded facet of water curved away from gravity, sluggish and lazy, as though it had another destination. Often she didn't have the patience and dropped the kettle in the sink, collapsing in a nearby chair, where she would remain for minutes or hours.

They had come to Ardnabrayba five years ago, and now they were leaving. Sinéad had insisted they move from Dublin in the first place, so she had only herself to blame. When the factory was being set up, Declan had spent a year shuttling back and forth, occasionally staying in the country for weeks on end. One Friday night, returning late to Dublin, he dozed at the wheel for a second or two outside Celbridge and the car ended up in a ditch. He was unharmed, but she was shocked into action and declared that they would begin looking for a house in Ardnabrayba.

For the first four years she was at home with Issie. Declan worked long days at the factory and was often abstracted when he came home. She could see the numbers and ideas turning in front of his eyes as he did his best to pretend to listen to her. She'd hung on to the idea that they were still in this together, but then, inexorably, the old feeling of abandonment returned, and it did its work on her with more malevolence and accuracy. The Parstelin that the doctor prescribed had no effect, and the drug he replaced it with made her feel as though she were in a thickly padded astronaut suit, walking on the moon. She stopped taking it after a month, preferring the rawness of the pain to the detachment of medication.

Wine seemed a better way to find temporary relief, and after a month or two she would usually have drunk half a bottle of Vintara before her husband returned in the evening. Because she rationed herself to a glass every hour or so, she never felt drunk the way she did after too much champagne at a dinner dance. It settled her nerves and allowed her to deal with the children more confidently. Declan didn't seem to notice any difference in her.

§

The house was sold. They were leaving today. Standing at the window, Sinéad registered the chaos behind her as Declan herded Issie and Owen out of their bedrooms along the hall (did they need to go to the toilet? Did they need a drink of water?). She could sense him trying very hard not to get angry with her for doing nothing. The noise and movement around her were a relief; the ghosts of the house, or inside herself, couldn't get at her now.

A removal van had taken most of the furniture on Friday. Sinéad had imagined a period of calm would ensue until they got in the car on Saturday, but even as the removal van was pulling away she realized that they might struggle to fit the remaining items and themselves into the car. Remarking on this to Declan, Sinéad said that at this stage she'd be happy to let the car drive itself to Dublin, to leave them to lie on the floor for a week with nothing to do but stare at the ceiling.

They'd had dinner the night before at the Poschiks, who'd bought an old three-bedroom house in the village, with its front door on the main street. Sinéad sometimes regretted that they too hadn't bought a house in the village and instead were relegated to the cold mountainside of Doolagar. Declan's idea that the children would have more space to play and explore out in the countryside had made sense at first, but Owen spent more time at the sports ground beside his school than he did in the fields near the house.

Eva had invited them over after hearing that they'd be in an empty house on Friday evening. Sinéad knew that Eva did not yet have the Irish habit of offering three times, and so she accepted immediately. The children were good friends and left the adults alone. They were interrupted on two occasions – by a neighbour dropping back a saucepan and then by a friend of Eva's who joined them all for a cup of tea, leaving before dinner was served. They talked about the Festival Day the previous weekend, and Declan was complimented on his idea of delivering the beauty pageant contestants to the main stage outside the Two Widows on seven Hibernian tractors. Declan smiled and said it had been Robert's idea.

Eva had prepared a large spread of goulash and dumplings, followed by what she called kolaches – pastries covered in curds and walnuts which she'd been taught to cook by her Czech grandmother. To ingratiate herself with the locals in their first year, she'd carried plates of these cakes from house to house. Now she supplied the tea-shop on the main street. The story went that a busload of American tourists had polished off two trays of kolaches after being told by their guide that the cakes were a Connemara speciality.

Well, they were now, as indeed was Eva, who had established herself as a part of the village. At the start, Sinéad had seen it as her role to get Eva settled in, but the German woman proved resourceful, learning English quickly and enough words of Irish for the shop and the post office, if not negotiations with the schoolteacher and bank manager. She taught a home economics class at the primary school and attended every match and competition her children played, remembering everybody's names, as well as their children's and ailing relations. Then last year, when Eva had pretended to be concerned about her, Sinéad had reckoned it was high time to cool the friendship down, if indeed they'd ever been friends at all.

Declan wanted to be in Moate by lunchtime: it was their custom to eat at the carvery there on family trips to Dublin. The house keys had to be dropped with Dara at the Two Widows and a signed contract handed in at the factory. Sinéad was mildly irritated by these delays, as the prospect of Dublin came into clearer focus. She hadn't seen the inside of the Two Widows in four years, since the death of Declan's grandmother, when they'd all stood around the spirit grocery and listened to the priest saying that one of the town's great people had gone and that it was hard to imagine what would be done without her. But now, he'd continued, her grandson was changing the place in ways, he felt sure, that would make her proud in the years ahead. Máire Babs uí Bhaoill had often spoken to him of the achievement of Hibernia Traktors, and it was only right that this was repeated at the occasion of her funeral. It was not a sad day, but one of celebration of a life well lived for eighty-five years, as daughter, wife, mother and grandmother.

Declan got out of the car, walked swiftly to the door of the pub, knocked and waited. Dara, who lived over the pub and never went to bed before two in the morning, materialized eventually, and nodded blearily at Declan as he received the house keys.

Sinéad breathed in as Declan waved goodbye and pulled out into the scant traffic. Now to the factory. The butcher was already open, the marbled meats laid out at an angle in the window, and a scarfed woman Sinéad didn't recognize going in the door. The limit of the village was marked by a petrol station, whose two pumps stood alone in a lake of newly laid tarmac. Aloof from it, but falling into disrepair, was the old sergeant's house, now occupied by two unmarried brothers. Then a field on either side, lined by stone walls and filled with clumps of thistles and marshy grass. Cement mixers and diggers sat around the field; four bungalows were being built, Declan had told her.

Just at the moment when you thought you were free of the village and swung around the bend, the Hibernia Traktors plant spread out in front of your eyes on the left side of the road. Sinéad had grown to hate the look of it, with its linked metal fencing, proud signage and corrugated iron roofing, all set in a sea of concrete. The wound the factory had made in the land was still so raw; even after five years it obviously didn't belong there.

Declan left the documents with the man at the gate. The plant was quiet today, the car park empty. He would be down again at the end of next week, and regularly thereafter, but he had turned the day-to-day running of the factory over to Seán Guilfoyle and had promised not to slip back into commuting from Dublin. Sinéad watched her husband gesturing, and the man, in his twenties, laughed appreciatively. Declan had learned how to be a boss, but also how to tell a joke or two, or make an enquiry into the health of a man's wife, his children's marks at school. He told her that he remembered the way his grandmother used to do it, and that he often recalled her tone of voice and gestures.

§

The move back to Dublin, having been a vague fantasy for Sinéad, had quickly come to seem inevitable. She and Declan had talked, vaguely at first, about the benefits of educating the children in Dublin. Declan had become involved in a couple of property investments in Dublin and Manchester, and complained about the difficulty of travelling from remote Connemara. He told her he felt he'd completed the real work of setting up Hibernia Traktors, which was now trading profitably, and she got the impression that he was getting bored. Then, in January, James Boyle had died unexpectedly while changing back into his clothes after an early-morning swim at the Forty Foot. For a period after the funeral, Sinéad was married to a man who was as lost and confused as she was. Declan couldn't concentrate on his work, didn't hear when Owen spoke to him, would leave his dinner untouched on the table while staring into space. Nursing her husband through his grief, she forgot her own. She listened to him for hours while he talked of how he always felt he'd disappointed his father's expectations. Why had the old man never visited them in Ardnabrayba? Sinéad didn't have the answer to that.

At the funeral he met several old friends from the neighbourhood, and soon he began voicing his concern that his mother would not be able to cope in the house alone. Sinéad could not conceive of her mother-in-law being unable to cope, in any situation, but she was surprised on their visit to Dublin a month later to see how diminished Catherine Boyle was. For most of the weekend she remained in the armchair by the fire, a rug over her legs, capable of talking only about her husband and what everyone had said about him at the funeral. Her face was pale and she seemed to have become physically weaker. Declan now worried about her living on her own. It had never occurred to Sinéad that moving to Dublin would mean moving into the big house on Mount Merrion Avenue, but for Declan this became an essential element of the plan, and she was so desperate to get out of Ardnabrayba she did not feel she could object.

She had tried to argue against sending Issie to Roebuck, where the nuns had taught her and her fellow students that their accomplishments in life must be merely adornments to their lucky husbands. Declan answered that there was no other good girls' school in the vicinity. He wouldn't countenance the idea of Sion Hill, and the Loretos were too far away. What about the new school on Newtownpark Avenue? It was going to be mixed and non-denominational, though it was run by the Church of Ireland. Or St Andrews on Booterstown Avenue, which, although Presbyterian, didn't shove religion down the throats of the students? He came back to her with reasons she couldn't now recollect – something to do with university places or the like – but she knew he wanted the children to go to a Catholic school, in the traditional way, without the distraction of the opposite sex. In so many other respects Declan was impatient with the past, but on this he was immovable.

Sinéad dreaded the slow queue of cars nudging their way into and out of Roebuck, for Issie, and Deerpark, for Owen, morning and afternoon, a primped and neurotic woman behind the steering wheel of every saloon and estate car. Two schools, twice a day, at least until Owen would be able to take the number 17 bus by himself.

They were in Moate by one o'clock and were coasting along a quiet Rock Road by half four. Declan depressed the indicator and they swerved right up Merrion Avenue. Owen pointed out Molloy's shop to Issie, telling her the exact kinds of sweets they had. Sinéad felt her hopes rising as they approached the house. This was a good place to bring up a family. Owen would like Deerpark: he'd excelled in Gaelic football at Ardnabrayba National School, and always enjoyed passing the rugby ball back and forth with Declan on Saturday afternoons. And Issie: the more she thought about her daughter, the more she considered that the Roebuck nuns might come off worse from the encounter. Even at six she was fiercely independent, not seeming to need the same cuddles and attention that Owen had craved.

The car crunched to a stop on the gravelled drive. Catherine Boyle opened the tall, heavy door and came down the front steps to greet them.

As they were dropping their things in the hall, Sinéad looked around the hall and saw herself framed in the large mirror; behind her was the door to the living room, letting in some light, and a glimpse of the bookshelves that reached to the ceiling and rows of generously spaced ornaments. The hall itself had neck-high wainscoting in the same dark wood as the floor. Plaster foliage braided the angle where the wall met the ceiling. She sensed the shades of the house arming themselves against her, bracing themselves for a struggle. She breathed in and announced war on them.

§

The first phase of her campaign was redecorating. In this she did not meet the expected resistance: Catherine Boyle had declared that Sinéad was now the woman of the house and, still evidently paralysed with grief, had withdrawn almost completely from the house to her bedroom on the second floor. Some days she didn't rise from bed, and Sinéad had to bring up her meals. For most of her life she had enjoyed good health, but was now the victim of one minor ailment after another. A tiny kitchenette was installed on the second floor to allow her to make tea for herself, and this was especially useful in the months when workmen were coming and going through the front door.

Sinéad had firmly instructed the architect to 'make the place fresh and new', and he'd set to work with enthusiasm, introducing as many modern elements as possible to the old Edwardian structure. She sighed with relief each time another feature of the old house was removed: a fireplace, banisters, the Aga. She paid especial attention to the new kitchen, imagining how she would expand her gastronomic repertoire on its brightly polished hobs and worktops.

The second phase of the campaign was to bring new people into the house. This was where Sinéad lost momentum. She didn't want her old friends from school and UCD, but she didn't know how to go about making new ones. The panic began to rise in her again, and she felt that although she'd inflicted significant wounds on the old house, it was now regrouping for attack.

In the end, Issie made new friends for her. Sinéad began sharing the school commute with two other Roebuck mothers, and when Jackie or Bronagh dropped Issie off just after three, Sinéad would often invite the other woman in for a glass of wine. When either Jackie or Bronagh left an hour later, Sinéad felt a need to clear away the evidence of what remained of the bottle. Owen often found his mother drowsy on the couch in the living room with the heavy curtains closed when he returned in the early evening after rugby practice, usually still in his kit with a school bag on one shoulder and a sports bag on the other. Iseult would be somewhere in the house doing her homework, watching TV or practising her writing.

Owen's arrival always cheered Sinéad. She would get up from the couch and slowly make her way over to him to give him a long hug, which he tried to return with equal intensity. Then she would tell him to sit down in the armchair and tell her what had happened to him that day. He felt it his responsibility to cheer her out of her sadness with stories of teachers, schoolmates and intrigues in the bike sheds. He told her things that his friends would never dream of telling their parents, and he was good at honing the details to a comic point. The conspiracy warmed Sinéad and she held on to it tightly. She loved Owen for the look of sympathy on his face, for the way it pained him that she was in pain. Why couldn't Declan ever see what was so obvious to even his ten-year-old son?

At some point, Sinéad realized with happiness that she didn't really need the excuse of Jackie or Bronagh in order to open a bottle in the afternoon and drink it all. She would hash up some kind of dinner and retire to bed while the children ate in the kitchen. Declan would often find her asleep when he got home from work, and this left him free to stay up late with his papers in the study.

§

Jackie Conroy and Bronagh Keane came to dinner with their husbands, Louis and Eddie. The men hardly knew one another, or Declan, apart from the occasional school drop-off or hockey match. They had no business interests in common and no mutual acquaintances they could discuss. Louis Conroy was in advertising and Jackie had been his secretary. Eddie Keane was an electrician, from Ringsend, who'd built his business by winning contracts to maintain the systems in the new office blocks that were springing up in the city. It was rare for a Roebuck girl to marry a man of his ilk, and Sinéad was curious to meet him.

The women retreated to the kitchen, leaving the men standing with G&Ts. Eddie Keane enquired about Declan's work.

'I set it up in 1968, and we lived down in Connemara for a few years,' Declan said carefully. 'Things weren't too great around the oil crisis, but they're looking up again, thankfully.'

'So how many people do you have working for you there, Declan?'

'About three hundred.'

'I don't need that many people myself, for the moment anyway,' Eddie joked. 'It's a lot of responsibility. And the next thing you know you'll be kidnapped by the IRA like that Dutch chappie in Limerick.' Keane gave the word 'chappie' ironic emphasis. 'He had about 1,400 people in his factory. So you're probably safely off their radar for the time being.'

Like everyone else in the country, Declan had followed the kidnapping case: the Guards were laying siege to a tiny council house in Kildare where a Dutch industrialist was being held by terrorists. As people said, the man had come to Ireland and brought economic prosperity to Limerick and this was how he was repaid. Declan couldn't avoid a sense of dread every time he picked up a paper or sat down for the evening news: perhaps this was the day the man had been killed.

Declan didn't like to be reminded of it, but he tried to run with the joke. 'We'll have to start using the IRA hit list as a measure of industrial success. No doubt it's fairly accurate.'

Eddie laughed. 'You'll know you've made it, Declan, when you're bound and gagged and giving your breakfast order to a lad in a black balaclava who's none too friendly.'

'I think Sinéad needs me in the kitchen,' Declan said. 'I won't be a moment.'

The three women were smiling conspiratorially when he entered the kitchen. They had all attended south Dublin convent schools, and they were trading stories of early smoking in risky locations. Bronagh and Jackie now explained to him that they'd discovered they'd had the same boyfriend, though not at the same time. Declan asked Sinéad if she needed any help.

'No, we're doing fine here, aren't we? You go back to the men.'

'Though we do need a refill, don't we, girls?'

'Yes, please!'

Two hours later the dessert was finished and the tone of the conversation was wheeling ever more wildly. Somehow they'd arrived at religion.

'Jackie, what do you think of the nuns? No, no. Not just the nuns, but the priests too, and all their old dope?' Sinéad directed a stare towards Declan as she said this.

'Jesus, Sinéad. I had a bellyful of them at school. Oh, they were boring, and you couldn't do anything to stop them, except maybe ask them a question that scandalized them completely and made them blush. At least then you'd have a bit of fun. But otherwise, Jesus—'

Eddie interrupted. 'The parish priest came to my parents telling them I had, eh, a "vocation". My mother was delighted, and she nearly had me signed up for Clonliffe. Now I don't—'

Sinéad hadn't registered a word he'd said, and she cut across him: 'Bronagh, Bronagh! What do you think of all that old dope? You'd have to be a right eejit to believe it, wouldn't you? I mean, we all send our kids to the nuns, don't we? But that doesn't actually mean that we believe all their old shite, does it?' She held up her empty glass towards Declan and wiggled it from side to side imperiously, without looking him in the eye. 'More wine, please.'

'Oho, it looks like your lovely lady needs a refill.' Eddie did his best to prevent his smile from turning into a leer.

Before Declan could respond, Eddie took the bottle of claret from the centre of the table, filled Sinéad's glass to the brim, then did the same to his own.

For a moment Declan fought the urge to rise from the table and tell Eddie Keane and his wife to leave the house. How much had he himself had to drink? He felt the heat suddenly go to his face and he realized he wouldn't trust himself to pour a glass for anyone, let alone his wife, who was very drunk, and had been very drunk for a long time. So when he told her, 'Perhaps you've had enough,' he not only meant that she'd had enough this evening, he was also thinking about the past few months, or indeed years. Her eyelids were red and puffy, and she had an expression of bovine stupidity, this woman who was so beautiful and anything but stupid. He could see the resentment she felt towards him. Where did that come from? What was going on? The evening was turning into a grotesque carnival. He had to do something, say something, to bring it back under control.

When Jackie and Bronagh heard his words, their eyes widened in expectation. Eddie leaned back in his chair a little, as though to get out of the way of the blast. Louis Conroy appeared to be asleep. Sinéad looked furious, but she said nothing, and the moment passed.

Eddie turned to the others with mock tact and said that perhaps it was time they were all going home. Louis Conroy awoke on that word and stood up abruptly and comically.

Declan showed them to the door, and when he returned to Sinéad at the dining table he could hear them outside, laughing on the drive as they fumbled with car keys and made arrangements to meet again.

'Perhaps it's time . . .' Declan began, but Sinéad cut him off.

'No, it's not time. I'll say when it's time. This was my dinner party, and for once in my life I'll say when it's time. God, that I don't have to sit listening to some government minister just because it's good for your business. I'm sick to death of what's good for your business. Do you hear me? Have you heard me once in all the years we've been married?'

'Sinéad . . .' Declan began again.

'Do you hear me? I've had it, do you hear me? You abandoned me.'

Sinéad had howled the last sentence, and pushed her whole body towards him. He was aware of her words echoing around the room.

He remembered the awful night in Ardnabrayba when Issie had wandered out onto the hillside. The wind-driven rain tore at him, blinding him and almost knocking him down. Eventually, he'd found her, cowering beneath a wall. When he reached down and took her in his arms, he felt such utter exhilaration and relief, as though with one gesture he had put to rights the wrongness of the universe.

He needed to do this again, for Sinéad this time, right here in their living room, but he had no idea how. He realized that the wine was allowing his wife to speak, and what she said made him confused and angry.

'What do you mean, I abandoned you?' He paused, anger growing in him. 'What do you bloody well mean?'

'You haven't even noticed, have you? You haven't even noticed how miserable I've been for the last ten years. I thought we'd be in it together. Do you remember that night in Jammet's? We were both going to be in it together, weren't we? But you betrayed me. I became somebody to bring up your children and to appear all dolled up by your side every fortnight or so at some God-awful dinner dance with a lot of God-awful people. I'm thirty-seven years of age and it's over for me. I'm finished.' And then, once again, more quietly as though to herself: 'I'm finished.'

'What did you bloody well expect?' he retorted. 'Did you think you were going to build tractors? Did you think you were going to go to the meetings? That was my job. Your job was to look after our children. And it's just as well for you that Issie doesn't need much looking after, isn't it?' Declan had never formulated the last thought to himself, but just as she'd sought out his most painful areas, he found himself instinctively doing the same.

Sinéad stood up and in one quick movement smashed her half-full glass on the floor. 'You're such a bastard,' she said slowly and quietly. She went to the door, her gait unequal to her determin-ation. Declan made to get up, but then sat down again.

He stared down the table at the dinner party's detritus – the crumpled napkins, some stained with lipstick, the dregs in the wine glasses, the dessert plates which hadn't been cleared away, smears of caramel and irregular small pyramids of crème custard strewn on them, the two ashtrays full, one candle guttering, the other coming close. The silence in the room was unnerving in the immediate wake of the word 'bastard' and also after all the loud talk of the evening. Declan thought he still heard the faintest echo of Sinéad's parting shot ringing back and forth across the room. But no. The house was completely silent. He couldn't hear Sinéad moving around, and his mother would have gone to sleep hours ago.

After about ten minutes the door began to open slowly. It couldn't have been Sinéad or Owen, as he would have heard their footsteps. It was Issie, in all the splendour of her seven years, sleep in her eyes and her nightgown on the wrong way round, the way she always liked to wear it. She said nothing but only looked all around the room and then at him.

'Issie . . .' Declan didn't trust himself to say anything else.

'Daddy, I woke up. Why are you here? I heard cars outside and people laughing.'

She took a step towards him.

'No!' he said. 'There's glass on the floor.' He went over to her. 'Issie . . .'

'Daddy, is everything all right?'

Declan stooped down and swung her up into his arms so that her chin was resting on his shoulder.

'Yes, everything is all right.' He carried her up into the darkness of the upper house, leaving the lights to burn in the dining room till morning.

§

When Sinéad woke the next day, it was early and no one was stirring in the house. Declan was asleep in the bed beside her. She put on her dressing gown and went downstairs to the dining room, as though to check she'd remembered the course of the evening correctly. Everything was as she thought it would be, and so she went to the kitchen to find the brush and dustpan, returning to the dining room to sweep up the pieces of broken glass. When she was sure she'd cleaned up every last piece, she set to clearing the table, bringing the glass and delf into the kitchen on a tray. Her hands were steady. She did the dishes, and when she'd cleaned all the worktops, she put the breakfast things out on the table. Then she made herself a cup of coffee and sat down to wait.

As she'd expected, Declan rose before the children. She heard his footsteps in the bedroom above and then how he made his way to the bathroom to have a shower. He came into the kitchen about ten minutes later, said good morning and sat down at the table. She returned his greeting and took a drink of her coffee. Then she asked him if he'd like a cup of coffee, and he said yes. When she handed it to him, he thanked her and she went back to her seat and looked out at the garden, which always caught morning light in ways that commanded attention. She thought she saw everything more sharply this particular morning: the house, the garden, her husband. She tried not to remember anything, but her own words kept returning to her. She did not feel sorry for saying them, but neither did she know what to say next.

Their life could not go back to the way it was, but they did not know what to do now. They said nothing for the next hour, except to offer more coffee, or orange juice. When Owen and Issie came down from their bedrooms, about ten minutes apart, they both seemed to sense the special atmosphere at the kitchen table, and they behaved as though they'd joined a solemn ritual which demanded their silence. Owen took the dessert spoon for his corn-flakes very quietly out of the cutlery drawer and did not complain that there was not enough milk to cover the cereal. The first crunching sounds he made seemed too loud, and thereafter he tried to crunch each mouthful slowly. Sinéad had to get up to pre-pare Issie's two slices of toast and honey, and her daughter waited patiently in her chair, looking at her father and swinging her legs back and forth beneath her.

After a little while, Sinéad noticed that Owen and Issie were exchanging conspiratorial glances and that Owen was ever so subtly moving his dessert spoon. Without moving her head, she looked down to see what he was doing. He made the spoon move cau-tiously and curiously out from behind the cereal bowl, as though to take a peek at Issie, and when Issie turned her head to look at the spoon, he whipped it back quietly behind the bowl. Then, five or six seconds later, the spoon, having gathered its courage again, would begin inching its head out to consider the frightening monster that was the seven-year-old girl. In the concentration of the game, both children had forgotten their parents and the atmosphere in the kitchen. Sinéad glanced towards Declan, expecting him to be abstractedly looking out the window, and she was surprised when she saw that he too was absorbed in Owen's dumbshow, a small shimmer of delight behind his exhausted face.

After five minutes of this, Issie could stand the tension no longer and burst out laughing. Owen looked up at his parents, worried that he'd done something wrong, and was relieved that they were both smiling and that he'd entertained them as well as his sister. He too then began smiling and asked Issie if she wanted to look at the car-toons with him. She jumped off her chair without answering him and ran out of the kitchen, Owen following after. Sinéad and Declan still did not know what they would do, but now at least they'd man-aged the first hour of the rest of their lives.

§

Declan had to go to London the following day and was due to return on Thursday, but he was able to cut the visit short, returning late on Wednesday evening. The children were in bed, and Sinéad was waiting for him. When he came into the kitchen, he could smell the potatoes and a stew that was rich and fragrant. On the table there was a bottle of Guinness, which he preferred to wine with his midweek meals. Again they ate mostly in silence, apart from asking mundane questions of each other now and again. How was the trip? How was Owen's performance? Was Declan's meeting all right? Did Issie still have a sore throat?

They finished eating, and Declan drank the last of his bottle of Guinness. He pushed his chair back a little from the table but didn't cross his legs. Instead he put his hands lightly on his knees and leaned forward a little.

'What are we going to do now?' he asked.

Sinéad answered that she didn't know, she just didn't know. They continued looking into each other's eyes.

Over the following weeks they remained careful in their dealings with each other and Sinéad cut back her drinking. Declan's property ventures were, as he said, at such a stage that he couldn't ease up for a few months, and although he was able to cut short some trips, he made no major changes to his schedule. He did not consider that a necessary consequence of what Sinéad had said to him. She had her job and he had his. Once that was accepted, and once she'd forgiven herself for what she'd said to him, then things would improve.

Sinéad in her turn waited patiently for Declan to understand the implications of her outburst. After several months, however, it was clear to her that the dinner party had provided merely another opportunity for them to misunderstand each other. This made her feel more bitter than ever. She'd given him a chance to understand her, and he'd not taken it, or had been unable to take it, which amounted to the same thing.

One day Declan received a phone call at work from Bronagh Keane to say that she would no longer be able to share the duties of pick-up and drop-off with Sinéad. At first he didn't understand why she'd called him and not Sinéad; nor did he understand Bronagh's reason for ending an arrangement that was convenient for everyone. He pushed her on the subject. She avoided a straight answer. He pushed yet again and, reluctantly, she told him that she'd received a phone call from the school at 6 p.m. the day before to say that the three children still hadn't been picked up. It'd been Sinéad's turn, and Bronagh was at home waiting for a plumber to arrive. She'd to go up to Roebuck and pick up the girls. When Sinéad opened the door to them, it was clear that she was, well, 'the worse for wear'. She didn't even thank Bronagh or apologize. 'I don't think Issie understood,' Bronagh reassured him.

Declan thanked her and said he understood her position.

He drove home and found Sinéad in the kitchen finishing a bottle of wine. It was around midday. He started telling her that she had to stop drinking, but he saw from the belligerent expression that came over her face that he wouldn't be able to persuade her. She began shouting at him. She shouted that she hoped his mother would hear her and find out the truth about her beloved son. After two or three minutes of this, she began crying. Declan escorted her upstairs to their room and put her in bed. He got up to leave, but she begged him not to go, not to abandon her, please. He said he wouldn't leave her, he just wanted to get a glass of water. She let him go, and he was back quickly and lay down on the bed beside her still in his suit and his shoes.

The house was quiet. He could hear the cars on the road outside, shuttling between Blackrock and Stillorgan. He presumed his mother was in her bed. They were alone. There was a strong smell of wine – sickly, rich – on Sinéad's breath, and she held on to him as they lay there in silence. The phone began ringing down in the hall. Declan listened without any impulse to answer it. He did not even wonder who might be calling. The sound of the cars outside counterpointed the phone's insistence. Then it stopped, leaving a larger silence.

Later that evening Sinéad promised him that she would stop drinking. For two months she kept her promise. When she began drinking again, she was better at concealing it, taking care to remove the empty bottles to the bin and learning Declan's schedule intimately so that he would never come upon her when she was far gone. She was confident that she'd regained the appearance of a good housewife running her family well, and so she was surprised one lunchtime when she opened the door to see Helen Creighton, asking if she could come in for a cup of tea and a chat.

They'd seen little of each other after the Boyles had moved to Galway, but Sinéad knew Helen had been having her own troubles. The Creightons' younger son, Stephen, who was born the year after Owen, had constant respiratory difficulties and remained the same height as his classmates grew larger. When the Creightons were eventually told by a specialist that he had cystic fibrosis, they had no idea what it meant. As they learned more and as the boy's prospects came into focus, Liam Creighton disappeared further into his work. Helen started drinking heavily, and eventually the specialist noticed her desperation and quietly gave her a number to call.

Sinéad put a cup of tea on the kitchen table in front of her old acquaintance.

'So I called the number, Sinéad, and I thought it would be some other mother who had a child with CF, but it wasn't that at all. The doctor had given me a number for somebody in Alcoholics Anonymous. The woman didn't say that at first, but just asked me if I'd like to meet for tea sometime. I agreed. When we met, she told me all about herself and that she knew the doctor not as a patient but as a fellow alcoholic. I told her I wasn't an alcoholic and that I had no idea what she was talking about. I paid for the tea and left quickly. But in about a month's time I found myself in tears for no reason, drunk as a lord at eleven in the morning, and I remembered her and picked up the phone. She refused to see me that day as she said I was drunk and there was no point, but she suggested we meet the next day, after we'd both dropped off our children at school. So I did. We talked. She told me once again she was an alcoholic. She didn't insist that I was one, but I knew damn well then that I was. I still couldn't say it though. I was too ashamed.'

Helen asked Sinéad if she'd be willing to go that evening to a meeting in Blackrock village. Sinéad said nothing, just nodded, wrote down the details on a piece of paper, thanked her friend for coming to visit and, as Helen was leaving, said, 'See you then.'

The afternoon was a long one. She picked up Issie at 3 p.m., and bought the paper and some groceries in Molloy's on the way back. The *Irish Times* was spread out across the kitchen table, a cup of tea was at her hand, but she was attending to neither. Her daughter had disappeared up to her room to do her homework. Declan's mother was in town for the day. After a while, she took a sip of her tea and found it was cold. She made another cup and tried to remember to drink it this time. The house was quiet, apart from the faint noises that Issie made above and the cars washing by on the road outside.

At half five she heard the key in the front door and turned in her chair to look out at the hall. She saw Owen putting down his school bag and his kitbag in the hall, and padding over to the door of the living room in his socks. She was going to call out to him when she saw his expression as he reached for the door handle of the living room: it was a mixture of fear and apprehension. Why on earth would he be frightened? Owen was the entertainer of the household, the one who knew how to turn every situation to lightness and comedy. He took a breath before he pushed down on the door handle.

When she called out to him cheerfully from the kitchen, she saw the transformation in his face as delight came over it – delight at the fact that she was not in the living room with the curtains closed, lying on the couch drunk, with the world, including him, gone dark in front of her eyes. Many years later, after she'd attended hundreds of meetings like the one that lay ahead of her that day, she would tell this story. How she'd watched her son come in the door. How she'd seen the fear in his eyes. How she knew that she'd created that fear. How she then knew she was an alcoholic and that she would never touch a drink again.

§

The rooms were awful. Since no one smoked in her home, what struck Sinéad was the reek of cigarettes, not recently smoked, but smoked in these spaces for years, the odour sunk deep in the carpets and curtains, colouring the walls and ceilings beige. She was offended, too, by the stackable plastic chairs in broken rows across the cheap carpet, the white paint applied over older flaking plaster, the large radiators that should have been replaced decades before. These rooms occupied neglected spaces scattered across south Dublin, unloved bits of libraries, rectories, civic offices. Newcomers had to do their best to find the rooms, as no one wrote 'Alcoholics Anonymous' on the roster. Still, everyone else knew and the French learners leaving the room and the yoga students arriving after them were more than usually curious.

Sinéad was surprised how many people in the meetings she knew from public life, people she considered infallible pillars of society, who pronounced sentences, wrote editorials. There was a singer-songwriter whom Owen liked, and Sinéad had to bite her tongue every time she came home after a meeting where she'd met and talked with him again. Some of them came from roads, groves, closes, arbours, parks, crescents in the area, where they pretended to be upstanding citizens; and then they arrived in this room where they admitted that they weren't. A man would not stand outside his front garden and tell his neighbour how he'd got drunk the night before, come home, beaten his wife, kicked a hole in the door of his children's bedroom, and then fallen asleep in the bath having failed to get all his vomit in the toilet. But when he stood up in the meeting, a few miles down the road, he would say it all.

Sitting there listening, she felt buried alive, her mouth full of moist earth, distantly hearing voices above her, talking about experiences and sensations she recognized but had never heard expressed. When, after a couple of weeks, she got up, said her name and what she was, she told her story not because she finally understood it herself, but because she wanted to find a way to that understanding. She simply said what had happened. If anybody had asked what the substance of her discovery was, she could only have responded by telling her story once again, from the beginning.

Compared to the other stories she'd heard – of beatings from drunken parents or husbands, or sexual abuse, or financial ruin –

Sinéad's story was more like a fairy tale. She tried to turn this into a joke to avoid the embarrassment at the start, but the only person who laughed was herself. What was the matter then? She was worthless, wasn't she? That was it. The day she disappeared, few people would notice. Her husband would mourn her for a few months and then take on more work. Owen was big enough to survive, and Issie preferred her father in any case.

The first to reply was Ruth, an older woman who reminded her of Mrs English in her father's office. She said, first of all, that Sinéad was not worthless. Nobody was worthless. She said that another person listening to Sinéad might ask what the hell she expected, getting married and having kids. But, she said, some women just can't do it all. Some women are built for other things. There's nothing wrong with that.

Ruth seemed about to add something, but then abruptly thanked Sinéad for telling her story, and took her seat again. When the meeting was breaking up, Ruth approached her and said she noticed that Sinéad didn't have a sponsor yet, and if she liked, she, Ruth, would be glad to do it. Sinéad could think about it. She smiled again and reached out to touch Sinéad's forearm. 'You did great.'

At the touch, she felt tears coming.

Helen had brought her to the first meeting, but after that she drove herself. Once, when her car was being repaired, Declan picked her up in Blackrock and they decided to go for a coffee out in Dún Laoghaire. They tried Ross's Hotel, but it was closed, so they drove back along the seafront to the Royal Marine. Beside the hotel were tall hoardings that stretched up to the main street – 'A new shopping centre,' Declan said.

'You know,' Sinéad said, 'I can't remember what was there when we had our wedding reception. We must have been driven past it. Were there houses or something?'

Declan laughed. 'I can't remember myself.'

They dashed through the rain and into the intricate, monumental Victorian portico, like a fortification the Empire had abandoned in its withdrawal. It commanded a view of the harbour, and the mail boats coming in and out at Carlisle Pier. The East Pier stretched around it like a protecting arm, but in the October darkness they could see only the lights on its promenade. They found a free table in the reception area, near a window, against which the rain broke in irregular waves.

'Someone joked today that if the country were run by recovering alcoholics, we'd be a whole lot better off than we are at the moment,' Sinéad said. The waitress had just put down the tray with coffee cups and pot on the table and walked away.

Declan frowned, his eyes on the back of the waitress, and shifted in his seat.

'What's wrong?' Sinéad asked.

'I don't really understand this business of "recovering alcoholics". You're not alcoholics any more. Why do you say you're an alcoholic, recovering or otherwise, when you haven't touched a drink for months?'

'I'm never going to stop being an alcoholic. That's what they explained to me at the very start. Ruth has been going to AA for twenty years.'

'I also don't see why it stops you having the occasional glass of wine, for God's sake, like the normal person you are. You'd be completely fine, I know you would.'

'Addiction doesn't work like that, Declan. It's more like a disease that could come back at any time, triggered even by a single glass of wine.' She'd explained this to him before, and was irritated at his failure to absorb it.

Declan was silent for a while, turning things round in his head.

'Yes, you've told me that, that having too many drinks is a disease. It seems to me that it's not my fault if I catch a cold, but there's no doubt that it's my fault if I go to that bar now and drink ten pints. What kind of a disease would make me do that, for God's sake? Those people just want to let themselves off the hook. It's not a disease – it's their *fault*, which is something completely different. Can't you see that? You don't need them and their old talk any more. You're all right again.'

Declan looked around the reception area of the hotel. Most of the noise came from the bar area: clusters of people trying to get an order in, and two well-dressed older ladies retreating to the next couch down with their Babychams. They settled themselves into their seats with clucks and shifts of satisfaction, clinking their glasses together as though they'd just received news about a will.

'I *am* all right again, love,' Sinéad said as she leaned over and put her hand on his arm to squeeze it. 'And it's thanks in large part to all the help you've given me. But I'm just not strong enough to take a drink again, and I need those people to help me keep that strength. And I need you too.' She squeezed his arm once more, and then sat back in the couch.

Declan released a long sigh. He looked out the window at the dark bay, and she followed his gaze. It was nearly nine o'clock and the rain had drawn off. The tarmac in the car park scintillated under the lamps and the mail boat was arriving. Off to the right, the lights of Sandycove, the house at the end lit up, the last human outpost before the enormous darkness of the sea and sky. It was his turn to follow her eyes.

'Listen, I'm sorry for what I said.'

'It's all right.'

'I think I'm more messed up about this than you, really. It kills me that there's nothing I can do to help you.'

'You know that's not true.'

'I mean, that you have to go to these other people. That it's not enough at home. That I'm not enough. But listen, I've been think-ing about what you said. Maybe you really do need something else. Your father was telling me again about those summers you worked in the office with him. He said you were a whiz at the accounts. Would you not think of maybe trying the exams?'

'You mean for chartered accountancy?'

'Yes.'

Sinéad laughed. 'You're joking.'

'I'm not. Your father said you learned quicker than anyone else. Why not give it a shot? If the property stuff expands in the next few years, my accounts guy will need help. What are you going to do otherwise? I can't see you running a boutique for the respectable wives of Foxrock.'

'Jesus save us,' she said with a laugh that had an edge of panic to it. Then she paused and looked at him. 'You really mean it, don't you?'

'Yes. Is there anything you'd rather do?'

She was so lost in thought, she didn't reply.

'You could take some night courses in the next year or two – nothing too onerous – and maybe consider the exams in a few years' time. To be honest with you, I've never been that good with the numbers myself.'

It had got noisier. Muzak filled the reception area – a song by Neil Diamond, his voice replaced by a string section. The paint was flaking off a pillar beside the entrance to the bar, where they were playing some kind of disco. The two sorts of music collided where Declan and Sinéad were sitting.

'Let's go out for a walk. The rain's stopped.'

They paid and walked down the middle of the lawn towards the seafront, the brightly lit hotel disappearing behind them.

'It's got a bit dowdy, hasn't it, since 1962?' Declan remarked.

'God, I expected Basil Fawlty to leap out from behind one of the potted plants.'

'Why don't I pick you up more often and we'll go for a coffee, only not to the Royal Marine? We'll find somewhere else. Maybe up to the Montrose.'

'Oh, not the Montrose. It's like a glorified motel. I like the seafront. Let's keep going to the dowdy Royal Marine.'

'You know Owen's playing out-half now, just like my father. Maybe that was my big mistake, to try for wing-forward. Or maybe the rugby talent just skipped a generation. I could see Owen making the Junior Cup team in three or four years.'

Sinéad laughed and said, 'I hope not. I don't want to think of him getting knocked to pieces on the pitch.' She said this with a pout, but meant it seriously.

He looked away, enjoying the prospect of his son running up the steps at Lansdowne Road to take the cup. He normally had no great interest in rugby, but he'd experienced a moment of exaltation the first time he saw his son score a try by virtue of his talent alone, weaving between the backline of their opponents and placing the ball casually on the grass between the goalposts. He'd converted the try as well, almost looking away as his boot hit the ball to send it flying straight between the posts. He was obviously a talent, but Declan knew that he frustrated the trainers by his lack of application. They were irked also by the knowledge that if they'd dropped him, Owen probably wouldn't mind. Not that he was apathetic; it was more that he was extraordinarily equable. They had no power over him. This made Declan even more proud of his son, even as he shared their feeling that some central core of the boy remained untouched by all that went on around him – both at school and at home.

They passed the bandstand on the right. A group of teenagers sitting on the high wall shouted an obscenity in their general direction.

'Did you see Issie's English homework last week?' Declan asked.

'Yes, I did.'

'The story about the ghost of Blackhall House? With the dragon in the cellar who tried to get an appointment at the hairdresser's after a hundred years? Where does she get it from? Neither of us was good at English. She's amazing.'

Sinéad was silent for a moment or two, then, looking straight ahead, said, 'Any time I offer to help with her homework she politely refuses, saying that she doesn't have any problems with it. She's a puzzle to me. I even checked it after, and she was right. She doesn't have any problems with it. Sometimes I wish . . .'

'What?'

'Sometimes I wish she *did* have some problems that I could help her with. She's so independent. She doesn't seem to need anybody's help.'

They drove home through Monkstown, and Declan stopped off in the late-night shop in Blackrock for a pint of milk for the morning. Sinéad watched a few customers inching slowly along the counter of the Central Café, like fish in a tank. The man behind the counter moved quickly between the till and the deep-fryers.

It was nearly ten o'clock when they swung into the drive, but a light was still on in Issie's bedroom.

'She must be reading again,' Sinéad said. 'I told her not to. I'll go straight up to her.'

'No, let me do it.'

Sinéad looked at Declan and nodded. The wind had come up again and the trees were tossing from side to side in the darkness. They walked up the granite steps, and after the front door was closed the porch light went out. Raindrops began to fall in irregular rhythms, flustered by the wind. After twenty minutes the light in Issie's room went out and the light in the main bedroom came on. Then it went out when Declan and Sinéad went to bed and made love in the darkness and the silence of the old house.

5
Lynch-Bages

1987

The Fitzsimonses' house, about the size of an English manor, was on the middle stretch of Avoca Avenue, surrounded by an acre or two of lawns and trees. Lily's father had inherited the family insurance business. To judge from his conversation, Issie put his birth date no later than 1750.

Issie's own house was spacious in comparison to those of some of her schoolmates, who lived in semi-ds or, in one exceptional case, a council house in Stradbrook; but Lily's house was on a different level. The swimming pool was only five metres short of the pool in Roebuck. The garden was more like a small park. And you could actually get lost in the house itself: there were, Issie estimated, about ten bedrooms scattered around the two extensions that the Fitzsimons had built. Small flights of stairs linked the corridors along the first and second floors of the house. Issie's favourite place was a window on a landing that looked over the garden and beyond to the semi-ds of Hyde Park Avenue, box after box stretching back towards Mount Merrion Avenue. One summer, when she'd stayed with Lily for a week, she went frequently to this place, taking a cushion and a book, remaining there for hours as the August afternoon refused to concede to night.

They'd known each other since primary school – Issie's speed, precision, and ability to dream up strange scenarios complementing Lily's loyalty and long deliberations about the smallest of matters. These differences had been reflected in their examination results through the years, and while Issie expected to be accepted into Modern English and Philosophy at Trinity College, Lily had convinced herself she was looking forward to resitting the Leaving Certificate after a year in a crammer college.

Issie had sat her last exam on Thursday. Now on Saturday, with Lily's parents away for the weekend, the Fitzsimonses' house and grounds had been overrun by Roebuck girls, and boys from Blackrock College and Deerpark and other schools in the vicinity. Around midnight, having spent much of the day coordinating visits to three different off-licences by young men and women, armed with their documents of identification, Issie found herself sitting on a deckchair on Lily's sloping lawn cradling a vodka and Coke on her lap and gazing at the sky. She turned to Chris Bondy and said, 'As the moon rose higher the inessential houses began to melt away until gradually I became aware of the old island here that flowered once for the sailors' eyes – a fresh, green breast of the new world . . .' Her voice trailed off, as her brows crumpled trying to recall the rest of the quotation. 'How does the rest of it go? Come on, clever clogs. Wake up, it isn't yet midnight and you're going to sleep already. You're such a fader.'

Chris pulled himself up a bit in the chair and looked around, dazed. He searched under the chair for his can of Harp.

She repeated the quotation for him again, with feeling. When she finished, he was silent for a moment and then spoke.

'What the fuck are you talking about, Issie? Some poxy poem from Leaving Cert English? Thank fuck it's over.'

'Chris, you may well be the best wing-forward of your generation, and you certainly are the best-looking boy I've ever gone out with, but, Jesus, you can be a pain in the arse sometimes. Look at the night, look at the garden.'

The noise of splashing came floating over the dark lawn, accompanied by the girls' high-pitched screams and the boys' rugby chants, which reached a crescendo before they swung one of their number, fully clothed, into the deep end of the indoor pool. One of the boys had half-jokingly proposed skinny-dipping earlier in the evening, and the girls had laughed, then primly proceeded to change into their one-piece swimsuits behind a screen, occasionally peeking over the top at the boys changing into their togs at the other end, one hand holding the knot of the towel, the other foostering underneath it for the jocks, all of them comically wobbling on one foot.

'Wait, wait,' Issie resumed. 'I've got it: "She had come a long way to this blue lawn, and her dream must have seemed so close that she could hardly fail to grasp it. She did not know that it was already behind her, somewhere back in that vast obscurity beyond the city, where the dark fields of the republic rolled on under the night." There it is.'

'Jesus.'

'I know, it's beautiful, isn't it?'

'No, Issie. I didn't mean "Jesus, it's beautiful." Come on, let's go back to the house.' He moved to get up, but she remained in her chair, regarding him.

'It is true, though, you *are* the best wing-forward of your generation, aren't you?'

Chris smirked and sat down again, puffing out his chest ever so slightly. 'Yeah, well, I don't know. That's what they wrote in the *Irish Times* anyway.'

'Right. Good. Well, I was thinking then that you should ask Ryan Devereux over there, who if I'm not mistaken is the best tighthead prop of his generation, if he would go back to the house with you for a while and let you stick your head up his arse, like you boys usually dream of doing.'

Before Chris had time to say anything, Issie continued, 'Oh, Chris, I didn't mean it.' Relief spread over his face, as the prospect of later delight came back into play. 'No, of course I didn't mean it,' Issie said in a purring tone, placing her hand affectionately on his arm, rubbing it gently. Then her face hardened. 'No, that was just another fucking poxy quote from another fucking poxy poem. You fucking dick.'

She got up from the deckchair and walked towards the pool. When she got there, she dared Lily and the others to throw her in. They screamed happily and emerged from the pool, the water streaming down their limbs, exhilaration in their faces. For form's sake, Issie put up a bit of a fight, but it was more fun to give in, and within a few seconds she was being swung back and forwards, held by the arms and legs. 'One . . . twoooo . . . threeeeee . . .' A half-second floating through the air, the blue water beneath her, the stained fibreglass roof above her, fully clothed and between worlds. Then splash. A new life.

About four hours later she set off for home with Aideen O'Malley. They dared each other to do a drunk test on the gapped line that ran down the middle of Mount Merrion Avenue. Eyes closed, arms outstretched, they ran; on opening their eyes they found themselves nearly at the kerb on the left-hand side, and sat down on the grass verge.

'We're probably sitting on five decades of dried dog shit right now,' Issie said.

'Well, it's comfortable enough for my bum.'

Down at the bottom of the avenue, about half a mile away, a car pulled off the Rock Road and swung towards them. They couldn't hear the gear changes, but they watched the speeding vehicle, mesmerized by the headlights, until suddenly in a rush of noise it zoomed past towards Stillorgan, becoming a ghost.

§

It was Issie who opened the door to the two guards at a quarter to six, with Aideen standing behind her holding her cup of tea. Their first thought was that something had happened at Lily's.

'Good morning, miss. Are your parents at home?'

'Yes. What's wrong?'

'It's your parents we have to talk to, miss, if you wouldn't mind. Good morning to you too, miss.' They nodded to Aideen.

'Come in then, and I'll wake them.' Issie went quickly up the staircase, glancing back once at the two guards standing in the middle of the hall looking around them. Aideen remained downstairs with them, but nobody said anything.

A few minutes later the guards were invited by Declan and Sinéad into the living room to sit down. Issie came in as well, and Aideen stood in the doorway. The guards told them the details of the car crash. When Owen was taken to James Connolly Memorial Hospital in Blanchardstown he was conscious and talking, but he died about fifteen minutes after that. The official identification had been made by one of his friends. They were very sorry.

§

The sun illuminated the people as they walked through the church gates on Booterstown Avenue. Most of them had waited in their cars for a few minutes to make sure they didn't arrive ahead of the immediate family. The short distance they walked was shadowed by copper beeches, birches, the occasional palm tree, privets and large rhododendrons, and so, on turning the corner at the granite pillar, they were dazzled by the sunlight for a few moments and raised their hands to their foreheads. Behind them, to the left, was Gleeson's pub, where some of the men would end up afterwards. The older people wore solid black, but many of the younger people, in their late teens and early twenties, seemed not to have such clothes at their disposal.

It was almost five o'clock and the early evening was still warm. Many felt the summer drawing them; the thought of a few months waiting tables before university resumed, or of two weeks in a French gîte or on a Greek island, or of the marvellous and frightening nothingness of July and August after the exams. Some of them might go for a swim out at the Forty Foot or the Vico later. Most, however, would go back to the Boyles' house and have one or two drinks and eat a sandwich as they stood around talking in subdued tones, then gradually raising the volume with shouts and laughs, telling stories about the deceased or other things.

Mick Guilfoyle, the recently appointed Minister for Justice, arrived with his brother Seán, chief executive of Hibernia Traktors. Then Hugo Donovan, another new member of the cabinet, for Industry and Commerce. Robert and Eva Poschik and their three children had driven up from Galway earlier in the day to be at the viewing in the hospital. From one side came Declan Boyle's secretary, Maura Brady, a woman in her late thirties. From the other side came Conor Larkin of Steinman Brothers Cohn, dressed in a suit that was obviously un-Irish. He'd arrived from London the night before, able to fit the funeral in before returning to New York that evening. He found himself in step with Winifred Bridgmuir, née McKenna, and although though the two did not know each other they nodded in recognition of their common destination.

Two middle-aged men emerged from Gleeson's and stood in the doorway adjusting their ties. They inhaled at the same time, as though bracing themselves for a minor but burdensome piece of business. After some cars passed, they made their way across the avenue, waving at Conor Larkin. To judge by the vagueness of that man's response, he didn't know the Coyle brothers, who ran one of Ireland's biggest construction firms. On the steps of the church, one of them inadvertently got in the way of an elderly couple, who graciously stopped to let the brothers by. The Coyles didn't notice this politeness and had quickened their pace to a little jog, perhaps in order to get a seat in the pew beside their old friend from America. Niall Falkner and his wife gave the builders a wide berth and then resumed their progress to the church door.

Inside the church, people talked quietly. Here and there a kerfuffle broke out between a parent and child, usually a boy, who was then yanked back into the pew, whimpering at the unfairness of having to wear a white shirt and tie and sit in a church in the middle of the week, looking at a box with a corpse in it, somebody he'd never met. There were two infants in the church who would not be hushed by their mothers, and their voices filled the vaulted space above the mourners. Gradually and unconsciously the people began to talk a little bit louder, and then there was a sudden hush when the three priests emerged from the sacristy. All rose. The priests, in densely woven embroidered cloths, stiff with ecclesiastical decoration, nodded to the congregation that they could now sit down again.

The last mourners were filing into the back of the church: Pez Driscoll, Mick Guilfoyle's political advisor, accountant and bagman; Liam and Helen Creighton; Declan's two cousins from Ardnabrayba, who hadn't been at the viewing, having driven straight to the church from Galway and got lost in Sandyford on the way; Declan's solicitor and his accountant; friends of Sinéad, some of whom she knew only by their first names; and the younger people, so many that they couldn't fit in the church and spilled out the door, gathered for the unusual occasion of the death of someone their own age.

Slowest to resume their seats were the immediate relations in the first two pews on either side of the aisle. Sinéad's sister Marie had taken the name Bridget for her decade as a Carmelite nun, but reverted to her given name when she left the convent in New Jersey to take up a job as a social worker in West Philadelphia. She was standing beside her younger sister, Fiona, Fiona's husband Bryan Cooper and their five children. Beside them were Sinéad's parents, Belinda and Malachy Grogan. Declan's sisters, Mella and Frances, with their husbands and, between them, five children, were on the other side of the aisle. Catherine Boyle, too infirm to leave the nursing home, was not present. Issie, flanked by her parents, watched Patrick Sutherland stride across the altar. He took up a position behind the microphone and welcomed everybody. There would be no Mass, only some readings.

After the short service, the afternoon's blue skies and light summer breeze seemed almost an affront. Issie, just short of six feet tall, had a good view of the crowd spread across the car park. To one side there was a small meadow, surrounded by white railings, and to another the foster home, freshly painted and as cheerful as Catholic institutional architecture could be. Beyond, on all sides, stretching to the distance, were estates of semi-ds, relieved by greenery at least twice the houses' age.

There were so many people she knew, or half knew. Most of the girls in her year at school, she reckoned, and most if not all of the Deerpark boys who had come to their house over the years and many more who hadn't. There were the Poschiks, whom she hadn't seen in years. That must be Kasimir, without a tie. She couldn't remember the daughter's name. Janek, the one in the beige jacket, leaned towards his sister and said something to make her smile.

It seemed strange to Issie that people were able to smile. It seemed strange to imagine that she would smile again at some point in the future.

Her father turned to say something to her mother, and Issie looked ahead unseeing, her arm still tightly grasping his sleeve. Fifteen teenage boys in Deerpark blazers were standing in formation across from the church door. Some were stocky and short, others rangy and slight; three taller boys stood at the back. Fr Sutherland, Declan's old schoolmate, came over to the Boyles to tell them that this year's Deerpark Junior Cup team, which had got to the semis, wished to offer their condolences. As the priest gestured towards the boys, all of them bowed their heads an inch. Her father walked over to them and their captain came forward and they shook hands.

The boy, so similar in stature to her dead brother at that age, was another strange phenomenon. She observed her father talking to him, his tall figure stooping slightly. Was the captain explaining how, when he was eight or nine years old, he'd seen Owen play in the Junior Cup final? Issie had been there in Lansdowne Road, on a Tuesday afternoon in March. Deerpark were up against Blackrock College, who routinely picked up the trophy. She sat with her parents in the West Stand, the Deerpark boys on the right and Blackrock on the left. Blackrock had five cheerleaders with megaphones spread out along the bottom of the stand, and placed strategically among the rows of seats were tall young men, probably from the Senior Cup team, with their backs to the field, staring up at the rows of younger boys' faces, shouting at them as hard as they could to make them sing louder, louder.

When the final whistle blew the Boyles leapt in unison, along with all the other Deerpark supporters, while the Blackrock boys sagged back into the seats in disbelief. As the Deerpark team were filing back down in euphoria, after they'd accepted the trophy, Issie was able to lean out and catch Owen by the neck and give him a kiss. She adored her brother, her protector and entertainer.

Now, this other, newer captain stood across the church probably saying words like 'condolences' and 'on behalf of the whole team'. Her father nodded his thanks. When he turned back to his family, she saw the tears streaming from his eyes.

§

Declan saw that there were now only a few people left, and on his signal the Boyles made their way to the car and drove for a few minutes in silence to the house. Cars were parked nearby, on the avenue and on the side roads, most people waiting for the return of the family before approaching the house. Declan parked in the drive and the four of them ascended the steps, feeling the eyes of their friends and relatives on them. Catering had been arranged, and they walked past the trestle tables to the living room, unsure where they should stand. Declan tried to concentrate on the Mass cards that someone – a relation? One of the caterers? – had arranged along the mantelpiece.

John Finnegan, chef-proprietor of the Pot de Vin, had recommended the caterers, and now stood quietly in Sinéad's vicinity looking over the food. The sight of Finnegan evoked mixed emotions in Declan. Owen had been working at the Pot de Vin for five years, and Declan knew he'd had a very high regard for his employer. But Declan had found it impossible to shake off the unwelcome fatherly sense that his son had chosen an aimless path.

The first warning had been the Inter Cert. When the results had come through, hot on the heels of Owen's rugby glory, Declan and Sinéad told the boy that it was time to buck up. Owen agreed. Eight months later, after the results of the Christmas examinations in fourth year, Declan shut down his son's extracurricular life: no parties, no television and no rugby. There was a telephone call from Deerpark's Senior Cup team trainer, who had his eye on the cup in two years' time, but Owen accepted it all without argument and pledged that he'd now apply himself to schoolwork. Then there was another set of miserable Christmas results in fifth year, and so the disaster of the Leaving Cert came as no surprise. Far from securing the points required for a place in Medicine in UCD, his first, unrealistic choice, Owen wasn't even offered a place in Arts, his second choice.

After the last exams, Owen had gone to London with three friends. They shared a room in the residences of the Imperial College in Kensington. Declan had found Owen a job as office boy in a property firm, and soon came the news that he'd found another job himself, working in a restaurant three nights a week clearing tables, to supplement his income. Two weeks later, when phoning home, he told Sinéad that he'd handed in his notice at the day job and begun working lunches and dinners six days a week at the restaurant, where the money was better. Declan had to call his acquaintance in the London firm to smooth things over, but it seemed that Owen had charmed him, and the man laughed it off. By early August Owen reported that he was working happily in the restaurant on the slow nights, and the sommelier had started to navigate him around the wine list.

Declan and Sinéad put pressure on him, and in the end he agreed to come back to Dublin at the end of August, for crammer college. He got a job clearing tables at Pot de Vin on Haddington Road, on the strength of his experience in London. The restaurant had been open only a few years, but already it was among the most famous in the city. Before Christmas, Owen moved out to a flat on Northumberland Road, to share with two of his fellow waiters. He was, Declan knew, putting distance between himself and Mount Merrion Avenue, and all that the place represented.

Now, as he observed the stricken face of John Finnegan, Declan understood that what he'd hoped was a passing fancy had become a way of life for Owen. He'd never resat the Leaving Cert, never gone to university, never moved back home.

§

People had been saying things to Sinéad since early on the previous Sunday morning. Some of them she knew very well and others she didn't. Sometimes hours went by and no one came, and she realized that was because it was night. When the sun came up, more people would come to her. Their faces would emerge out of a general blackness, hover for a little while in front of her, making noises, forming words, twisting their expressions, and then they would fade, making the silence perfect again. She knew she should say thank you to them all, and sometimes they were puzzled by that, but mostly they weren't. Her legs had slowed down again, as they had before. The wind-tossed trees had slowed down again, as they had before. The blackness she knew. The blackness was almost like an old friend.

§

Declan now found himself by the mantelpiece talking to Liam Creighton.

'How are you holding up, laddie?'

'We're doing our best.' Declan put his empty glass on the tray of a passing waiter and asked for another G&T.

'Issie's grown up into a fine young woman,' Liam remarked, looking in her direction.

'She has though, hasn't she?' Declan agreed. It kindled a warmth in him to see Issie tall and straight-backed, perhaps a bit uncomfortable in the formal clothes the day demanded, but able for anyone in the room.

'We were never quite as confident as that, I think,' said Liam.

'Jesus, I don't know what we were, to be honest.' Declan sighed and paused a while. 'How are things with Helen?'

'Ah, you know. There's some things that can be fixed and some that can't. You know the way.' Liam paused. 'But it's not you who should be asking about me today. Are you and Sinéad taking some time off work?'

'I'm back in on Monday. Sinéad is going to be at home with Issie for a few weeks. And then we'll see. Issie's original plan was to work full shifts at the Pot de Vin for the rest of the summer. I suppose she'll stick to that. Then she wants to swing her rucksack on her back for a few weeks to taste this freedom she's heard all about before university starts. And who are we to stop her?'

For the few moments of their conversation, Declan had managed ever so slightly to escape from under the weight that had been bearing down on him for the past few days. It felt like a heavy block of concrete, the edges of which his fingers couldn't reach. His knees would snap beneath it and all the light would be shut out. Here it was again, as Issie came to his side, saying nothing but with tears welling in her eyes. Liam nodded in acknowledgement of her. Declan placed his drink on the mantelpiece, put his arms out and said, 'Come here to me, love.'

§

Her face buried in the breast of her father's dark suit, she inhaled deeply the smell of wool, aftershave and faint sweat, and remembered how she used to hurl herself into him when he came home in the evenings. The strong bones of his chest could never be broken, it seemed. She stupidly thought of the expression 'a pillar of society'. That's what he physically felt like at this moment, and she grasped him even more tightly in gratitude.

'How long will this last?' she asked.

'I suppose another half an hour or so.'

She was unable to imagine how she would get through that time. Eventually she told her father she was going upstairs. She kept her head down and walked purposefully through the people to the door, then ran up the stairs to her room. It had been her father's when he was young, and then Owen's. She'd been so mad with her brother for moving out after he'd come back from London that she'd invaded it a week later and dumped all his stuff in boxes in her old bedroom.

She closed the door behind her and walked over to the window. The noise coming up through the joists, planks and carpet of the floor was so loud that she felt she was walking on that muffled sound alone, held up by its buffeting strength. The notion of lying down on her bed suddenly seemed absurd. She went out again and was confronted by John Finnegan coming to the top of the stairs and looking round uncertainly. She nodded in the direction of the bathroom and he thanked her quietly. She went back down to the main room, determined to see the rest of it through.

A couple of years ago, Owen had talked Finnegan into giving Issie a job clearing tables. Their father had made groaning noises of complaint, but he knew that not even the adventure of working in a restaurant would distract her from her studies. Théo, Owen's fellow waiter and one of his flatmates, treated her like a younger sister but made ribald jokes to wind Owen up, even in Issie's company, which she found thrillingly adult. Occasionally she'd been unsure about Théo's intentions towards her, but he always and boringly decided to be a good citizen, and she was left to her virgin's daydreams. Owen always made sure she was out the door and on the last bus to Blackrock on week nights, and on Saturdays he would order the taxi for her himself.

'No guff, sis,' he would say to her ceaseless pleading. 'I'm serious. I promised Mum and Dad.'

'Oh, come on! You can't boss me around just because you're a trainee sommelier.'

'No, but I can boss you around because I'm your big brother. Look, if the old dears even heard you were taking drags of Théo's fags, they'd go crazy. That's bad enough as it is. No – out you go. No chat.'

She hated him at such moments, for the whole put-on of authority. And then she hated herself for making him do it. And then she smiled, and got the taxi to Blinkers, way out in the suburbs, where Owen never went these days, and met her friends. Or sometimes she'd meet a friend at Bo Jangles on the strip, when she was sure Owen would be elsewhere.

She still wasn't sure about John Finnegan, wasn't sure if she liked all his talk. He was a working-class Dub who'd been given a start in the kitchens of the Blenheim Arms Hotel at the age of twelve and had spent three years there prepping veg after the war. The way he told it, when he reminisced to his staff after service, he couldn't have given a fuck about fine dining at that stage, but when the hotel was shut down he got a job at Jammet's. He prepped veg for another three years there and thought they were a pile of pretentious pricks, until one night he overheard Louis Jammet mention the night's takings to the manager. He did the sums quickly, estimating the staff salaries, food costs and rent, and realized that the dandified Mr Jammet was a sharp businessman who was raking it in. Finnegan would look around at his exhausted kitchen staff slumped against the worktops and walls, the sweat drying on their foreheads, the smoke streaming from the tips of their cigarettes, and tell of how, armed with a reference from Jammet's, he had gone to train in Lyons, with Paul Faetar. After a few weeks working in the Pot de Vin, Issie could have recited the whole monologue easily.

The newly restored Taoiseach frequented the Pot de Vin – its wine list could not match that of Le Coq Hardi, but its food was better – and had the bills sent to his office to be paid a week later. The atmosphere of Empire decadence fitted his image well: he liked to be perceived as a *bon vivant* – as his supporters implied, not because he thought himself better than the rest of us, but because the rest of us, and Ireland in general, deserved better. The chef, though, was not impressed. 'That fucker is nothing but a North-side guttersnipe like myself. Joey's of Marino. Yet here he is, lord of the fucking manor. Far from it he was reared. Him and all those other fuckers.'

Issie hadn't been working the night of Owen's recent run-in with the Taoiseach. The private rooms were being refurbished, and so the great man and his female guest were seated in the main dining room – corner table, beneath the Napoleon portrait, as his secretary had specified. When the two had taken their first sips of Kir Royale, Owen approached them to ask if a choice of wine had been made yet. Usually this would be the sommelier's job, but Deegan, like the rooms above, was being refurbished, in St Vincent's Hospital for appendicitis. The Taoiseach looked up, irritated to be interrupted so soon, and told Owen to come back in five minutes, 'no more, no less'. Owen stood looking at his watch in the service area and began walking towards the table again at four minutes fifty-five seconds. The Taoiseach was in full flight, telling a story, as his guest leaned in enthralled. Owen hovered at a polite distance, saying nothing, before finally approaching.

'Where's Deegan?' the little man growled. 'His night off or something?'

'Taken ill, sir. With appendicitis,' Owen replied, as deferentially as he could manage.

The eyes sharpened when he heard Owen's accent.

'A Southside boy, I hear. I thought you were a Frenchman. The last time I was here I heard you chattering away with Théo.' This was not said in a tone of polite interest.

'Yes, sir,' Owen replied.

'Yes, what?'

'I am from Blackrock.'

He started laughing: 'Jesus, I don't know if I can afford to eat in a restaurant where the waiters are from Blackrock. Anyway, posh boy, we'll have that wine,' he said, pointing to the bottom right-hand corner of the list. 'Do you think you could pronounce that for me nice and clearly in your fancy French accent?'

Owen swallowed. 'Yes, sir. *Romanée-Conti.*'

'Say it a little louder.'

'*Romanée-Conti.*'

The people at the other tables were listening to the exchange, and there was at least one low gasp when Owen pronounced the name of the wine. As he was returning with the bottle, a man at a nearby table asked if he could look at the label. Owen hesitated and then lifted the bottle for the other guest to see. At that moment the Taoiseach looked over, saw what was going on and said in a loud voice, 'Who's that fucker, and what's he doing with my Burgundy?' Owen hurried over to the table and got to work on the cork. He was worried that he'd mess up the procedure, but it went well, and the wine was deemed satisfactory. As Owen was about to withdraw, the Taoiseach motioned for him to bend down closer.

'And you, you jumped-up little shit, the next time you bring the wine straight to me, do you hear?' The Taoiseach's guest tittered, as though something witty had been said. Owen nodded curtly and withdrew.

Owen had told the story as an amusing anecdote, reproducing the man's growls, his emphases and his accent with admirable comic accuracy. But Issie imagined the Taoiseach's cronies listening to the same story told by their boss and laughing so hard that the buttons on their shirts, the belts around their waists, and the stitching that held the sleeves to the torsos of their suits might burst. The idea of the laughter of such men made her shiver. What she loved about Owen was his ability to take everything as he encountered it. For all that he was her elder, for all that she liked his protection, for all that she positively nestled into his flank whenever he called her 'Sis', he gave the impression of floating on ambient breezes. But in one short exchange he had been shot down, and seemed to shiver with the awareness. She was pained for him.

By that time, Owen had relented on the matter of Issie going clubbing with him and the other waiters. The breakthrough came on a Saturday night when their parents were dining in the restaurant. Their father had booked a table for fifteen after some deal had been closed, though it was obvious that the restaurant had not been his choice. He had dined in the place with their mother a few times, but with Owen and now Issie working there he usually chose Le Coq Hardi or the Russell Hotel for business occasions.

Declan had to introduce his two children to the table, and jokes started going around about him being a successful restaurateur; Issie dreaded the prospect of working the table for the rest of the evening. But to her surprise the adults ignored her subsequent incursions, and their readiness to demote her to invisible servant irked her ever so slightly.

The Americans were picking up the tab, in thanks, as they said, for all the hospitality they'd received in the preceding week. Their main man asked for the wine list when they sat down, to indicate that there would be no argument in the matter. When Deegan was taking his order, this fellow turned to the table and joked that he was going to order the only Irish Bordeaux that existed – Château Lynch-Bages – in honour of the fine country they found themselves in and where they looked forward to working in the years ahead. Declan chimed in to say that the original Lynch himself was from Galway. 'Well, that confirms it,' the American said, as he closed the wine menu and returned it to Deegan.

After the main course, Issie saw her father whisper to Théo to hold the dessert for five minutes. He then stood up to address the table. Most of the restaurant was on coffee, liqueurs and petits fours by now, so Issie's main responsibility was to circulate with the pot to offer top-ups. She'd been trained by the head waiter to do this with increasing frequency after midnight as a gentle way to ease the customers out the door. Having just completed a round, she was free to linger at her station, half obscured by a curtain, and observe her father. She'd never seen him give a speech before, stretched to his full height in front of other people.

His suit of grey pinstripe sat well on his solid frame. She saw him touch the upper button on the jacket, making certain it was done up, and then his large hand returned to his side, resting against his thigh. He did not put his hands in his trouser pockets, but neither did he seem stiff or serious. A smile played over his features, a lively and enlivening amusement and interest. Her father and her brother were so different, but this vein of amusement ran uninterrupted through both of them, and made her love them both.

Her father was talking about some phone call to Conor Larkin at the beginning of it all. How he'd been sitting in the Two Widows, waiting to be connected, when he was trying to set up the factory in Ardnabrayba. The people laughed warmly and naturally. Having got them with a joke, he now turned serious, thanking the Americans.

'When I was growing up in Ireland after the war, the best prospect a young man had was the boat to England or the boat to Boston. Here at this table this evening, indeed, we have the oldest son of Brian Larkin who succeeded in America, when it was impossible in Ireland.'

Issie's eyes drifted to her mother, who was smiling admiringly at her husband. The numbers lady. The anomaly among her friends' parents. How many other Southside mothers worked as accountants in big companies? Issie had sometimes wished that her mother were a typical pink-tracksuit-wearing platinum blonde, ferrying herself and Owen around Blackrock from school to music lesson to ballet. She wondered what it would have been like to come home and smell apple tart in the oven and see a kitchen table set for dinner instead of covered with accountancy books or files. She was curious about what that type of normality would have been like. This evening her mother looked like any other executive's wife, gazing up at her husband, adjusting her necklace slightly.

'The agreement we have reached is not about banking, finance or other vague abstractions. It's about people. People coming together to share experience and friendship. People who will live together and become neighbours and sometimes even relations. "Welcome home to Ireland," is what I say in thanks to our hosts this evening.'

There was gentle applause, and Declan took his seat again. Issie's hand was on the coffee pot as Owen came up behind her.

'How's it going there with the old folks?'

'Dad just gave a speech.'

'Get out of it. How come they're all awake?'

'He wasn't bad, you know.'

'Ah, sure the old man's a cracker when it comes down to it,' Owen pronounced lightly as his eye traversed the table. 'That'll be a whacking great bill. With Lynch-Bages 1982 into the bargain. Anyway, sis,' he continued, 'with the folks distracted by these Yanks, why don't you come down to the strip with Théo and myself this evening? Stéphe will meet us there too when he's finished at the Coq.'

This was a first and Issie smiled.

'Just don't go pretending you're new to it all, OK? Panda down at Bo Jangles told me that you're not unknown in those quarters. Of course, only when da big brudder is not in attendance.'

She smiled at him again, with added winsomeness.

'So go on. Tootle around with the coffee pot again and tell the old dears it's time they went home for their cocoa. There's a good girl.'

They ended up, after Bo Jangles, lying on the grass of Dartmouth Square at six o'clock in the morning, smoking a joint. Théo's arm was lightly resting against hers and Issie was trying to work out what implications that might have in the next few hours. They said nothing. On her other side, Owen had his hands under his head and lay there unblinking, as though receiving an extremely important communication from the panorama they faced: the midsummer sun had started colouring the sky above them with extravagant swathes of pink and bright blue, flecked here and there with grey.

Issie could sense, but not see, the trees and Victorian houses spreading out from beyond the edges of the lawn they lay on, and then the canals, the office buildings, the shopping centres. The odd bus, braking to a stop, was audible two streets away, but now that the sun had arrived the birds were mostly giving it a rest. Owen took a breath as though to say something, but then subsided again, observing the sky.

§

Around 9 p.m., after the last people had left the house, Sinéad went out to the garden and began digging furiously at the flower beds. The physical work allowed her to stop thinking, and even feeling. She gritted her teeth and dug in further. Only when her arm brushed the small rosemary bush she'd planted years before and its pungent fragrance reached her nose did she stop.

6
Witches' Night

1995

She had an apartment all to herself: fifty square metres on the third floor of a turn-of-the-century building, in the part of the city where everyone now wanted to live. In the past month the cherry and almond trees had exploded into blossom, and the scent, held in by the other apartment buildings surrounding the courtyard in the back, spread through her rooms and made her dizzy. Having spent the dismal winter wrapped in too many layers of clothing, Issie now felt herself shedding all her scales. She'd never experienced spring-time so intensely in Ireland.

With the warmer weather, the courtyard had become a play-ground for two toddlers. Their mothers brought out cheap plastic chairs and sat in the yard smoking, while the boys made clay explode in the air, shared toys and occasionally shoved each other around. In another part of the yard an old man tilled a patch for vegetables, slowly and laboriously turning the earth and putting in seeds. He didn't seem to acknowledge the mothers, though she saw him wink at the boys. The blossoms fell from the trees and accumulated like snowflakes on the ground, making Issie's own ceiling a few watts brighter.

When she looked up, most of the facing windows were open, as people let the fresh air into their room and lungs after the winter. Wet clothes were now hung out on racks from window ledges. Flower pots were brought out onto the small balconies. She loved sitting out on her tiny balcony, observing it all, a cigarette in her hand. What had she ever seen from her bedroom window on Mount Merrion Avenue? A few old trees that only got in the way.

By now she knew Prenzlauer Berg well. 'What Islington was to

London in the '60s . . .' She had written that in an article and now cringed at the memory. Artistic cooperatives. Tattoo parlours. Industrial foundries repurposed as cafés. Electric guitar repair shops. Flyers on the pavement with instructions about how to reinvent socialism. Organic food stores, at least one of which kept its own chickens in the backyard. Holistic this, chakra that. She still hadn't made up her mind about most of this stuff, and the main reason she'd moved to Berlin, after a couple of years teaching English and doing freelance journalism in Prague, was for the low rents. But in contrast to Ireland, where nothing seemed to have happened in her lifetime, and even more dramatically than Prague, East Berlin had been turned upside down, in the process liberating the strangest compulsions and the most arcane hobbies. Simply to walk through it all was one of her great pleasures.

The first article she wrote after arriving in the city was about white witches, most of whom seemed to work as yoga instructors and assistants in health food shops. She'd made an appointment with one of them, and found herself knocking on the door of a basement apartment not far from her own. There were potted plants beneath the high window in the corridor, which overlooked the courtyard. To the left of the door were two wooden shelves, seemingly home-made, which held slippers, and three pairs of women's shoes were lined against the wall.

The door was opened by a woman in her mid-forties who wore sandals and a floral print dress, and had her hair tied up in a bun. She held out her hand. 'Resi Lehmann.' Nothing witch-like at all about her. There seemed to be only a kitchen and a living room, but part of the hallway was cut off by a long curtain – if not a gateway to Narnia, then probably for storage. Shelves of books ran from floor to ceiling, and there were many more plants. It could have been the apartment of a schoolteacher, and unlike most of the other apartments she'd seen in the area it gave the feeling of having been continually inhabited for a long time.

Issie told the witch that there was nothing wrong with her and that she was merely writing an article. She would pay for her time anyway. The witch was amused.

'You mean, you want to write about all this things going on after the Wall came down? From a witch's eye?' Her English was more or less correct, but had a machine-like quality due to the concentration required to produce it.

'Yes.'

She laughed. 'Well, I will be disappointment to you then. Things are not really changed for me in last thirty years. People come and I try to help them, whoever is in power' – she paused while she thought of the word – 'upstairs.'

Issie smiled at the description and began writing in her notebook.

'I was asked a few questions now and then in the past, but it might surprise you that some people in important positions came to see me also.'

The tea was ready and Resi poured it. The pot was made of glass, and inside it was a decoction of mint, sage and rosemary. The greenery swirled around, staining the water gently and releasing the leaves' aroma into the small room. Issie drank and it was refreshing: she could feel the pungent vapours race through her sinuses.

'Look, Issie, I would not feel good if you pay and I am just talking. Why don't I give you a massage? That is part of what I do. And we can talk at the same time.'

Issie was uneasy. She didn't like the idea of exposing either her flesh or her mind to the woman whom she, the journalist, was supposed to be investigating, or at least writing about.

'You need not be concerned. I have been doing it for twenty years.'

She had to strip down to her bra, and turned in her chair with her back to the witch, who started on her upper shoulders. After a few minutes it seemed to Issie that the border between the skin on her back and the skin of Resi's fingers had dissolved. Knots long tangled were now undone, as the fingers slid along the ligatures and cross-hatching of the muscles.

Resi whistled. 'Wow-whee! What you got there?' She seemed to be trying to extricate a very small animal perhaps the size and speed of a silverfish and with the armour of a pangolin from between the muscles; it hurt Issie when it moved. The creature kept slithering away from the witch's quick fingertips. Having failed in one place, Resi would start from a long way off again to corner it and take it out.

Issie didn't need to hear Resi's sigh of satisfaction to know when the beast had been caught: there was a spasm beside her shoulder blade, and it felt as though all the muscles in her back had suddenly been released after years of being stretched tight as a bow. There was a terrible pain, but also relief.

'Jesus fucking Christ!' Issie shouted.

'I know, I know. That was something.'

'What was it?'

'I don't know. I'm not that good. Put your shirt back on. Have some more tea.'

Issie reached for her dish of tea and drank a draught of the liquid. It tasted clearer and stronger than it had before. Her senses were sharpened. Resi started asking questions about her family, and Issie, still surfing a wide wave of relief, answered without hesitation. When she left an hour later, she felt that the witch had seen her more clearly than anyone had seen her before. Not her parents, her lovers, not her closest friends from school. It had been a shock to hear herself described so dispassionately by this woman. Yes, on every count. It wasn't what the witch had said about her future that was surprising – an Irishwoman in Berlin was obviously 'searching for something' – but what she'd said about her past, and her father and mother. And mainly her brother, whom Resi said she'd found knotted in the weird arrangement of muscles in her back.

§

At the Lebanese restaurant near her apartment, with its Formica tables, pictures of Lebanon's national football team wedged between the mirror and a row of unfamiliar spirits, faux wainscoting and fluorescent lights, the owner, in his mid-thirties, could be heard talking on the phone in fluent Russian. What about the hummus and dolmades on her plate? Had they been prepared by a Russian also? She'd read an article recently which explained that in Berlin the Turkish restaurants were run by Bulgarians, the Italian restaurants by Greeks, the Greek restaurants by Arabs, the Chinese restaurants by Vietnamese, and so on. The only exception was the Bulgarian restaurants, which were run by actual Bulgarians, the ones left over after they'd staffed the Turkish restaurants. The article ended with a joke about how difficult it was to find German restaurants in Berlin. And, Issie thought, Russian restaurants too.

This morning she had to get out the door and onto the trail of Russians in Berlin. She'd pitched the idea to a British broadsheet that the city had been invaded by Russians once again; the first wave was émigrés in the 1920s and '30s, then came the Soviets in tanks, and now there was a new bunch completely: mechanics, writers, punk rockers.

The evening before, she'd gone to see some performance art in an old factory in Mitte. The sign said M+R FARBEN. There were tall clerestory windows, with a grid of square panes, stretching up about three metres from street level to illuminate the shop floor inside. She took the cage lift to the seventh floor. When the door was whipped back she was nearly blinded by six klieg lights, three on each side; a red carpet ran between them towards a large doorway to a room full of people. From a flyer she found at the bar she discerned that the event was an ironic take on Hollywood – first the performance art, then a party. Sandwiched between the two, bizarrely, there was to be a poetry reading.

The first two poets read in German. The third was dressed in a morning suit, and while he wasn't wearing a monocle, he may well have had one in his breast pocket. He read in Russian. The programme said that his name was Volodya Sirin.

Issie approached Sirin when he'd descended from the platform and was making his way to the bar. He looked at her quizzically when she began explaining who she was and what her article was about. He said his English was much better than his German. Excellent, Issie thought. He was tall and had a long face, smoothly shaved and girlishly pretty, with blood-red puckered lips. He displayed little emotion except to smile in a slightly superior manner at what she said. He reached into his breast pocket and took out not a monocle but a silver cigarette case, and offered her a black Sobranie. OK, she thought, let's play the game, and she took one. He reached into his side pocket for a lighter. That was the only crack in the façade: it was a plastic lighter with the insignia of a German football club.

He saw the crinkle of amusement in her face and whipped the lighter back into his pocket as he exhaled a long plume of smoke into the air over her head. Before Issie had a chance to ask him for his contact details and arrange a proper interview, a young woman in a black ballgown, about the same height as Sirin, slid up to his side, locked her arm around his elbow and whispered something in his ear. Sirin nodded in agreement, then said to Issie that he'd be back in a few minutes. He did not come back. The beauty in the black ballgown had led him away, no doubt to a villa in the Grunewald with bay windows overlooking the lake, where they would be offered ices and sorbets, sweet Russian liqueurs and more Sobranies by a short, bald, muscular butler.

So it was that this morning she had looked up the address of Berlin's only Russian-language newspaper, which turned out to be a kilometre away from her apartment. She would call around in person, present her credentials as a fellow journalist and hope they could put her in touch with Volodya Sirin.

Weeds held dominion over the pavements of Prenzlauer Berg: nettles, docks, pigweed and, in more sheltered corners, goldenrod. They seemed beautiful to her in Berlin, an assertion of what was underneath, taking advantage of every crevice and flaw in the concrete to twist themselves towards the light. For her, the weeds of the city heaving their way up were a more potent symbol of the failure of communism than all the images of the Wall collapsing.

The office of *Rul'* was a single room with two desks, above a sandwich shop. The woman there knew Volodya Sirin – though his real name was Yuri Odarchenko. Perhaps Ukrainian, the woman said sniffily. V. Sirin, the woman explained, had been the nom de plume used by Nabokov; and *Rul'*, she added proudly, took its name from the newspaper that Nabokov's father founded in Berlin. Issie hadn't known that, but now she remembered from third-year English that Nabokov had lived here before moving to America.

'Would you have any idea where I could find Sirin, I mean, Odarchenko?' Issie asked her.

The Russian woman seemed resentful of the question, as though Sirin had once failed to show up at a long-promised assignation in the green shades of a city park on a warm April night, to read her his poetry and swear his love.

'Everyone wants Sirin! What do I know? He once told me he worked in a bike repair shop, but he always lies. Mystification, always mystification.'

'Do you know where the shop is?'

The woman looked at Issie with exasperation; then, as though a balloon had popped inside her, she copied an address in Prenzlauer Berg on a piece of paper. Issie pocketed it, thanked the woman and made her way to the address she'd been given. It was indeed a bike repair shop, with artistic graffiti over the sign. A man was kneeling beside a bike with a wrench in his hands. When he looked up, there was a shadow of a smile indicating – what? – curiosity or amusement, she couldn't say. What was amusing about her? She took a breath and lined up the German words in her head before attempting to speak them: 'Hello, how are you . . . I wonder if you . . . I'm looking for a . . .'

The man started laughing when he heard her German. 'So, you are not somebody from immigration or social welfare?' he said in good English.

'Are my clothes as bad as all that?' Issie asked, unsmiling.

'Ah, German bureaucrats now have perfect taste in clothes, so that was a compliment.'

She smiled. 'I'm looking for Yuri Odarchenko. The poet.'

The man started laughing again: 'The poet. The bike repair man. The bespoke tailor. The man who owes me two hundred marks but can't give it to me because he needs to buy yet more Sobranie cigarettes so he can pretend to write yet more poetry that no one will translate. Yurochka. Why would you like to talk to him?'

'I'm writing an article on émigré Russians in Berlin and he seemed interesting. You know, like Nabokov in the 1930s.'

'And Tyutchev in the 1830s. So Yurochka is now a classic of our literature, as well as being as good as any Savile Row tailor? The man has everything. God's gifts are shared out unequally at birth.'

The man put down his wrench and got up. 'I have seen you before,' he said. 'At the Hollywood party in Mitte. I was the DJ. You talked a little with Yurochka, but he was as usual led astray by Zina.'

'You were the DJ? What's your name?'

'I am DJ Kat.'

'Well, nice to meet you, Mr Kat,' she said, smiling. 'I'm Issie Boyle.'

'It amuses you, my name. It is not quite as cool as it sounds in Ukrainian. That was my mistake. In Ukrainian a *kat* is an executioner, so you see: much more menace than your little kitty.'

'Do you know where I'd find Yuri?'

'Oh, no one knows where Yurochka lives. In the skies. In the wind. And anyway the man is so secretive. His biggest secret of all is that he doesn't write poetry.'

'But I saw him read . . .'

'Ah, yes, but whose poems was he reading?'

Issie watched this man puff out his chest ever so slightly and smile.

'You mean you wrote them?'

He nodded sheepishly.

'But why don't you read them?'

'Oh, it's a little game we play. And anyway, Yurochka is so much more handsome than me.'

Issie hesitated.

'It was the poet you wanted to talk to, wasn't it?'

Issie nodded. 'OK then, Mr Kat. Let's get down to work.'

He yanked the old metal roller shutter down in one loud flap, but it came only three-quarters of the way. He waved his hand. 'Who's going to steal a lot of broken bikes?'

'Can't we talk here?'

'No! For this we go to a café.'

They went next door and ordered *Milchkaffee*. DJ Kat's real name was Vassily Shishkin – Vasya. He'd come to Berlin with his preposterous friend in 1990 because Russia – well, she hadn't been there, so she couldn't know. His family were all in the Party, and he'd studied law in St Petersburg. 'Who knows? If I'd stayed there I might be a member of the new oligarchy, writing no poems, and my wife might be one of those you see with shopping bags around Friedrichstrasse.' He'd done his military service, like everybody else, and had hated it, like everybody else. Peeling potatoes, marching up and down, eventless weeks punctuated only by the sadism of their commanding officer. But he'd learned to fix bikes there, as well as engines, and got to drive a tank now and then.

After living in Marzahn for a few months, he and Yurochka found a big empty apartment in Prenzlauer Berg. 'We simply took up residence there,' he said. 'We thought we'd eventually be thrown out, but no one ever came. In Russia, amazing things also happen, but they usually have bad outcomes – like someone gives you a bottle of vodka and you go blind. In Germany, it's the opposite. But then I moved out, to a *Hausprojekt*, in Wedding.'

'What's a *Hausprojekt*?'

'It's a kind of co-op where West German kids pretend to be communists. I know, I know. The irony of my living there. It's called Zinni, after some Italian union leader who was shot in 1913. He probably has some school named after him in a provincial Russian town. In our *Hausprojekt*, we're just one big happy communist family. You should come and see it sometime. It might be good for a story.'

'I'd love to.'

'We're having a May Day party on Monday night, in fact.' He paused. 'And of course, if you have a boyfriend, he's welcome too.'

Was Vasya interested in whether she had a boyfriend? As she hesitated, a smile of curiosity spread across his face. She took the address in the end and promised to come.

§

She'd agreed to meet her friend Eglantine at a street party in Prenzlauer Berg on Monday afternoon, when May Day festivities were going on all across the city, and wanted to check out the concert in the Mauerpark beforehand. As she approached the park, she had to walk under a bridge, and she could hear the music increasing in volume; it echoed off the walls and roof of the overpass. Reggae. German reggae.

The park was a strip of embattled greenery about a kilometre long, edged on one side by a sports stadium, its floodlights standing high in the sky. The Wall had run somewhere along here. Besides the grass, the only other elements were concrete and sand. The concrete had been folded into steps, paths and bunker-like structures, then every one of its surfaces had been graffitied by at least three generations of young Berliners.

At a distance from the crowd, she noticed a group of five or six heavy-set men standing together on a street corner. All in their thirties. Three with moustaches. Not friendly. Not here for the reggae. Their eyes ran back and forth across the concert-goers. Perhaps these men were from a provincial town, somewhere in Thüringen for example, where she had spent an awful day researching hiking trails. One of them saw her considering them and leaned over to speak to another, then resumed his survey of the crowd. Finally it clicked: plainclothes.

Further down the street she saw the vans – about ten of them – and riot police standing around smoking. What were they doing here? She looked around her. The people flowing into the Mauerpark didn't look threatening. Some were smoking pot or sipping from bottles of beer, but this wasn't a football crowd; these were the type of people who would doze off on the grass, looking at the sky and pondering questions that had no answers.

She was to meet Eglantine in a square nearby, at 3.30. Mademoiselle Bellegarde was in her first year of doctoral studies at the Free University – something about American diplomacy in the Cold War. They'd met at an event at the French Cultural Institute. Issie found herself looking forward to Eglantine's flirtatious condescension, and how it usually gave way to actual conversation. They mostly spoke French together, and this allowed Eglantine to adopt the role of knowing seductress. On one occasion, out of deference to an American at a party, they'd spoken English, and Eglantine had become demure and shy. Since then, whenever Issie felt that Eglantine was presuming a little too much, she would switch to English to restore the balance.

Issie found a currywurst stand and took her food and a bottle of beer to the shadow of a poplar tree on a grassy slope. She lay back on the grass and tried not to think of syringes, broken glass, dog shit. Another band had plugged in their jacks and launched into a set. Ska this time. The singer had a terrible voice, but the band was decent. Her muscles let go a little as the beer went to work.

Soon it was time to make her way to Kollwitzplatz, the little square where she'd agreed to meet Eglantine. The uniformed police were still gathered where she had seen them earlier. Green uniforms, white helmets with the visors flipped up. They had a kind of Darth Vader aventail, made of thick dark padding, to protect the backs of their necks. Batons lolled at different angles from their belts – simple cylinders of wood. One or two eyed her appreciatively but didn't make any untoward noises.

She found Eglantine at the appointed place; *bisou-bisou*, and then, as she'd been taught, *bisou*. On a corner opposite the square, at a safe distance from the cars and shops, people were piling material for a bonfire: cardboard boxes, dead branches, newspapers from recycling containers. A teenager was trying to prise apart the slats of a wooden fruit crate, the nails fighting back, twisting in resistance, before finally giving way. People carried babies in papooses, and passing cyclists saluted the bonfire builders, wishing them a good something night.

'*Walpurgisnacht*,' Eglantine said, seeing Issie's quizzical look. 'The witches' night. It's a part of May Day here. The witches go wild and dance around the fire.'

Loud music was coming out of the back doors of a VW van parked nearby – more reggae, but this time with Jamaicans singing. Catching a whiff of hash smoke, Issie made a gesture to Eglantine and they looked around the square. There was a likely looking man, but he wouldn't sell them anything. 'No capitalism today,' he said, smiling. 'Here you are.' He handed them a lump of hash. Eglantine had the rest of the necessary material, and they sat on a carousel in a children's play area, smoking. After they'd finished the joint they moved to the swings, throwing their heads back to watch the world flung back and forth – apartment buildings, blue skies, sand and trees.

They went to lie down for a while, head almost touching head, spread-eagled on the grass. Eglantine was probably her best friend in Berlin, but although they'd confided in each other about romantic entanglements, they'd rarely mentioned their families. Now Eglantine spoke of her father's death the year before, and of having received a letter from her mother, asking her to move back to Nice.

They were silent for a while, observing the sky. Then they propped themselves on their elbows and looked around the park and playground. Through the trees and railings they could see that more people had arrived and were dancing to the music coming from the back of the van. The bonfire was finished. Issie had no idea of the time, but it was still bright, still too early to light it. They slumped back down on the grass.

'What about *your* parents, Mademoiselle Boyle?' asked Eglantine, turning playful again.

'Oh, just the usual.'

Eglantine started to laugh and flicked a few leaves of grass into Issie's face. 'What does that mean?' she said.

'I mean, just the usual boring, Irish, middle-class family. I went to a boring, Irish, middle-class convent school, my parents had a boring, Irish, middle-class crisis in their marriage in their forties. They got over it in a boring . . .'

'All right,' Eglantine shouted. 'I get the idea: you're bored by your family, that's why you're here.'

'Oh no, it's a much bigger problem than that. I actually quite like my parents, especially my father. No, the problem is I'm bored by the whole country.'

'Wow. What an ego! For other people, it's enough that they have problems with their parents, but you require a country.'

'If you saw the road we live on, you'd understand. Nothing has moved on it for a hundred years. I remember when I read about the French Revolution at school, and I thought that's what our place needs. It needs to be turned . . .' Issie couldn't think of the French expression – *boulversé? basculé?* 'I don't know how to say it. Inside out? Back to front?'

Eglantine told her the word.

'Yes, that's it. Turned upside down.'

'So that's why you went to Prague and then came here. You like places that have been turned upside down. And what about brothers or sisters?'

Issie took a breath. In Dublin, everyone knew. Dublin was too small, but she realized now that it was a great advantage not having to explain. She felt a pain in her chest, so deep that it didn't even push up the tears.

'My older brother died eight years ago, when he was twenty-three.' Out of the corner of her eye, Issie saw Eglantine nod.

'I'm very sorry.'

'That's all right. It was a long time ago.'

'Was that your parents' crisis? The one you mentioned?'

'No, no,' Issie rushed to say. 'That was all done and dusted. He died just before I went to university. Do you know what a witch told me?'

'Wait, no. I don't. But what do you mean, a witch?'

Issie explained about Resi Lehmann. 'She basically told me everything about myself from when I was born, and then she said I have to find my mother.'

'But you don't actually believe all that stuff?'

'I know, I know. I burst out laughing when she said it. I said to her that there's sometimes a question of paternity, but that every mother knows her own daughter. But no, she just repeated that I have to find my mother. I've been thinking about it ever since and can't make sense of it.'

'What's your mother like?'

The question knocked her off balance. What *was* her mother like? For the first time in her life, from a distance of thousands of kilometres, Issie caught a glimpse of her mother as just one human being, who was born in Dublin, grew up there and gave birth to her in August 1968. She knew these facts, but lying half-stoned in a children's playground in the middle of Europe helped give her distance from them. The image that came to her mind was of her mother at night in the kitchen, a cup of tea and spreadsheets arranged before her. With the house quiet, the road in darkness, her father asleep, these were the moments her mother would often try to coax her into communication.

Issie knew what was going on. Her mother went to AA and felt somehow guilty towards her and wanted to make up for it. Thus the repeated requests to 'have a talk', 'go to town for lunch', 'a walk up Killiney Hill, just the two of us'. Issie didn't see what her mother's troubles had to do with her. She didn't feel scarred, traumatized or bitter, and no, she didn't want to go up Killiney Hill on a wet Sunday afternoon.

'She's just the usual bored housewife of a rich businessman who doesn't have enough time for her,' Issie said eventually. 'And I can't really blame my father for that. She had a problem with drink when I was small, but she got over it. Then, because she was bored I guess, she started doing accountancy, and my father – probably out of pity – got her a job in his company.'

It didn't sound right as she said it, but the degrees of the inaccuracy were hard to gauge.

'It doesn't sound as if you like her very much.'

It surprised Issie to hear it put like this.

'She basically ignored me when I was a small child and I learned fairly soon how to look after myself. And Owen, of course – he was my brother. She loved him most of all. I just get frustrated with her bullshit now and then. I don't see why she had to stay home when she would have been more happy getting a job. I mean, feminism started in the '60s, didn't it?'

'Perhaps not on the little island of Ireland,' Eglantine said.

'No, you're right. It was probably too late for her. But all the same, she could have done something for herself, couldn't she?'

Before Eglantine had a chance to answer, they were interrupted by a loud cheer from the street. The bonfire had exploded into flame, and the effect was thrilling as the fire leapt up to the height of the lower trees. It was twilight now. Issie and Eglantine hauled themselves up off the grass and walked out through the park gate towards the fire. Three women, all with dreadlocks, dungarees and sandals, began howling and dancing. It was good, Issie thought, to see a bit of life again after all the spacey talk of the last two hours. The atmosphere was inclusive, generous. The witches didn't seem to take themselves too seriously, laughing as they went around the fire, and trying to get others to join in. Issie and Eglantine looked at one another, then hopped together into the circle. A *haroo* of happiness went up from the other women at this, and more people followed, men and women both.

It was all such fun that Issie didn't feel the least bit frightened when, taking a rest on the kerb, she saw a row of policemen, three deep, stretched from one side of the street to the other, about fifty metres off. For a brief moment she thought somebody might be kind enough to pass them a joint or invite them over for a beer.

The police were saying something through a megaphone. Then they began beating on what she now saw were riot shields, slowly and regularly. They stopped, and the noise of the megaphone could be heard distantly again. No one took any notice. The police resumed beating the shields, faster this time. There was a squawk from the megaphone. At that the ranks began disassembling, the policemen breaking into a trot, shields in one hand and – she could now see – batons in the other. They were running.

A boy failed to get out of their way quickly enough and one of the policeman swung his baton as he ran, as though in a polo match, bringing it across the boy's torso. He fell to the ground. The rest of the police were suddenly here, a couple of metres from her, the batons going up and down, whacking the people regardless of whether they were sitting on the ground or standing up. Girls started screaming. Eglantine, who had remained dancing when Issie sat down, was caught in a surge of bodies moving off to the other side of the square, followed by the main body of the police. In their dark green uniforms and white helmets they were like a swarm whose movements were caught in strobe-cuts from the streetlights, the flames of the bonfire and the police's own searchlights.

What was going on? Why were they doing this? It had been so

harmless. The police had come to the end of their charge and were now dragging people along the road surface. Suddenly, Issie couldn't find Eglantine. The police had regrouped and she thought they were getting ready to charge again, but this time they cleared a space down the middle for a large green truck. What was going to happen next? As the truck got closer, a long spear of water shot across the square from the upper-right-hand corner of the truck's cabin, raking the people whom she now thought of as protesters. Some were knocked over by the force of it. One man taunted the truck, daring it to shoot at him. The blast of water swung around to reward him, and just before it arrived he stepped behind a lamp post, which took the force of the blow.

The police were jogging behind the truck, not swinging their batons so viciously as before, but still working on the crowd with them. Suddenly, Issie felt scared. It was time to get out of here.

She began walking down a side street, but stopped when she saw a group of policemen striding quickly towards her. She turned and ran back to the square, then ducked into the next side street. All quiet. She ran as fast as she could for a hundred metres or so. On her left was a Thai restaurant, the owner at the door. She hurried into the restaurant and sat down.

Three other tables were occupied – one by a group who looked like fellow refugees from the square, and the other two by normal customers out for an early evening meal. The noise of the police grew louder. The owner took out a key and inserted it in a lock that activated the shutters. They took about thirty seconds to close. Outside, somebody seemed to be banging a car and shouting. There was a rush of boots across pavement, and the sounds of more scuffling and shouting. Eventually the noises faded. The owner came over to Issie to ask if she would like a drink. Yes, she would like a drink.

§

Before setting off for the party in Wedding, Issie made a detour past Eglantine's apartment and found her safe and well. She tried to talk her friend into accompanying her to Vasya's, but Eglantine said that she'd had enough adventure for one day.

Issie wandered alone through the dark streets of Wedding for about half an hour before she found the right building. It looked like all the others. Two or three minutes passed before someone came to open the door – a girl in a print dress, her blonde hair tied back. She had good English. They introduced themselves, and Mirabel led Issie through the passage to a courtyard. Fifteen or twenty people were sitting on benches on the far side. The sounds they made suggested that the party had reached the point when people had relaxed in each other's company but were not yet tired or drunk. Their laughter was caught by the canyon of the court-yard, twisting on itself in runs and salvoes, the echoes rising to the sky; trailing behind them were streaks of smoke, dead straight in the windless space and illuminated by the fluorescent light.

Vasya wasn't there – that was the first thing she noticed – which didn't matter at all, but it left her without an obvious connection to these people. What had she to do with them? Housemates and friends of a bike repair man she'd talked to briefly the other day. But here was a glass of wine in her hand already. Maybe they could tell her why the police had attacked a peaceful street party in Prenzlauer Berg.

Mirabel handled introductions. 'Ralf, Thomas, Alison, Pierre, Åke, Yasha, Horst, Andreas, Gudrun (but no Ulrike!) . . .' at which every-one laughed, Issie didn't know why, 'Hanno, Zina,' whom Issie remembered from the party in Mitte, 'Matthias, Clara, Liz, Christian, Carl, Denise, Gary, Josh, and me, Mirabel, which literally means "wonderful". Everyone, this is Issie, Vasya's friend.'

Issie hadn't actually told Mirabel whose friend she was because Mirabel had talked all the way through the passage and the yard, saying that Pierre was an installation artist ('That's why you'll see him going round with a video camera now and again – we're prob-ably part of his project'), Åke was just visiting, Yasha had two small children, Horst was writing a novel about the state of Germany ('even though Pierre keeps telling him the novel is dead; Horst says not *his* novel'), Andreas worked in the same government office as

Gudrun, Zina was Yurochka's girlfriend ('though no Yurochka tonight'), Josh was a cook at a Mexican restaurant ('he introduced me to *mole*'), Matthias, Clara and Liz were Horst's friends, Christian, Carl, Denise and Gary were her friends, and 'I'm the daughter of the original co-op people, which makes me an aristocrat around here.' All this was delivered in a quiet, conspiratorial voice, a little breathlessly, a pleasant barrage of information which said, 'Don't worry, it's all OK.' Issie appreciated it and smiled accordingly. What was her accent? The woman wasn't German, Issie was sure of it. Anyway, Issie thought again, no, definitely, she hadn't said anything about being Vasya's invitee. She had only given her name and asked if this was the Zinni *Hausprojekt*.

The group continued talking in German at a speed that was way past her level. Mirabel translated the highlights: 'Basically, Horst and Pierre are having the "novel" argument again. Pierre says that after modernism, there's no point in trying to write novels that encompass the course of a nation. Nationalism is dead. The real drama now is of consciousness. By the way, you see the side of the building there?' Issie looked over at the black and white silent movie that was playing on the tall face of one of the apartment buildings in the yard, the images ruckled by the ledges and windows. 'Pierre did that as an alternative to background music – background imaging, he calls it.

'Anyway, Horst says that he's not a nationalist. He couldn't give a damn about Germany. It's just that for his first novel he wants to write about what he knows. He also wants to write a novel people will read, unlike *Ulysses* or *Mrs Dalloway* – do you know those books? – which he says are too boring.'

Issie bridled a little at the denigration of the Irish national classic and looked at Horst sharply. She had to admit to herself, however, that she would never have read it outside the classroom. Although she knew one or two people who hadn't studied literature and had read it, they were always so bloody proud of the fact.

'Pierre says that the point of novels is to make the middle classes feel they are sensitive and have taste, unlike the plebs below and the rich bastards above. Horst is saying the great German novelist is early Mann, *Buddenbrooks*. And the great English novelists at the beginning of the twentieth century were Conrad, Forster and Galsworthy. That's why Pierre laughed so loudly, because he heard the name Galsworthy. Do you know him?'

'Not really. My mother used to listen to the dramatizations on the radio.'

'Well, I don't understand any of this, but you seem to. Are you a novelist too?'

'No, but I studied literature at university and I write for a living. Journalism.'

'Everyone! Issie's a writer too!' Mirabel announced to the table in English. Pierre and Horst stopped in mid-shout and mid-gesture, and turned their heads.

'That's right,' Issie said, 'and my journalistic instincts couldn't help but be aroused by the riot I just came from.' She had their attention with that line.

'What riot?' asked Mirabel.

'Down in Prenzlauer Berg, in Kollwitzplatz. We were all just sitting around, or dancing, at a bonfire, when suddenly the police went crazy and beat the hell out of everyone.'

Andreas said, 'It's because there was a big fight in the Mauerpark, about an hour earlier. Some anarchists started stirring everyone up and the police made over a hundred arrests. The bricks were flying through the air. Then there was a stand-off on a street nearby: they wouldn't move, and neither would we.'

Hmm, Issie thought, wasn't he the civil servant, or was that Pierre? He seemed to enjoy presenting his accurate-sounding facts, but also his partisanship.

'So we're looking at each other across twenty metres and someone in an apartment above threw open their windows and started playing "Hey Jude" at full volume. Everyone – except the bulls – sang the chorus, "Nah, nah-nah NAH-NAH-NAH NAAAAH!" Hilarious. Then I took off, when the same guy put on "Back in the USSR" . . .'

'No wonder they were so worked up when they got to the square. Nobody wanted any trouble.'

'Last year the trade unions came out looking for trouble, and had a go at the police,' Andreas said. 'So I think the bulls were on the lookout this year. That's why they went in so hard with the anarchists and then down in Kollwitzplatz.'

'They didn't even give a warning,' Issie said.

'They're legally obliged to give three warnings,' said Andreas.

'I heard the megaphone squawking in the distance, but I don't think anyone could make out what they were saying.'

'How did you get away?' Gary this time.

'I ran down a side street into a Thai restaurant. The owner closed the shutter right after me.'

'Red walls? Small little owner and a smaller wife?' asked Pierre.

'That's it.'

'I know where you mean. It's run by Laotians,' said Pierre, who seemed to be German.

It must have been close to 1 a.m. by the time Vasya arrived in the courtyard, holding a beer. He was especially happy to see Issie. 'You came! I was telling Mirabel I didn't think you would.'

He sat down in an empty chair beside her and proclaimed, 'I have a good story to tell.' All turned to him. He took a drink of his beer.

'I had planned to get back earlier, not least because I wanted to welcome our Irish guest,' he said, gesturing to Issie. 'But I was distracted by a curious thing. You know that old freight yard near Humboldthain, on Scheringstrasse?' Several people nodded. 'Well, as I was walking by around midnight, I hear a sound I know very well from my army days. Tanks creaking and rumbling along. Here, on the quiet streets of Wedding. About ten of them.'

Everyone was leaning forward.

'I stayed to watch them. And they turned off into the yard. The drivers jumped out. They had some bottles with them and clearly intended to finish them off in the guards' building. I think they'd had a bit already. They were in very good humour. It seems they'd been driving them around a field all day as part of some exhibition of vintage Soviet tanks.'

'And?' Pierre asked.

'And they didn't bother to lock the gate after them. I thought I'd just go in and have a look at the tanks. And they left the tanks open so I had a look inside one of them. The good old T-34. That tank has no keys – just a start button. If I'd had with me nine others who'd done Russian military training, we could have taken them all and surrounded the Bundestag. As it was, I had to be happy with one.'

'What do you mean?' Issie asked.

Vasya sipped his beer, reclined in the chair and crossed his legs, observing the group. 'It's parked outside.'

'You're joking.'

Vasya put on a solemn expression. 'A Russian never jokes about his tank!'

They all got up immediately and went out to the street. There it was: a smallish one, with a long cylinder attached to its side, and the barrel pointing at the third floor of an apartment building further down the street. Vasya had parallel-parked it neatly.

'What in hell are you going to do with it? If the bulls find out . . .' Mirabel, the aristocrat, was clearly concerned about her estates.

'Oh, I just thought I'd take it for a little drive before returning it. I'll have it back in the yard way before those gentlemen wake up to their hangovers.'

'You mean you're going to drive it around?'

'Yes. And I would like to invite our esteemed Irish guest, if she would like a guided tour of Berlin by night. And by tank.'

They all looked at Issie, who swallowed and said yes quickly.

Vasya turned to the others. 'We people on the mainland know all about tanks driving in and out of our countries, but our guest from the island . . . Well, it will be a new experience for her.'

Vasya scrambled up from the wheels and disappeared into the turret. His voice emerged echoing, telling Issie to get in the same way. A metal flap at the front flipped open, and Vasya's head appeared. Issie was now up on the turret looking down into the tank's innards. Ammunition racks, big heavy switches with angular edges, a radio bristling with further switches and wiring – all this seemed to bar her way, but with the streetlight above them she could just about see a path to a small seat in the turret. She lowered herself down. Mirabel started to say something to Vasya, but he started the engine and the whole machine shuddered into life. Then, slowly and carefully, Vasya brought the tank out onto the road, and Issie felt its enormous weight put in motion. It was as though the entire ground floor of an apartment block had detached itself from its foundation. Vasya shouted, 'All clear?' From the turret she looked around to check that the others were standing well back, and shouted, 'Yes!' He released the throttle and she waved back to the group on the pavement.

Vasya swung the tank onto a wider boulevard with a grassy median that had steel rails for trams scored through it. There was a red light. He stopped and waited for it to change, then let out the throttle and the machine roared in response. Issie's head and shoulders were sticking out of the turret and her hair whipped back. They must have been doing thirty miles an hour. One or two cars pulled level with them, but what could they do? Try to find a payphone and call the police? The police were no doubt too busy back in Prenzlauer Berg, and anyway wouldn't believe the story.

After about ten minutes they crossed the river, making for the Tiergarten. Vasya manoeuvred the tank onto a roundabout and suddenly she could see the Brandenburg Gate ahead. The thrill of the vehicle, trundling its way through the sleeping city, and her on top of it, made Issie feel as though everything – the whole solid world – was suddenly fluid.

Then she became a little frightened: police vans were approaching, and three of the larger trucks with water cannons. Her parents would be delighted to see their daughter in the *Irish Times*, leader of a failed coup in Germany. Vasya kept up his speed, chopped his hand in the air twice as a kind of salute, or statement that they were pressing on. The police drivers waved back at them. And they were gone.

Owen. He would have loved the fun of this. He didn't give a fuck about 'getting on'; he did what he liked. The pot, the beer, the adrenalin of the riot, the happiness of seeing Vasya again, and the fact that he was driving her through Germany's capital in a Russian tank, made her say, rather solemnly, to herself, 'I dedicate this ride to you, my brother.' Then once more, this time shouting it into the night. A retching sob found its way up from her guts. She couldn't even hear her own crying over the engine's terrific noise. Just as fucking well, she said to herself. Such a sentimental cow. Resi Lehmann had found this wound in her and said straightforwardly that it was awful but there was nothing to be done about it. It was true, she realized.

Vasya let out the throttle a little more and the tank roared on through the warm Continental night.

The Dark Fields of the Republic

2002

Boyle Holdings had one floor of a 1970s office building near the Stephen's Green end of Leeson Street. Mark Turpin looked up at the monolith of ageing concrete, with rust stains and cracks here and there, old aluminium window frames and a general air of neglect; some of the blinds on the topmost floor were broken and seemed to be winking ironically at him in the dim late-afternoon light. He jogged up the steps, pushed through the door into the reception area and was struck, as he had been when he came for the interview, by the disconnect between exterior and interior. The reception area was cool, and not just cool for Ireland. You could tell that they'd got somebody very expensive to do it, somebody who'd been sent to a quarry in Italy to scope out the right marble, talked to the workers, eaten spaghetti with them and then flown back first-class.

He was about to start his first real job in Ireland. With an undistinguished Arts degree from Trinity, he'd drifted to Budapest to teach English, and wangled a job as the in-house teacher at a real-estate company set up by an Irishman ten years his senior. Tom Hyland had got in early, privatizing nineteenth-century apartment buildings after the fall of communism. It entailed getting alternative accommodation for sitting tenants, then renovating everything and selling on quickly. Hyland began throwing Mark ever larger chunks of responsibility in the business, and taking him on Friday evenings to a swanky bar to spend the night talking about the old country, which he both hated and loved. Gradually Mark had got the hang of the business. For his last few years in Budapest things had gone so well that he couldn't remember the last time he'd taken a bus or tram.

Mark had been here in December for his interview, so he knew that after the foyer the lift was like a time machine that whipped you back to the 1970s. He'd half expected, on that first visit, that the boss's crusty old secretary would offer him Marietta biscuits. But he'd accepted Miss Brady's offer of a San Pellegrino (unshabby), and drank it as he sat in the hall in a mahogany armchair with brown upholstery – the same type of chair (shabby) he'd seen in his father's office in the bank in Raheny. He couldn't put it together: how could such armchairs be in the office of a company that was doing so well?

He'd heard, from his uncle Liam, that Declan Boyle, who was not getting any younger, was looking to hire someone to work on developments. Mark's last deal in Budapest hadn't gone optimally, and the news from Ireland was better and better. The idea was to work for Boyle for a couple of years, get the lay of the land, establish contacts and then set up on his own. His first real day would be Monday. Today he was here to sign papers, see his desk and be introduced around the place.

'Mark! Mark Turpin. You're here. I didn't know you were coming in today. I'm Sinéad Boyle.'

'Mrs Boyle, hello.' Well, that wasn't right. The words had come out of his mouth quicker than he could think. His parents had trained him to talk to his elders this way. If he'd been anywhere else in the world, working in such a small company, he'd have shot out a brusque, 'Sinéad. Very good to meet you.'

'Please call me Sinéad.'

And now, what was worse, he had permission to use her first name, when he didn't want her permission at all. 'Sinéad. And please call me Mark.' What a berk, what a total berk of a thing to say.

'Yes, well . . .' she said, smiling. 'I'm sorry I missed your interview, but my husband was very impressed. And of course you come with the warmest recommendation from our old friend Liam Creighton.'

It probably wasn't the right time to tell her that he'd also gone to bed with her daughter while they were both at Trinity. He could see where Issie got her looks. Sinéad Boyle was tall and smartly dressed. Her hair was well coiffed and a scarf set off her brown eyes. He wasn't sure what she actually did in the office, but she was poised there in a prepossessing way, a slim sheaf of papers in her hand, and looked like the sort of person who made decisions. Perhaps she was making a decision about him at this moment. His hand went instinctively to his tie to make sure it was knotted properly and also to keep it slightly out of her gaze.

The tie was the weak point in his armour. When unpacking, he'd discovered that he'd left all his Brown Thomas-bought ties in his apartment off Andrássy Avenue. So, pressed for time, he'd had to grab one of his father's, which, under the fluorescent lights of Boyle Holdings' offices, was forensically revealed to be totally naff. He might as well not be wearing the Lobb shoes and Zegna suit.

She continued: 'My husband and I spent four days in Budapest a couple of years ago. It's a beautiful city.'

He didn't want to be known as the guy from Budapest. 'Yeah, I never really felt at home there myself, you know.'

'Oh, really?'

He could see that she wasn't interested in his feelings about that city, and that she had already glanced down at her papers.

'Yeah, it's good to be back.'

She was turning away, and smiled encouragingly by way of farewell.

Boyle Holdings dealt in property mainly, apart from some tractor company in Galway. He knew from his uncle that Declan Boyle had been involved in the push to get Steinman Brothers Cohn involved in Ireland – and that was not to be sniffed at. Again, the armchairs: how did the armchairs fit with that kind of achievement? He wasn't due to see the boss today, but Declan waved at him from his office as Miss Brady, the secretary, led him to his desk. There was no fun in her. Mid-fifties, still a 'Miss', obviously devoted to the firm like a nun to her order. Probably had a scattering of nieces and nephews out in Kells or some other satellite town, who bled her dry for Game Boys, PlayStations and light sabres. His Budapest secretary, Orsolya, had been twenty-three, fluent in English and German, and had the ability to distract the toughest business negotiators merely by levelling her eyes, brown as mountain lakes, in their direction.

His plan was to be gone within the hour, just when everyone would be descending on the Shelbourne bar. He was all set for a good few scoops, then maybe on to SamSara afterwards, if the right people were there. Well, if the right *person* was there. He'd met a girl the other night in Kehoe's who was devilling for a friend of his from Trinity, and he'd succeeded in getting her number. With any luck they could go back to her place. Certainly, there was no chance of bringing her back to his parents' gaff, where he was still embarrassingly billeted until he found his own apartment.

His hopes for a view of Stephen's Green from his desk were not fulfilled; instead, there was the rain-stained concrete wall of the office building next door, and, at the bottom, a rubbish-strewn alley. In Budapest he'd had a view of the Danube, and on a fine day he could see all the way to the front clasp of Orsolya's brassiere.

After signing the necessary documents and being introduced to the fifteen or so employees of Boyle Holdings, he made his way to the lift. The doors opened to reveal Issie Boyle and a small, plump boy – seven, maybe – with unruly hair curling out from underneath a backwards baseball cap and a mightily dissatisfied expression on his face.

'I will not go to Granddad's and Grandma's again. I HATE it there.'

'Max, I thought we were friends,' said Issie softly. 'And friends are nice to one another. Can you give me a hug and tell me that there'll be no more trouble today?'

The boy was softened by this and moved towards his mother's outstretched arms.

'Come on, my man. Come here,' his mother further coaxed.

Mark was embarrassed to be a witness to this. It would have been more fun if the argument had escalated, and he would have been curious to see how Issie had dealt with it. This wasn't the right time to renew their acquaintance and he hoped to slip into the lift unnoticed, but mother and son blocked his way.

Issie now stood up and recognized him. Mark wondered what she remembered of the night they'd spent in her rooms.

'Hi, Mark,' she said. 'I heard you'd be working here.' No fond reminiscences were evident in her features, which was probably just as well. It had been a case of mutual misrecognition: she'd weirdly taken him for some bohemian character, and he'd thought she was like all the other Roebuck girls he'd bedded in the past. The grey morning light had revealed their errors.

Sinéad Boyle was now out in the corridor and bending down to her grandson.

'Max,' she said cajolingly, 'just listen what we're having for dinner . . .'

'I don't want anything that's cooked.' The boy's tone was plaintive.

'But everything's cooked, Max.'

'Can we have chips, Granny? No one cooks chips. You *buy* them in McDonald's.'

'Well, tonight we're going to have pizza, and we're not going to cook it. A man will bring it on a motorbike. How's that?'

Max cheered up at this and unclasped his arms from his mother's legs, edging closer to his grandmother, who was still hunkered down at the child's level.

Mark had by this time manoeuvred himself into the lift, and said his goodbyes as the doors closed. The two women strained to smile back at him, and Max was already stomping into his grandmother's office.

Through the plate glass of the reception area he could see that it was raining. No umbrella. No raincoat. Fuck. He'd be drenched between here and the Shelbourne. But his mood was light. He had a chance with Zoë Standish, the 22-year-old devil he'd met the other night. And while he felt he hadn't yet got everything he deserved in life, he was certainly lucky in that – thank the good Lord – he didn't have kids.

In the shelter of the Shelbourne portico he sent a text to Zoë before launching himself into the melee of the bar. 'U in the Shelbourne? Meet at the staircase in hr?' Nothing too fancy. Now the revolving doors flipped him into the embrace of Verry McVeigh, a girl he'd known at Trinners.

'Mark Turpin, you hound! What are you doing here?'

'I'm back to stay, Verry. This is where it's all happening.'

'So they say. Hey, these are my friends from the bank . . .'

Mark looked histrionically at a loss.

'First Irish Trust,' she said.

'Oh, great stuff. You guys are doing well, I hear.'

Verry gave the impression that she wasn't sure yet if she needed the compliment from him in particular.

'But not as well as Anglo,' he said, and watched the shot sink in.

'Yes, well, we're hot on their heels, I think you'll see. But what about you? What are you up to?'

'Boyle Holdings.'

'Oh, really? Now that *is* interesting. We don't do much business with them. Here's my card. Let me buy you lunch sometime.' Her tone turned a little flirtatious. 'You're going to need someone to look after you in this town now. It's not like it used to be. I wouldn't like to think you couldn't keep up.'

As she spoke, he clocked the chief executive of First Irish, Martin Thornley. He recognized the face from a profile in *Bloomberg*. Close friends with the great and the good – but mainly the rich. So, Verry was out drinking with the boss. Interesting.

Thornley had cracked a joke and the others were lapping it up. They were standing beside the staircase – the Horseshoe Bar, as always, jam-packed on a Friday night. The men around him – and they were all men, apart from Verry – were of a type: ruddy complexions, expensive shirtware, Italian handmade shoes. One of them wielded a long Cuban, but the stronger fragrance around them was that of money.

Mark wanted in on this conversation. He wanted to be able to walk up to any one of these men and shake his hand and be recognized. He wanted them to know his name in advance and say his name on seeing him. He wanted to be acknowledged and get a cut of the biggest business they had on the go. He could taste it almost, a few inches away from him, the mix of the men's aftershaves in his nostrils, the weave of their shirts distinguishable.

Making a phone gesture with his hand and pointing at Verry's card, he took his leave of her and pushed his way through the crowd. Verry would probably have introduced him to these men if he'd hung around, but he had a sudden instinct to play it cool and he still didn't even have a drink. What's more, he'd spotted his old friend – and, more importantly, Zoë's master – Maolseachlainn Ó Dúgáin.

'So where's your devil, Mal?' he asked, having got himself a pint on the way.

'Oh, that's why you're talking to me, Mark. Very good, very good. Why do you think she'd be interested in an old man like you? She's only twenty-three, for God's sake. And you're what, thirty-five? Have you no shame? You know the rule: half your age plus seven.'

Mark did the sums in his head and saw the beauty of it.

'All the sweeter then,' Mark said.

'But what you're not getting is that the *rule*,' Mal was rather drunkenly emphasizing his words at this stage, 'is there as much to protect *you* from boring conversation as the *minors* from your unwanted . . . *attentions*.'

'It's not conversation I'm interested in.'

'But you'll have to explain what *The Magic Roundabout* was. The Clangers! The Lark in the Park. Leslie Dowdall. Believe me, I know, it gets really tedious after a while educating the youth in return for a torrid time between the sheets.' Mal smiled, perhaps at the memory of such times. Mark wasn't interested in reminiscing about the old days, but he reckoned he had a better chance of finding Zoë if he stuck with Mal.

Time passed; pints were drunk; the crowd ebbed and surged. At one point Mark found himself talking to the acquaintance of an acquaintance, who turned out to be a filmmaker with the preposterous name of Phineas Copeland.

'So what do you make films about?' Mark asked him from a height.

'About you, for a start,' was the answer.

'What do you mean?'

'Well, at the moment I'm working on a documentary about all you people riding the tiger.' Jesus, if this little man only knew. Maybe he should invite him back to his parents' place for some of the shepherd's pie his mother would be reheating.

'Yeah, well, it beats the fuck out of what this place used to be like.'

Your man seemed to be taking mental notes. Mark was about to disengage when he realized that his way was blocked by Issie Boyle.

'Phineas, hi!' Issie cried, across Mark.

He had another look at Issie. Not bad. Not bad at all. She didn't have the burnished and Botoxed looks of the wives and girlfriends of some of his acquaintances – Issie relied on being naturally attractive in ways that most women in their mid-thirties couldn't. Where was the hubby? he wondered. Away on business, perhaps?

'So, Issie,' he drew himself up, 'Max get off OK then?'

Issie turned to him as if noticing him for the first time that day.

'All good, thanks.'

'I didn't know you were married. When did that happen?'

'I'm not. It didn't.'

What a gobshite he was. Just because he'd been away for ten years didn't mean everyone here was stuck back in the last century.

'No, no. Of course not.'

'Max is my son. You got that much right. But his father's not on the scene. Not even in the country.'

Mark raised an enquiring eyebrow.

'You want my whole life story, Turpin?'

Fiery as always. He liked his ladies a bit more demure. But it was fun all the same.

'Just making conversation, Issie. No sweat, OK. He seems like a nice fellow.'

Mark felt a hand on his shoulder and heard a booming voice from behind: 'Is that the unmistakable scent of TURPITUDE?'

Mark steeled himself and turned. 'Seanie, how are you?'

'Turpitude, yes, the lowest kind,' Seanie repeated.

'What turpitude is that?' Issie asked, seeing Mark squirm.

'Oh, not turpitude really. I heard you just landed a job in Boyle Holdings – hi, Issie – telling them how you'd become a Russian oligarch or something. Where were you, anyway? Moscow?'

This was an unavoidable hazard of being back in Dublin: bumping into arseholes who'd gone to school with you, and thought it all in good fun to slag you off.

Mark took a sip of his drink and said nothing.

'Oh yes, Turpitude. You know, it's all very well you hopping around there and making a pile of roubles or crowns or whatever they have there. All funny money, isn't it? But you're back in the real world now, Turps.'

Mark knew this was routine slagging, but he was out of the habit of dealing with it, and felt his body stiffen.

'Why don't you just fuck off with yourself now, Seanie? Maybe you could find some more paedo priests to defend. I hear your firm does a great line in that.'

Seanie began laughing. 'Oh, the fangs on him. Isn't he great, all the same?' Seanie looked around at the others. 'It'll be great crack altogether having you back,' he said, 'great altogether.'

Seanie drifted away then, having had his fun, and Mark realized that Issie was looking at him with new interest.

'What was all that about?' she asked.

'Oh, Seanie and I go way back to when I stole his Skittles and he told the teacher.'

They were silent for a few moments.

'I'm tired,' she said.

'Yeah,' Turpin smirked. 'And I'm not drunk enough. What are you having?'

§

It was always the same: after Issie left the office, Max would calm down and ask questions about what they'd do in the evening. Would there really be pizza? Would Granddad read to him? Did Granny want to see his new game on the Game Boy? What about Häagen-Dazs? Yes to all of the above.

Sinéad seated him in her office and told him to play his machine while she made one more call and cleared her desk. The boy's face twitched and winced now and again as he pressed the buttons and avoided, she supposed, bullets, flails and dragons. He still had his baseball cap on – he only took it off at night – and it looked as though it'd been a while since his hair had last been washed. But Sinéad knew, having occasionally dropped him at school, that Max adhered strictly to the sartorial conventions of his peers.

The school was called the Kimmage Project, but the location was the more salubrious Terenure. It had a strong language component, including German, which Issie was insistent Max learn. Could she be thinking of going back there? Did the father, whoever he was, speak only German?

As far as she could find out, they used some newfangled educational method that entailed a complete overhaul of the school hierarchy and decor every year. The students would elect a new headmaster, colour scheme and curriculum. Every month or so the teachers would take a day out to bring the students on field trips to meet designers, engineers and fire-regulation officers in order to witness and often participate in the deliberations and negotiations. They had to learn skills of consensus, compromise and criticism. Sinéad wasn't sure how well the school was doing with Max in this department.

'There's my little man!' Declan had entered. Max pressed a button on his console to pause the game and leapt up into his grandfather's arms. How did Declan do it? It was hardly fair. Of the three of them, it was Declan who got along most smoothly with Max, despite putting in the least effort.

They were not the last people to leave the office; some of the employees would be there until seven or eight. It was raining heavily and Declan said he'd bring the car round. Max plonked himself in the middle of a large couch in the reception area and resumed his game. Sinéad sat down beside him and tried to figure out what he was doing. Without removing his eyes from the screen, he explained the different protocols, worlds, levels and points, pausing his narrative occasionally while he negotiated a difficult transition.

When Declan pulled up outside they hurried out through the rain into the new black BMW. Its predecessor had been on the road for over twenty years, and Sinéad still wasn't used to the glossiness and smell of the new model. Declan had taken a perverse pride in the shininess of the old one, especially when he parked alongside other property developers' cars in the K Club. It was, she knew, one of his ways of indicating he didn't run with the herd. If she asked what model the new car was, he wouldn't be able to say, though she knew it was the top of the range.

The traffic snarled up at Bective. The rain and the headlights gave the bodywork of the Mercedes and BMWs an even higher sheen. There was no conversation in the car for a few minutes, just the windscreen wipers, so smoothly engineered that their rhythmic sound was close to silence, marking time.

'Mum says cars destroy the world,' said Max.

Declan turned around and smiled. 'But I presume you'd rather not walk home this evening.'

'Oh, no! I think cars make the world more interesting.'

When they reached the house, Max dumped his Game Boy on his overnight bag and it clattered to the floor. He didn't care – he was out the back door to the garden; they didn't have one in Harold's Cross Road.

'You'll be filthy!' Sinéad shouted after to him, to no effect. 'Change your clothes at least, Max!' The rain had stopped only as they'd turned onto Mount Merrion Avenue.

'Come on, let him go. I'll make you a cup of ginger tea and we'll have a kind of cocktail hour.' Declan embraced her. It remained a pleasure for her to have his body all to herself. His arms were crossed at her back and his large hands clasped her shoulder blades. She exhaled, as though she'd been holding her breath all day.

They went into the living room and Declan placed the glass teapot on the table; lozenges of sliced ginger and two leaves of mint swirled around inside it. He had made himself a gimlet.

She'd never overcome her dislike of the room. Back in the days when she was at war with the house, Sinéad had tried changing the sash windows, the drapes, the colour scheme, and banished the bibelots to a cabinet in the dining room. But it remained a stolid Edwardian temple, its view out to the avenue framed by two tall ash trees. The first time she'd walked into it, James Boyle had been the ostensible lord, but over the years Sinéad had learned the degree of quiet mastery that her mother-in-law wielded and that it was truly her domain. Although Catherine Boyle had died over a decade ago, this would always be her room.

'Cheers, big ears,' she said to her husband, clinking her teacup against his cocktail glass.

'I had Conor Larkin on the line again today,' he said.

'Does he still want you to flog HibTrak to the asset strippers?'

'That's not quite how he puts it. But he told me yet again that owning a marginally profitable tractor manufacturer in the west of Ireland makes no sense for a Dublin-based property developer.'

'It's true you hardly ever get down there.' She herself never visited any more, and didn't miss it.

'I know, but the place still makes a difference. Or at least I like to think it does.'

He retained it, she felt, out of a feeling that he had created those jobs in Ardnabrayba out of nothing.

'Anyway,' he said, 'it was pleasant to talk to Conor again, and the call came after a less pleasant call.'

'From who?'

'Seán Guilfoyle. It looks like his illustrious brother is going to be called up in front of the Tribunal.'

'Surprise, surprise. What did they get him for?'

'Political contributions. Some of them made by myself after we set up Hibernia Traktors.'

'But there was nothing wrong in that.'

'Except that I don't think that Mick declared them as such. Certainly, I never saw a receipt.'

She was certain Declan had done nothing wrong and her instinct was to reassure him, but she knew immediately that he'd be tainted if it became known that he'd made payments to a cute-hoor local TD who was now Minister for Finance, and for a moment she said nothing.

'Seán was all very friendly on the phone,' Declan continued, 'but I could feel his brother breathing down his neck.'

Sinéad took a sip of her tea.

Declan continued: 'He said that Mick was looking forward to returning all those *loans* he'd received from me in the old days. I asked Seán what loans, and he said all the funds that I'd given to Pez Driscoll to hand on to him.'

'Oh, Pez . . .' She remembered meeting Mick Guilfoyle's sidekick at the GAA club in Ardnabrayba, dispensing new kit to Owen's football team out of plastic bags with the logo of a Galway supermarket printed on them.

Declan explained that Driscoll used to approach him regularly on Mick Guilfoyle's behalf, seeking funds for the upkeep of the Clubhouse or some other local cause, or to fund the next election campaign. The local causes always seemed worthy, and Guilfoyle had done Declan's company great service by helping to secure state guarantees and by getting the new road. He'd never dealt with Guilfoyle on any of these matters; Pez said it was his job to look after that end of things so that the TD would be able to concentrate on matters of state. Years ago, Declan told her, an investigative journalist had started asking questions about preferential treatment of HibTrak by the government in return for contributions to Guilfoyle. Declan knew, because Pez had told him, that the journalist had gone to Ardnabrayba and been received cordially at the Clubhouse, but nobody would tell him where the money came from or where it eventually went.

Declan was now repeating what she already knew. That Ardnabrayba village had been transformed since the arrival of Hibernia Traktors. That builders were at work on an estate of twenty houses just beyond the church. That the town had featured in a national newspaper as a story of rural success, bucking the trend of emigration and economic failure. He paused then, and continued, thoughtfully, 'Seán has another couple of years to go as chairman of the board. He said that if Mick goes down, it won't do anyone any good. Relations could get very tricky.'

The January darkness outside had deepened several degrees. It seemed to Sinéad that the Guilfoyles and their friends ran raven-ously through distant forests, never coming near this house. This was where they were safe. She got up and turned on a second lamp. As she did so, she could see that Max had entered the room, and was watching his grandmother carefully.

'What is it, young fella?' Declan asked him. 'Do you want to come in and have a cocktail also?'

'No, thanks. When's the pizza coming?'

'We're going to finish up here and order,' said Sinéad. 'Go into the kitchen and you'll see the flyer on the counter. Have a look and see which one you want.'

When the boy had gone, she said, 'He reminds me of Owen, playing out in the garden.'

'I know,' said Declan, breathing in and then taking a long sip of his drink.

'He doesn't look a bit like him though, does he?'

'No.'

'Why won't she tell us who the father is?'

'I don't know.' Declan shook his head. 'It's her business in the end. I wish she'd just get her life together. She's still not earning a living wage.'

'You know how hard it must be to be a single mother. And it's not easy trying to break into journalism in Dublin.'

'But she's worked for the best papers in the world – the *FT*, the *New York Times* . . .'

'She didn't really work for them,' Sinead said. 'She was just a free-lancer. And if you ask me, I think the editors here resent her for it.'

The irony was not lost on Sinéad: always at such junctures she protected her daughter from Declan's disapproval, arguing that she should get a little more money or that they should help out with her rent, and always Issie thought it was her father's doing.

'And I'm not sure what she's up to with Max,' said Declan.

'How do you mean?'

'That ridiculous school for a start. I'll be damned if he learns any-thing there. I still don't understand why Deerpark wasn't good enough for her. Sutherland's there now and he's doing a great job.'

He would never say these things to Issie's face. She melted him every time. His resentment found expression only when he sat down with Sinéad.

'Here, listen, let's get these pizzas rolling,' Sinéad said. 'Which one would you like?'

§

The wrong man was in her bed once again.

The night before, Issie had been introduced to a very fit friend of Phineas Copeland's before she'd even had time to order a drink. This guy – ponytail, tan, earrings – was heading to the bar and offered to get her something. She'd looked him up and down. The tight jeans were a bit naff, but he clearly did not belong to the suits.

His name, it emerged, was Giedrius, and he came from Lithuania.

Giedrius was the man she'd wanted to wake up next to this morning. She gazed at the suit and shirt draped on a chair, the jocks to her left on the floor. Where had she gone wrong? The morning light poured generously through the window. If it had been the Lithuanian, she would have blown off the house-viewing she had this morning, run out to the bakery, brewed a massive pot of coffee and spent another three hours with him in bed.

This was, she realized, a recurring problem for her. The fling with Vasya had lasted no longer than it'd taken him to get her pregnant. He was nice about it, but said that he'd thought she was using protection and that he'd never wanted to get into all this. All what? Children: all that. He wasn't even legal in Germany. Issie nearly said, 'But if we got married . . .' That would have sent him running out the door of the co-op.

Would she have an abortion? he'd asked. Well, she'd answered, it seemed like it was none of his business now. Before he left the room they'd shared in the *Hausprojekt*, she hugged him hard. And then he was gone.

She'd been able to cope with single motherhood in a foreign city for about a year, and then gave up. Freelance journalism was good fun and paid the bills when she was on her own, but with a child she found herself constantly anxious about time and money. Dublin, where the economy was booming, began to seem like the promised land. How hard could it be to get a full-time job at a good paper with a CV like hers? And there'd be free childminding from her parents.

But it turned out to be difficult to land a job with an Irish paper. She thought of some of the people who worked in those places who wouldn't get within spitting distance of the *New York Times*. Issie had once even had a 'Talk of the Town' piece about an American cartoonist living in Prenzlauer Berg, and yet here they were deciding that she wasn't good enough for them. Lurking behind the three or four conversations she'd had with the editors was the unspoken question: if you're so good and could get a job anywhere, then why *don't* you?

Eventually, a friend had been able to help her get work from one of the quickly expanding property sections. Jules DeVesci, the deputy editor, had said how great it'd be to work with someone as experienced as Issie: 'I tell you, some of the people that walk in our door haven't a clue.' Issie remembered some of the articles that she'd read when prepping for interview, and thought, yes, the writers didn't have a clue, and neither did the editors.

The pathetic thing was that she was now grateful to be writing about semi-ds for an Irish paper. God, how she'd sunk. Dublin was humiliating her systematically for all her grandiose ideas. It was saying: we know who you are, we know where you live, don't think we don't.

The body in the bed beside her moaned complacently. Mark Turpin. She'd been drunk, and the two of them had got a little drunker, and suddenly sleeping with this man had seemed like the answer to all the questions she'd been asking. Everything would be wonderfully and immediately *solved* by getting in a taxi with him (if she could only make him shut up talking for the duration of the journey) and fucking his brains out on the queen-sized bed which took up most of the floor space in her bedroom.

And here he was in her bed at 10.30 a.m.

Jesus Christ. Had he worn a condom? Uh, yes, she now remembered. Well, there was something to be grateful for.

'Up, Mark. You've got to go.'

'What?'

Oh, so droll. A moment ago he'd been all geared up for a bit of mid-morning rumpy-pumpy. Now he was pretending to be half asleep. If she hesitated for a second at this juncture, he'd be pawing the knickers off her once more.

'Out, Mark. I mean it. I have to go to work.'

'But it's Saturday.'

'Yeah, well. I've got to see a house I'm writing about.'

'What?'

'You know, my job. That you were so interested in last night.' In one movement she was out of the bed and over to the pile of his clothes on the floor. Pick up and throw at man in bed. Remove man from domicile.

'Oh, come on, Issie. Come back to bed.' She observed him critically. He wasn't bad-looking, but he wasn't her type: for one thing, he'd been very careful to hang up his suit before bed. Then he'd started jawing on about Budapest, letting her know what a major player he'd been there, as if she cared. Why had he been trying to impress her, when she hadn't shown the least interest in his career? And then he'd stopped abruptly, as though realizing he'd left a cake in the oven. He'd been having a conversation but it didn't seem to be with her.

'Listen, I'm serious. My father's coming in fifteen minutes to pick me up.'

It was a joy to observe the speed with which Mark Turpin was dressed and out the door, though not before he peeked out the window to see if his new boss's car wasn't parked outside. Slam. Thank Christ. Anyway, that was her good deed done for employee relations in Boyle Holdings.

Her father wasn't coming. The house she had to view was on Idrone Terrace in Blackrock, and she'd arranged to meet her parents in Blackrock Market around lunchtime. The bike was her usual means of transport to viewings, even if she had to haul herself out to Foxrock or beyond. But today there was Max to pick up, and only twenty minutes to get to the viewing. And she was still in her undies. OK, then: no shower, no breakfast and a taxi. The fare would cost her one-twelfth of her fee for the piece, which wasn't good accounting. But that was her mother's forte, not hers.

She spread the email printouts relating to the property across the back seat of the taxi as she tried to get herself acquainted with the house. When the car pulled up at the address, Issie grabbed them all and stuffed them into her handbag. Then she had to take them all out again in order to find the fare. Then she stuffed them back in again.

The estate agent was standing at the gate, watching sceptically.

Bottling out straight at him, hand outstretched: 'Hi, I'm Issie Boyle. You must be Will LaTouche.'

He paused and said yes and hello, then turned to walk up the steps.

'Beautiful property.'

'We think so.'

'Edwardian terrace.'

'Victorian.'

'Didn't Def Leppard live in one of these?'

'Not that I know.'

'Right, right. Must be awful noise on weekend nights from the Wicked Wolf.' Issie gestured towards the pub nearby. She would rain on his parade a bit.

'Oh, no. It carries out to sea.'

'Still, the trains, eh? They make a bit of noise.'

'The owners never complained.'

LaTouche gave the impression that he was doing her a favour letting her write a puff piece that would swell his commission by a good few grand. He took out the keys and opened the large Edwardian – no, Victorian – door. Like most such houses coming on the market, this one had been scrubbed to a high gloss by teams of cleaners and then finished off with a vase of flowers and lifestyle magazines fanned out on the coffee table. She couldn't find fault with the place, apart from the price tag. The interior decoration was done superbly: it managed to feel state of the art and still respect the architecture of the house, unlike the renovations her mother had inflicted on the house in Blackrock – they'd been an act of vandalism. All those 1970s features that Sinéad had put in were so triste now, and the draught from the hideous conservatory got worse every year, nipping at you from all sides on cold days.

Cecil King, Ireland's only abstract modernist, had also lived a few doors down. That would provide a good intro. Contrast with the view from the bay window. On the second floor there was a children's room, uncluttered and perfect. If only Max's were like this. The small door of a closet was slotted in under some kind of sloping feature in the ceiling. She tried the door, and it was stiff. Will LaTouche waited, long-suffering, in the hall. The wood of the door had warped out of shape – obviously poor workmanship, especially when you compared it with the original doors, which were still solid and straight after a hundred and fifty years. She jerked it again and it opened, releasing an avalanche of children's toys: cuddly dogs, monkeys, frogs, zebras, crocodiles, guns and Barbies. They tumbled across the thick-pile white Cadogan carpet. Some of the animals caught her eye and looked at her optimistically.

Will LaTouche came in, sighed and then hunkered down to shove the things back into their dark cell. 'Are we all finished for today, Issie?'

'Yes, thanks, Will. You've been just great.'

She hadn't arranged to meet her parents in any particular place in Blackrock Market, and they weren't picking up when she tried to call. There was brisk trade already. Crates of books at waist height lined the tunnel into the market, and the people there were her people, Saturday's *Guardian* and the *Irish Times* under their arms, relaxed, interested in the artisanal cheese and bric-a-brac. There was no one she really knew, but lots of people she knew to see. Some had kids trailing from them, others were still limbering up for that experience. Their clothes were expensive but second-hand-ish-looking at the same time.

'Mum! Mum!' There was Max, her parents behind him. It looked like he was in a good mood. She couldn't lie to herself: her heart actually leapt when she saw him.

'I am Maximus Meridius, General of the Felix Regiment of the Roman Army and servant to the Emperor Marcus Aurelius! I learned it off by heart! He's called Max too! And he won!'

The three adults were laughing. Sinéad reached out her arm to touch Issie's.

'It was all grand,' her mother said. 'It was great having him, as always.'

'And I'd say it was no chore for you, Dad, to watch *Gladiator* again.'

'I hope you had a good time last night,' he said.

She fought off the image of his newest employee in her bed.

§

Arriving in winter darkness at 7.30, Declan could see a light on in Mark Turpin's office. The new man had had a good first week: drawing on an old school contact, he'd been alerted to three emerging possibilities to the north and west of Dublin. He could be found sitting at his desk every morning before Declan, and he was usually still there when Declan was leaving.

Declan also liked the adventurousness in Turpin that had brought him out to Hungary. He thought of Liam Creighton's older son, Enda, who had stayed tucked up safely in Ireland, his father arranging a good job for him and a down-payment on a house. He had an irritating air of entitlement, an apparent inability to imagine that things could be otherwise than just dandy. Declan found it difficult to listen to Liam's prideful talk about his son, but maybe that was only because it reminded him of Owen. Would his own son have adopted that same air of entitlement? Declan didn't think so.

A text came from Issie, probably in the midst of the morning hassle: could he pick up a piece of furniture for her in the evening from a salesroom off Camden Street and drop it over to her? He could. Chances to be alone with Issie came rarely and he savoured them. They'd sit for a while in the little house in Harold's Cross and have a cup of tea. He might even be able to help Max with his home-work.

They could have bought her a house or an apartment, but Issie had insisted that she was going to stand on her own two feet. This she did most of the time, but now and then Declan had to lend her a month's rent; they called it a loan, but the money was never returned. Although that wasn't a problem, he hated to see his daughter so unsettled and with no clear future.

He spread the *Irish Times* across his desk. First, the inside back page, to check the death notices. Maura Brady brought him his coffee, his post and his schedule for the day. As she left his office, she said he might want to look at the top item.

He opened the letter, which stated that Declan Boyle of Mount Merrion Avenue, Blackrock, County Dublin, was hereby required, pursuant to the Tribunals of Inquiry (Evidence) Act 1921 (as amended), to attend as a witness to give evidence at the Tribunal sitting at the Upper Yard of Dublin Castle, on Tuesday the 20th of May at 11 a.m., and on such further days thereafter as may be directed. A list of questions was attached, under the heading of 'all correspondence and accounting materials relating to payments to the O'Bride Cumann, in the constituency of Galway North West, from the years 1968 to 1983, including any additional correspondence with Michael Guilfoyle TD and Patrick Driscoll that might have bearing on this issue'. The letter went on to state that the Tribunal was empowered to summon him to its proceedings and require him to present his information orally, as well as undergo cross-examination by Tribunal counsel. It further advised him that he should consider seeking legal counsel himself. Mr Justice Cyril Murtagh, 'sole member of the Tribunal', was sincerely his.

§

Verry McVeigh called a couple of weeks after they'd met at the Shelbourne. 'How about that lunch, Mark?' He sat back in his chair and smiled. The attention was pleasant. She was evidently serious about getting some business from Boyle Holdings, and the image of her figure, expensive fabrics folded around her body, in the Shelbourne bar had stayed with him. His only conquest since returning to Dublin had been Issie Boyle, and that experience would evidently not be repeated. He told Verry he didn't like to eat a big lunch on a working day – how about a drink after work?

As they sipped cocktails in a new bar on George's Street, she laid out the case for Boyle Holdings doing business with First Irish. The figures didn't sound bad.

'But how about you, Verry?'

She smiled quizzically.

'How long have you been with First Irish?'

'I started last year. Before that I was in London. And you? By all accounts you were doing nicely in Budapest. You could have set up your own company there . . .'

So she'd done a bit of homework.

'If I'd done that, I'd never have left the place. The plan is to work for Boyle Holdings for a while and get the lay of the land here.'

'And then set up your own outfit?'

He wondered if he'd tipped his hand too much, but she was smiling in a good way. 'I'm glad we're having this conversation then,' she said. 'I can get in on the ground floor. A few years down the road, we could be doing a lot of business, you and I.'

Now Mark began to wonder why he'd signed up with Boyle at all. If he was having this conversation with Verry after just a few weeks in the saddle, perhaps he should have set up on his own from the start.

Her apartment was at the Harold's Cross end of Rathgar. He took his time removing her clothes – wouldn't like to rip that couture work – and she giggled when he ran his fingers over her silk undies. She was moaning in a low voice, which seemed a bit premature – even he knew that – but it was satisfying to hear her pretend that she'd wanted him for so long.

§

Turpin had called and texted several times, but Issie let him hang. No other gentleman friends had been entertained since that episode. Now she was focused: she was going after Giedrius, and she would plan and research the move as though it were a feature article for the *New York Times*. She wasn't going to leave this kind of thing to chance any more.

She rang Lily and asked her if she'd like to meet on Friday. Yes? Good. Then she rang Phineas, who she knew was at a romantic loose end at the moment, and asked about Friday.

'Is this a date, Issie?'

'You should be so lucky.'

'What's the story?'

'Let's leave it mysterious for the moment. How's your fit friend Giedrius?'

'Is he what this is about?'

'Well, if he wanted to come along that'd be great.'

'OK, OK. I get the idea.'

'Look, Phineas, you won't be disappointed either, I can tell you,' said Issie. And it was true: Lily was a fine thing.

Her mother knocked off early on Friday and picked up Max directly from school. That gave her the chance to finish the article on the house she'd visited the day before and send it by five. She attached the file and watched the progress bar fill as it winged off to Jules DeVesci's computer. She'd figured out what they liked at the paper, and Jules was talking about having kids, so maybe, just maybe, she'd have a shot at a job there. She just had to keep being a good little girl, and eventually Dublin would pat her on the head and reward her.

She slapped down the lid of her laptop, spent a short while making herself up and banged the front door behind her, the knocker confirming it with a brass tap a moment after. Tomorrow she'd agreed to go to Mount Merrion Avenue for lunch, but for now she had the evening ahead. She wasn't even aiming to bed the man tonight, but he should know that she was closing in.

The Stag's was filling up when she arrived. A few people were out on Dame Court already, pints in hand, the joy of Friday evening in their faces. When the night was over, the people around her would return to both shoebox apartments in bad parts of town and spacious villas overlooking Killiney Bay, but for the moment they all suffered the democratic humiliation of trying to catch the eye of the barman, arms squashed up against their chests, a banknote like a corsage held beneath their chins.

Giedrius and Phineas had taken possession of a table in the back room. A third man was with them, wearing a suit, his fringe swept with business neatness to the side. Some banker, probably, that Phineas was milking for funds. As she approached, she felt Banker Boy's eyes on her.

'Issie Boyle!' he said. When she looked puzzled, he said, 'I'm Caz Poschik. Kasimir.'

'No!' Issie must have been about seven when they'd last met properly, and she remembered clocking him at Owen's funeral. She'd heard about him from her parents in the meantime. He'd made a career in . . . what was it? Married, but there was some fuck-up. And was there a child? Something, something, something.

He was on his feet, shaking her hand. He was not quite as tall as her, and stocky. Not great looking, but not a total write-off either.

'Yes, really. I'd heard that you're back in Dublin with your son.'

'Yes.' Issie groaned. Why did he have to mention Max right now, with Giedrius listening in?

'What's the problem?' asked Caz.

'Oh, it was more fun in Berlin. But I couldn't hack it as a single mum all on my owney-o in the middle of Europe. So back I came like the prodigal daughter.'

'I'm sure your folks were happy to see you.' They'd sat down, and Phineas and Giedrius were leaving them to it.

'Well, my father at least. What about your parents?'

'Still to the good. My father's retired. Won't go back to Germany. In fact, hasn't been back at all since 1968.'

'That was some stunt they pulled off then,' said Issie.

'I still remember your father on the tarmac of the airport in Vienna, telling me how all the snakes of Ireland had been chased into the sea.'

'Well, it took a lot for your parents to leave their lives behind,' said Issie. This was all very well, but catching up with a childhood friend was not at the top of tonight's agenda. A text arrived from Lily – she'd been held up but was on her way. It gave Issie an excuse to address the others and start working on the Lithuanian.

'So, Giedrius, what's up with you?' she asked, taking a sweet sip of the cider Phineas had brought her.

'I was on set with Phineas this week,' he said, smiling. 'We were out in Darndale. Most of the time I had to keep an eye on three young boys who were – how to say? – a little too interested in our equipment.'

Phineas chipped in. 'Yeah, they kept asking us if we were from *Fair City*, and eventually I had to tell them that, no, we were filming *Star Trek* and to get lost. Then they said, "Yeah, and you're the fucking Klingon."'

'Nice one,' said Issie.

'We all got on after that. I told them what we were actually doing and they started telling stories about the junkies in the neighbourhood. After a while, I was able to nudge the camera in their direction and flip on the switch and we got about forty minutes out of them.'

'And it was just the two of you out there?'

'I can't afford more people at the moment.'

'You know, I've never been to Darndale,' Issie said.

'And you the property correspondent. You should do a Darndale special. You know, something on a bijou council house that can snugly accommodate at least fifteen welfare recipients.'

'That's not very funny,' said Issie.

'Hey, Issie, I'm the one who's actually been to the war zone.'

She turned to Giedrius. 'And what do you make of all this, Giedrius?'

'What do you mean?'

Issie wasn't completely sure what she meant. 'Well, Darndale is a bit different from the Shelbourne. Do you think it's unfair?'

'No. Those people who live out there are losers.' Giedrius didn't say it with animosity, or pity; he merely stated it as a fact.

'Oh, come on, Giedrius, you don't think it's that simple.'

The man's face was unperturbed. She'd seen the type before in Prague and Berlin: young men who were so relieved to escape the care of the communist state that they scorned all forms of welfare.

'So, boys and girls!' Lily breezed in and informed them that they were already late for their booking at Ar Vicoletto. Caz Poschik had to be somewhere else and said his goodbyes. Issie looked over at Giedrius, who was finishing his drink and gathering his jacket. There hadn't been much of a chance to lay the groundwork, but she'd make up for it in the restaurant.

It was a short walk, across Dame Street, to Ar Vicoletto. They ordered two bottles of red – 'Let's not waste time!' said Phineas – and platters of starters to share. This was what she'd been looking forward to all week, food and drink and the Lithuanian beside her. Lily and Phineas seemed to be hitting it off, and Issie was happy for her friend but couldn't help feeling disappointed. Disappointed by what, you dizzy cow? she asked herself. Giedrius was now enquiring about her job. She nodded to acknowledge the question, answered it, then answered his next, and so on and so forth until the stroke of eleven o'clock, when she asked for the bill, told everyone how much they owed and said she was terribly sorry but she'd an early viewing the next day.

Giedrius offered to go back with her in the taxi, but that seemed like the answer to no question she was asking. She jumped in the taxi, waved goodbye and set to wondering what in God's name was wrong with her.

§

They'd set aside the best part of a Saturday to go through the documents Declan would require for his Tribunal deposition. The company accounts had been prepared in the office, but payments had also been made to Mick Guilfoyle from Declan's personal account. He had kept all his chequebook stubs, but they had been thrown in tea-chests in the attic a long time ago.

Sinéad stood in the hall holding the ladder steady as Declan disappeared into the attic. He switched on the torch and a blade of light cut through the darkness and dust. A furred musk of ageing wood and clothes wafted down from the square of blackness above her. She was tempted to climb up and at least stick her head through the aperture, but a kind of superstition kept her down. The house was hers as much as Declan's, but in the attic there must be junk belonging to his parents that had remained there untouched for sixty years or more. She expected no skeletons were in residence above them, just archaically styled coats and hats; perhaps an old vacuum cleaner snaked round itself in a box; an ironing board with a frayed cover; her father-in-law's tax returns and bank statements from when Declan was a child, playing below in the garden.

Dull noises ranged above her as Declan shoved unknown objects around. Then a pause. She heard the distant riffle of papers. Silence for a while. It was taking longer than she'd expected. In the office, Declan was always able to put his hand immediately on a required document or file. She called up to him to ask if he was OK. Yes, he answered distractedly. Then she heard him moving around again in the darkness of the attic. The cars on the avenue were inaudible from this side of the house.

Now she could hear energetic shoving. There was an enormous bang and she called up to him. He answered that he was OK, that he'd only cut his arm.

'Not enough light for this,' he shouted then. 'I need to get this down.' A tea-chest edged into the light.

'Can you hold it there?' he asked. 'No. Stop. Wait. This is no good.'

At sixty-six, her husband was not as strong or as steady as he'd once been, and she was nervous for him now. It was clear that she could not take the weight of the chest herself. He pulled the box back from the edge and angled his own long form out of the darkness. Then, slowly descending the ladder, he tilted the box out and took its full weight. Red-faced, he wobbled a moment and she moved forward to help him with it; but he steadied himself and got it down.

They took a breather before carrying the chest downstairs and excavating its contents. Declan took the chequebook stubs to the front room while Sinéad made a pot of coffee. When she returned, he looked his normal self again, with papers around him, in control of the situation. He was studying one of the stubs, and she looked over his shoulder to see it: a cheque had been made out to McGuiney's Bike Shop in Galway – 29 October 1973. She remembered: they'd bought a Raleigh Chopper that Owen had dreamed of for over a year. He had done odd jobs around the house and saved his pocket money until he was eventually able to pay for about half of it himself; they'd made up the difference for his birthday.

It was never gone, the pain; it just hid beneath the surface sometimes, before slamming back into her. Occasionally, as now, there was no warning. At other times, Sinéad saw it coming from a long way off. At a dinner a month ago, she'd been seated beside a man who wrote film scores. Conversation had moved easily, to her relief – the man put on no artistic airs – and despite her enjoyment of his turns of phrase and the way he told her about growing up in Bray, she could see the question approaching long minutes before the man himself thought to ask it. As on all such occasions, Sinéad's first impulse was to make an excuse and leave the table, but at the same time she realized that she *wanted* to be asked the question. She studied her cutlery in order to steady herself, and the man, interpreting this as a lull in the conversation, launched them on a new tack.

'So do you and Declan . . . ?'

Sinéad's answer to the question was not always the same – it depended on how she felt and who she was talking to. Sometimes she couldn't resist the impulse to let Owen's name be heard, even though it could create an awkward moment and often left people floundering for a follow-up. At other times she responded that she had one daughter, and then felt as though she'd betrayed Owen's memory.

Declan placed the chequebook on the table and put his arms behind him to touch her. He didn't look around; they both faced forward towards the mantelpiece. Then she saw a trickle of blood curling around his arm.

She went to get a plaster and he suffered her to put it on. He leaned forward again and picked up the stubs, eventually locating a payment of £450 to Mick Guilfoyle, dated 3 March 1974. She switched on her big laptop and they got down to work.

Sinéad had envisaged an intense two hours of transcription, but after the first hour they'd done only one year. It wasn't because there were so many payments to Guilfoyle – there'd been just three so far – but because the cheque stubs were not unlike family photographs and they found themselves pausing over some, to piece together the whys and whens.

Their reminiscences consolidated all the talk they'd had with Robert Poschik just a week before. He'd been staying with them while Eva was undergoing treatment in St Vincent's Hospital. Robert, now retired, was still active in Ardnabrayba, having twinned the village with Mato's Hermsdorf and also helped organize an EU heritage grant to repair a medieval oratory on the side of Doolagar Mountain.

Robert told them that the locals had been rallying strongly behind Mick Guilfoyle in advance of his grilling at the Tribunal. Everyone down there thought it was just some big Dublin conspiracy. It did not seem irregular to them that Guilfoyle had built himself a huge ranch outside the town and wore expensive suits.

And now Seán Guilfoyle had been on the phone again, trying to find out how Declan was going to answer the Tribunal's questions about his payments to Mick. It had implications for HibTrak, and as chairman he needed to know. Declan had been evasive. Sinéad felt she needed to know the answer to Seán's question too, but she did not press it.

By six o'clock they had got through the first decade and a clear picture had emerged. In the early 1970s the contributions amounted to around a thousand pounds a year, but around 1980, Declan was surprised to see, the amounts started moving into five figures.

They sat back in their chairs and looked at one another. The coffee pot and cups lay in a mess on the tray at their feet.

'You know that this is going to cause an almighty row?' Sinéad said. 'You'll be all over the news. And it'll finish Guilfoyle for good.'

Declan's eyes ranged over the pictures in the room. The Jellett still hung on the back wall and there was a portrait of his mother beside it. Sinéad followed the direction of his gaze and inhaled at the sight of Catherine Boyle's beauty, caught at the age of twenty-eight.

They looked at each other again and he said, 'Yes, it will.'

They didn't speak for a while. Sinéad rose and moved to the thermostat, drawing her cardigan around her.

§

Verry had spent the whole day helping him move into his new apartment. Most of the boxes and suitcases were full of clothes, and she made various humorous remarks about the vanity of men. For her own part, Verry wore a battered pair of 501s and an oversized Oxford shirt she said she'd filched from her father. Mark was turned on by her casual clothes. They usually socialized in their business best, and this was an interesting change.

The apartment was on the fourth floor, with a great view over Portobello and the roofs of Camden Street. He'd be able to walk to work. His window stretched floor to ceiling and he imagined himself gazing out, a drink in his hand, after a hard day stacking up cash. The contrast between the clean lines of the apartment and the mess and junk of the old houses below was pleasing.

They collapsed on the sofa and cracked open cans of beer.

'So what about tonight?' Verry asked.

'How about I order a pizza and we settle in here?'

'You're a genius, Mr Turpin.'

When the pizza had been consumed and the grease-stained box tossed on the oak floor, they sat on the couch, sipping beer.

'When are you going to take it to Declan?' Verry asked.

The Clonskeagh deal – a large office and residential development. Verry had tipped him off to it: a consortium was forming, but there was room for Boyle Holdings to get in. He had been looking forward to entering Declan's office with a perfectly organized PowerPoint presentation laying out the figures and the site issues. Declan would say that was all very well, but Boyle Holdings liked to work with consortiums. Mark would then click the pointer and a list of the other potential investors would appear on the screen. Then Declan would maybe say for one reason or another that this wasn't the kind of deal they usually got finance for. Another click: First Irish's specific conditions for the deal would pop up, Verry McVeigh's name at the bottom of the screen. And at this point, Declan would sit back and smile, and Mark would try not to smile. They'd meet the other investors, and Verry and Mark would be sitting in the middle, explaining, helping, pointing things out. He would have arrived.

'Oh, I thought I'd wait a while longer,' he said. 'I don't want him commandeering the whole thing.'

'I'm looking forward to meeting him myself,' Verry remarked casually. 'I never have. I used to see his daughter around at parties, but we didn't know each other.'

'Well, he's not a barrel of laughs, I can tell you.'

'Thornley seems to respect him.'

Mark was looking out at the city lights. He got up and went towards the kitchen.

'Do you want another?'

'Why not?' she said. He threw a can to her and went back to the window.

'It's just a shame, I'm thinking, that this deal won't be mine completely. I'd love to run the whole thing to the end, and not have Declan looking over my shoulder.'

Verry sat up and took a drink from her can.

'That time's going to come very quickly for you, Mark.'

'I know, but I'm starting to think I was stupid to take a job with Boyle. I should have just set up shop on my own. This'd be my deal then.'

'You've done really well very quickly.'

Mark turned around to her and put his beer down on the table.

'I could, you know, just chuck it in at Boyle Holdings. Nothing's holding me there. In Budapest I started using the name MT Properties.' He felt the beginnings of a rush of adrenalin, but he kept his tone tentative. 'I'm sure I could sweet-talk Tom Hyland into getting involved.'

'You mean the guy in Budapest?'

'Yes. I think he'd find it fun. And he knows me.'

Verry started laughing. 'You really are ambitious, aren't you?'

'Not a crime, as far as I can see.'

'Not in this town. But look, I want to bring in Boyle Holdings. That's going to make Thornley very happy and my position's going to be all the stronger. You hang in there for a while, and before long I'll be able to give you all the money you need. This is going to set us both up very nicely. I'll make it clear to Thornley who was behind it all on the Boyle Holdings side.'

Mark picked up his can and took a slug.

'Don't pout. Come over here to me.' She patted the sofa. 'We'll talk about business on Monday.'

He stretched back on the couch, still looking out the window as Verry opened his trousers. It was surprisingly exciting to do this in the new apartment, with the lights on, only a few feet from the window. It was possible that they were providing entertainment for the neighbours. He tried to work out the street names from the pattern of the lights. After a minute or two he could no longer see the actual lights for the streets that he imagined. His mind moved down Dartmouth Walk, Mespil Road, Leeson Street Upper, Burlington Road, Wellington Place. He came in her mouth on the long, tree-lined stretch of Clyde Road, with its tastefully lit front rooms in redbrick townhouses, expensive cars parked on the gravel drives.

§

Issie was going to get her shit in one bag at last. She'd got Giedrius's number from Phineas, who was blissed out after hooking up with Lily. On Monday she'd called Giedrius, apologized for her hasty departure on Friday, saying she'd come down with a stomach bug (a lie), and would he be willing to let her make it up to him by buying him dinner this Friday? He sounded happy to hear from her, but couldn't make it on Friday as they had a shoot that would run late. How about Saturday?

That meant she had to pay a sitter: she'd learned by now that

Sinéad was inflexible about looking after Max any night other than Friday. It was going to be an expensive evening. It also meant that if she finagled him into her bed, she'd have to kick him out before Max woke up in the morning. And now she remembered that Max had to go to a friend's birthday party on Saturday afternoon. Issie was always tempted to Xanax-up for such occasions: they were excruciating. The conversation tended to focus on house prices, and the other mums looked to Issie for the inside track. She'd grown so bored writing about property that she was beginning to eye the paper's gardening column with envy.

On her free Friday night, she stayed in and worked on a pitch for the features page. It'd be good to squeeze a further toe in the door. Perhaps interview people who'd returned home now that the good times were rolling? But when she went through the stack of old newspapers that she kept in the living room, she discovered some-one had done that already. The Irish language as the new cool? Already flogged to death. Parents who didn't speak Irish but sent their kids to *gaelscoileanna*? That might be a fresh enough variation: generational divide, new money, cultural snobbery. Maybe find out what the *echt-gaeilgeoirí* made of it all – some crusty old granddad who vehemently didn't approve and started sentences with, 'In my day . . .' The Kimmage Project taught biology, history and French through the first official language; she could use the hideous birth-day party as a research trip.

The road was familiar to her: she'd written about a house nearby a few months ago. Hannah's parents seemed cool enough: he worked in IT and she was part time at UCD, something in business studies. On turning onto the road, you could tell where the party was by the cluster pattern of SUVs and MPVs in the vicinity of the house; the balloons on the gate were of secondary importance.

Ferdia Hamilton opened the door, declared himself delighted that Max could make it, and gave Issie a kiss on each cheek. Hmm – he barely knew her. He was wearing an incandescent, rough-weave linen shirt, through whose open upper buttons a bit of chest hair peeked, and very cool Paul Smith trousers.

'Come on in, guys. They're all out the back.'

It was a warmish March day, a bit overcast, but no wintry edge to the temperature. The kids, going nuts in the bouncy castle, had stripped down to T-shirts, and as they walked around the generator, careful not to trip over the wiring, Issie recognized a number of the mothers from drop-offs and Parents' Committees. To her surprise she also recognized Kasimir Poschik. He waved to her across the garden and then resumed his conversation.

'Can I get you a glass of something, Issie?'

'Is that Prosecco over there?' She gestured towards the ice buckets.

'Well spotted! One of those, then?'

'Thanks, Ferdia.'

Solicitous, without being a drip. Nice. Slim arse on the man also – which she was considering when his wife, Daisy, came over to greet her.

'Hi, Issie! Great you could come, and Max.' She nodded in his direction. He was pogoing in the bouncy castle with a boy Issie didn't recognize.

'Hey, thanks, Daisy. Your house is beautiful!'

'Coming from a pro like you, that's a compliment. Thank you. Is that husband of mine looking after you?'

Ferdia approached with the Prosecco and passed it to Issie. He put his hand affectionately around Daisy's back.

'We were just telling the others,' he said with a proud look on his face, 'that Hannah is going to have a sibling soon. Can you believe it?'

It took a beat for the penny to drop. Ferdia was waiting for congratulations, which Issie then dutifully provided: 'That's great! Good for you!'

'Come over and meet the others,' Daisy said. 'Though you probably know most of them.'

The mothers were formidable at a distance of ten paces. They were dressed beautifully, and most of them had clearly had their hair done for the occasion. The make-up was piled on thickly in some cases, but the overall effect was lustrous and prosperous-looking.

At five paces their scent arrived – a mixture of fragrances whose head notes assailed her first with a shock of flowers in full bloom, followed by the lush complexity of sandalwood and ylang-ylang. At two paces, as she stumbled on one of the bouncy castle's cables, the women turned their heads en masse in her direction to assess her.

They both pitied and envied her. There was no husband, she was scrambling to make a living, holed up in a pokey house near the canal, no car for the school run. On the other hand, they knew her well-heeled family wouldn't let her starve; also, she led the romantic life of a freelance journalist, and they imagined (inaccurately) that she was intimate with the artists and writers of the city. Most of the women had yet to negotiate the difficult middle stretch of their marriages and so were – or so it seemed to Issie – happy with hubby. But the idea of going out alone into the city on a Friday night, with a free house behind you, to which you could bring back anyone you liked – well, their fantasy worked on that a little.

And she was also to be watched, as she was single and attractive, 'in spite of how she dresses'. Issie didn't have to dress well to get men's attention, and the women carefully measured that effect.

The alpha mum, Emily, brought Issie up to speed on the conversation.

'We were all just raving about Rudy. What a dish. And so committed. All the kids are completely *inspired* by him.'

'He lays it on a bit thick occasionally, in my view.' Issie glanced around the group for agreement, but none was forthcoming. Rudy, as the kids and parents alike called him, was Max's homeroom teacher. He'd sent home a brief letter detailing difficulties he was having with Max's attitude: inattentive, uninvolved, apathetic about the issues the class was covering. According to Rudy, Max was liked by many of his classmates, but only because he set a bad example. Despite the amusing letter that Issie wrote in response, things only got worse between Rudy and Max. Issie thought she'd move laterally, and approached one of the other teachers after a Parents' Committee meeting. When she said Max's name, the woman stiffened and then repeated many of Rudy's points. It felt as though a conspiracy was forming. She was painfully aware that she didn't have the back-up of a husband in a sharp suit with a hot-shit job who'd reluctantly left the office early and was distractedly checking his phone the whole time. The other wives, Issie noticed, used their hubbies like nuclear missiles: the strategic advantage lay in restraint and the occasional display of their existence.

'How do you mean, Issie?'

'All that stuff about Tibet, for God's sake. And just the other day he gave out to the kids because of the logos they have on their clothes. A bit of a fanatic, isn't he?'

'Well, I reckon it's good to get the children thinking about this stuff,' another mother chipped in.

Issie looked around the garden for a way out of the conversation. Children were tumbling out of the castle towards the house; a magician was coming, apparently. Three hours of this before she could escape, drop Max with the sitter and skate off to Dunne and Crescenzi for her date with Giedrius. She mumbled something about going over to see an old friend, disengaged herself and made her way towards Caz Poschik.

'Hey, I didn't know you'd be here,' he said happily.

'Nor I you. You don't have a child at the Kimmage Project, do you?'

'No, Matt's not there. He and Hannah went to the same playgroup.'

'And Phineas told me that you're a butcher! Can it be true?'

He laughed. 'It's sort of true. I'm in the organic lamb business. Sometimes I wear a suit to meet supermarket buyers, but I'm in wellies a good deal too. I do a lot of work with the farmers in Wicklow and Rathfarnham who supply us.'

'So where's Matt at school?'

'He's at Scoil Lorcáin,' he said, switching to Irish. 'It's handy for his mother.'

She didn't want to pry into the story of Matt's mother, and she wasn't used to speaking Irish in the middle-class gardens of south Dublin, but she rallied. 'Point him out to me,' he said. She still hadn't seen this man's son.

'He's over there, with Max.' It turned out that he was the boy Max had been pogoing with in the castle. The resemblance to his father was strong – must annoy the hell out of the baby-mama, Issie thought. The boys had lost interest in the magician and seemed to be plotting something beside the garden shed.

'Do you think they know each other?' Issie asked.

'Not that I'm aware.'

It was something of a strain for her to keep up with his Irish and to formulate her own sentences. Everything took longer to line up, especially nonchalance. She couldn't shake off the feeling that they were putting on a show, but Caz seemed unaware of that aspect. His clothes also suggested a lack of self-consciousness. In fact, it looked as though he'd been tramping through farmyards: his jeans were streaked with mud.

'Working this morning, were we?' she nodded down at his jeans, switching back to English.

'I'm a bit of a mess, I know,' he said with a laugh. 'I don't think the kids disapprove though, do you?'

'But the yummy mummies might.' They laughed, and then were silent for a while.

'How are your parents?' he asked.

'Good, good.'

'You know my mother was always a huge admirer of Sinéad?'

'Get out of it! An admirer of my mother?'

'No, I mean it. Why wouldn't she be?'

Issie was tempted to enumerate her mother's faults, but held back.

'An independent woman who brought up two kids well,' he said. 'Right?'

Issie told him that a German witch had told her that she had to go in search of her mother.

'Why were you talking to a witch?'

'You mean you've never?'

'Not that I'm aware of, though I have my suspicions about some of the ladies here.'

Issie laughed deeply. 'I was doing an article. I don't believe all that New Age shite, but it was an incredible experience. I trusted her completely. Resi Lehmann was her name.'

He was silent. What was he thinking about? Witches, Germany, mothers, his own parents, journalism? Was he thinking about her?

'You're quite intrepid,' he said eventually.

'How do you mean?' She assumed he saw her weakness – that she'd tried very hard to buck the system, that she was still trying: that was what looked intrepid. But it was a pleasure to be weakened in this way; it made her come closer to him.

What was going on? Here she was, only a few hours from the date she'd been dreaming of, attracted by a different man. His directness unnerved her. Irishmen never went at things head-on like this. All her usual stratagems were useless to her.

She straightened her back and exhaled. 'I'd better go in,' she said.

'No, wait a moment,' he said. The tone was unclear – not supplicating, but not casual either. Then he segued into humour: 'You can't leave me at the mercy of the Rathgar coven. I need protection.'

So they remained in the garden, and Issie had another glass of Prosecco, while Caz, who was driving, drank juice. They found plastic chairs and sat down on them. Through the French doors they could see the cake being brought into the dining room, the children's faces illuminated by the seven candles on it. Hannah stood demurely observing the ceremony, then took a huge breath and blew them out. Led by Ferdia and Daisy, the children sang 'Happy Birthday', each in his or her own key, and the ragged melody carried out into the garden.

'This feels like the first day of spring,' Issie said. 'I'm a couple of years back in Dublin now, and I still haven't got used to the fact there are no hard winters and no sweltering summers.'

'Do you regret coming back?'

She sighed. 'Depends on the day that's in it. The country changed so much when I was away. Everyone's driving Mercedes now.'

'I'm not,' Caz said, laughing.

'OK, not everyone, but the place is heaving with cash. And I can't find a proper job. I feel like the hired help at someone else's party. The medical system is beyond shitty, and schools in south Dublin are a minefield. I couldn't get by without occasional help from my parents. It's kind of humiliating.'

'Yeah, but you're not the only one. And at least here you've got your family . . .'

'Oh, yeah, I know. My mother drives me nuts and I love my father. I suppose I like seeing them, all things considered. And my old friends. It's weird: I walk into somewhere like the Shelbourne, and on the one hand it feels like the old days when we were all just having pints in an overcrowded pub. But the thing is, their careers have moved, but mine's stalled.'

'But you've a child, and a fantastic CV. I heard about all the stuff you've done, and places you were published.'

Issie wondered how he'd heard, and was pleased by his interest.

He continued: 'Things go slower for women in your position for a couple of years, and then it all starts happening. Obviously your career can't move at the same speed as everyone else's when you've a child to care for. It's an achievement to have brought up your boy, and kept your work ticking over, *and* changed countries. Give yourself some credit. From the outside, it looks like you're a very capable woman.'

No one had ever said that kind of thing to her before. From her mother all she heard was how she could do things better. On her father's part, beneath the warmth, there was always some reserve regarding her decisions. Her childless friends, like Lily, had no inkling of the issues she'd to deal with. She exchanged emails occasionally with Eglantine, who was still in Berlin, still chasing twenty-year-old anarchists in miniskirts, but who sympathized with her situation, and it was a relief to absorb the understanding that shimmered off the computer screen. But who else was there? In Berlin she'd been intimate with other mothers of her age, whereas in Dublin the mothers seemed cut off from her by walls of shining automobile metal. The loneliness of her life came flooding in on her.

Who was this man who had opened those gates? God, it was so un-Irish the way he talked. She suddenly felt hostile towards Caz for laying open her wounds. The evening had been waiting for her, replete with pleasure, and now it seemed that it was merely an escape – part of the problem and not its solution. With Giedrius she'd have to keep up the pretence of being free and laid-back. He didn't look like the type for walks in the park with another man's son, or even contemplating the possibility of his own son.

'Everything OK?' Caz asked.

'Oh, yes. I'm just trying to work out if I've got my head screwed on as much as it seems. Most of the time I feel I'm just an inch ahead of the chaos.'

'What chaos?'

'You know, getting your life together, looking after things. To be honest, it feels like failure most days.'

Why was she saying this to him? Was she going to explode in tears on his shoulder? She was damned if she would.

'Well, an inch ahead of that kind of chaos is more than most people have.'

'But what about all these yummy mummies?'

He laughed. 'I'll tell you, in my opinion they *are* the chaos.'

A laugh exploded out of Issie – she was so surprised by the accuracy of what he said.

'I'd really like to see you again,' he said then.

She felt they'd been walking up to a brink, beyond which might have been some kind of understanding; and now a new brink presented itself. She reached into her handbag and dug around, without result. He laughed and pulled out his phone. 'Just tell me your number and I'll put it straight in mine.' She did. He pressed the final number with a flourish and put the phone away.

The party was breaking up. Mothers were prising their kids away from the hub of noise and movement. Three children were slumped in bean bags, their faces bluely illuminated by Game Boys. A DVD had been put on. What was Issie going to do now, tonight? In a previous existence she would have stood up Giedrius. No: she'd go in, buy him dinner, let him down gently and be tucked in bed *toute seule* by eleven o'clock. At such an early hour, she'd probably come home to find the sitter with her knickers around her ankles on her couch, and her boyfriend hard at work. Better let her know in advance.

'Can I give you a lift anywhere?' Caz asked.

Issie looked at her watch. They had half an hour, time enough to walk back, and the evening was still mild.

'That's OK. See you soon, though.' It would spoil it all to get in the car with the two tired and irritable boys. Max would be complaining about going home so soon, and spill the beans about God knows what else.

The castle had been deflated – Ferdia said it was being collected this evening, presumably to serve at another party tomorrow – and Issie downed the last of her Prosecco and went to find Max. The garden was dark, but the sky was corrugated pink, turquoise and grey. Contrails threaded the expanse here and there, people leaving the island or arriving, and people merely passing over, who would see a small ragged tab of land before, or after, the Atlantic. A tiny space of little importance in the world – and this garden where she stood reduced in that gaze to a grain, or less than a grain. In a few seconds she'd have to knit herself into the weave again: the leave-takings, promises of play-dates, the birthday parties to come in the weeks and months ahead. But for now she stood buoyant and alive on the grass, her head in the sky and her hair sifted by the light breezes circling the earth.

§

The barrister retained by Declan's solicitors was Martin Cahill, who shared a name with a famous gangland boss who'd been assassinated a few years before. Thus his colleagues at the bar referred to him as The General, which was the gangster's nickname; the coincidence was comical, as there was nothing thuggish or general-like about the bony figure of the senior counsel. But the man was formidable in his own way. During the preliminaries of the session in Dublin Castle, Declan saw that Mr Justice Murtagh followed Cahill's every remark as a hen watches a fox.

The eighteenth-century façades of the Castle had become familiar on the evening news, as witnesses scuttled from cars past granite pillars, balanced mullions and beautiful transoms into the chamber where they were to be interrogated thoroughly at the pleasure of the state. Many fine professionals – civil servants, accountants, solicitors – were found to have lacked the strength of character to confront endemic corruption, even though it was evident from their depositions that their intentions were of the purest. Blind eyes had been turned. Shoulders had been shrugged. Lives had been got on with. Yet again, solid, responsible people who had administered the affairs of state had unaccountable lapses of memory, while others remembered too much for other people's good. Occasionally, probity was revealed when least expected. Now it was Declan's turn to be tested.

The hearing began with the Memorandum of Information Sought, which was projected on a screen to the right of the sole member. This related to payments that Declan and Hibernia Traktors had made to Michael Guilfoyle since 1968. Declan took out his papers and read his list of payments into the record. Xavier Briden SC, for the Tribunal, then asked Declan whether that was, as far as he knew, a complete list. Declan glanced at his documentation and confirmed that it was. Briden then asked him how the payments were made, and Declan said they took the form of a cheque, never cash. Two stenographers typed quickly into computers, and Declan saw Cahill glance occasionally at his own laptop where, he'd told him, the live feed of the transcript appeared.

'Now, Mr Boyle. You referred to those payments as "contributions".'

'I did.'

'And not loans?'

'No, Mr Briden.'

'And there was no way that they could be construed as loans by any party to these transactions?'

'I don't see how that would be possible, Mr Briden. There was no discussion of repayment, interest or dates. I never wrote to either Mr Driscoll or Mr Guilfoyle referring to these payments as loans, or requesting the return of the money. If I had been loaning money, then thirty years is a long time to wait for repayment.'

'And yet I am informed that repayment was made.'

'It is true that I received a personal cheque from Mr Guilfoyle a month ago, but I am at a loss to understand its meaning. Thus I did not lodge it to my account.'

'Could it not be meant by him as repayment of these loans?'

'It's possible that he understood the matter in that way, but I can only repeat that it was not, and is not, my understanding. And we had no discussion in the period in question in which these payments were referred to as loans.'

'Do you know what the money was used for?'

Declan paused before answering. 'On some occasions,' he said, 'Pez Driscoll – Patrick Driscoll – asked for a contribution for a worthy cause, usually to do with the community. Other times he sought contributions to campaign funds.'

'So it was not your sense that these payments were for the personal enrichment of Michael Guilfoyle?'

'That was not my sense. But if you're asking me if some of the money went on Savile Row suits for Mick Guilfoyle, I can't guarantee that it didn't. You'd have to ask him about that.'

There followed an hour of further questions and clarifications, which were conducted in a desultory fashion; at one point Declan suspected that Mr Justice Murtagh was asleep. The upper windows behind the sole member and counsel were open, and birdsong floated in.

The prospect of giving evidence had kept Declan awake more than one night, but now that it was finishing he found himself wondering why he'd worried. He knew that trouble would follow for Mick Guilfoyle, but he felt detached from the whole thing. A lightness flowed through his limbs, as though they were buoyed up by the waves of the Forty Foot, rocking him back and forth. He'd stayed away from the place for a few years after his father had died there, but he had grown fond of it again. He might even be able to persuade Sinéad to come out for a quick dip, or at least accompany him, and they could go for a walk on the pier after.

At the back of the hall he heard the rustle and whisper of people milling at the entrance – journalists, by the look of them. Issie had told him about a place nearby that did a good cheap lunch, and it struck him that he might go across afterwards to eat there. He might even sink a quiet pint, which was not his habit at lunchtime.

Declan realized how dark it had been in the hall only when he stepped through the large doors into the daylight of the Yard. There was a group of about twenty journalists and two TV crews standing in his path. The first question was almost shouted out by a young woman, whose face was flushed with excitement: 'Mr Boyle, was it your intention to try to bring down the government today with your allegations against the Minister?' Declan would have retreated a step if it hadn't been for the fat stone column at his back. The journalists, as one, followed his flinch, their circle tightening. The microphones were all pointing at his head.

§

Declan was finished at the Tribunal, but the country was not finished with Declan. The *Irish Times* editorial the morning after his appearance set the tone at the more sober end of the spectrum. After considering the precarious position of the Minister for Finance, Mick Guilfoyle, whose testimony to the Tribunal was now eagerly awaited, the piece turned its attention to Declan Boyle, property developer and owner of Hibernia Traktors. Mr Boyle had done the state considerable service in revealing his contributions to Minister Mick Guilfoyle to the Murtagh Tribunal. But would he ever have achieved his many successes if he had not made those payments? The careers of the two men could be seen as interdependent: Boyle had built his tractor factory in Guilfoyle's constituency in 1968, with the TD's brother as his second in command, and this clearly boosted the politician's popularity among his constituents. Talk to anybody on the main street of what was once an impoverished country town, stricken by emigration, and you would hear nothing but good of both Boyle and the Guilfoyles. But a full inquiry had to be made into the nature of the relationship between Declan Boyle and Seán Guilfoyle over almost three decades. Mr Boyle contributed generously to the politician's coffers, for purposes not wholly clear. What did he get in exchange?

Declan and Sinéad were leaving the house that morning when they were approached in the driveway by a woman holding a microphone and a man holding a TV camera.

'People say that you've profited nicely from your close links with Mick Guilfoyle,' the woman said. 'Would you comment?'

At first Declan was too shocked to say anything, and stood there amazed that these people had had the nerve to invade his driveway. Sinéad had to step forward and gently press the woman back so that they could make their way to the car. The woman's foot caught on the cameraman's and she stumbled. Sinéad reached out her arm to her.

When she had regained her balance, the woman was back at them: 'Do you think bribery is the best way to do business in Ireland?'

Declan stopped and looked at her. She must have been about twenty-three, ready to take on the world, but without the slightest idea of who he was and what he'd tried to do for Ardnabrayba and the country in general. What did she know? How dare she? How fucking dare she?

Declan squeezed the car key and reached out to open the door.

'Are you proud of your part in the creation of Ireland's culture of corruption, Mr Boyle?'

'How dare you, you . . .' He nearly said it. He nearly called her a 'fucking bitch', but something checked the words. It didn't cross his mind, even now, that he would be on national news that evening. Rather, her pertness, her willingness to take him on, reminded him of Issie; it was a flicker of tenderness for his daughter that stopped the words as they were about to explode from him. In that moment his anger was deflected into his eyes, which he felt must be burning. He stood there, his hand on the lock of the car, staring at her over his shoulder for a second, and then got in and drove the car out.

As the day progressed he decided that he'd given them nothing to warrant the station putting it on the news that evening. But Nick Anderson, his solicitor, told him to brace himself.

'What for?'

'They were just getting pictures; they don't need words. Even if you'd merely said good morning and calmly got in your car, they'd have enough material. What we have to do is watch the report this evening and see if they step over the mark in what they say about you. They usually get their legals to pick through it beforehand. In all likelihood they will all but say that you are the cause of Ireland's every last woe, but without giving you grounds to sue. I'm sorry, Declan.'

Nick was right. Declan and Sinéad sat down in front of the television to watch the news that evening and saw themselves – their faces, their bodies, their clothes, their house – spliced into the story of people they didn't recognize. It began with the house, which was described as 'a mansion in one of Dublin's most affluent areas'. The voiceover of the journalist – Mary Flood Jones turned out to be her name – enumerated the successes of Boyle Holdings, paused, then asked, 'But was the culture of corruption at work? We asked Declan Boyle this morning for comment.'

They then cut to Declan's face as he stared furiously into the camera, then to Mary Flood Jones tripping, and Sinéad reaching out to her. The editing, and the sound of the gravel crunching under their feet, made the incident seem like a scuffle, as though Sinéad had pushed the journalist out of the way. The camera lingered on the car, and Mary Flood Jones noted that it was a top-of-the-range model that retailed at €137,000.

Declan turned off the television. He and Sinéad sat side by side in silence, in front of the grey, dead screen. Inside the house it was quiet, but the windows were open, letting the May evening breezes traverse the rooms. Cars went by on the avenue. Birds were still singing. Sinéad got up and went into the kitchen, asking Declan if he'd like a cup of tea. He said he would.

It struck him that in the course of his adult life he'd come to know the country well enough – the people, the political system, the way money was made, and how economic prosperity transformed a town, and a county. But the country had not yet had a good look at him. He sighed. Now it would.

§

Mark felt a bit bad about plotting his escape from Boyle Holdings during the very weeks when his boss was going through a shit storm. A week after Declan's appearance at the Tribunal and the media coverage that followed, he'd had a meeting in an office in Fitzwilliam Square with two of the other parties interested in the Clonskeagh deal. The mood wasn't upbeat. No one mentioned the Tribunal, but difficulties were mentioned that had not been seen as difficulties before. Mark's impression was that they were spooked by Declan's performance at the Tribunal and its possible implications. He called Verry the second he stepped out the door.

'I've just come out of a meeting with Gordon and Leshmian,' he said. 'They're getting cold feet. They've been spooked by Decco's sudden attack of integrity and are thinking twice about closing the deal with him. I'm telling you, this is the time for me to break away from Boyle Holdings and join the consortium on my own.'

She was silent.

'Verry, I can't do this without you, but I'm beginning to think you might not be able to do this without me. If you insist on keeping Declan involved, the whole deal could be fucked, and what will you have to show Thornley then? We can still make it happen. You'll be happy, I'll be happy.'

'Look,' she said, 'it's nearly twelve. Meet me at La Stampa in half an hour.'

As he walked down Leeson Street, he decided to head straight on towards the restaurant rather than kill twenty minutes in the office. He secured a quiet table and read a newspaper until he saw Verry enter the high-ceilinged dining room. She stopped at a table to exchange greetings – a light hand on the shoulder, a relaxed smile. When she got to the table he didn't get up to kiss her, and her face became serious when she sat down.

'OK, here's the deal,' she said. 'I talked to Thornley just now to sound him out on the Tribunal. He thinks it could be a problem too.'

Mark smiled.

'But hold on for the moment. He wasn't surprised that the others in the consortium are getting antsy, and he doesn't want the deal going down the drain.'

The waiter came to their table, and they glanced at the menus and ordered.

'So what does Thornley want, then?'

'He doesn't want any rash decisions. And our business is not merely to launch your career. He said it's a bad time for Declan, but that it's not all clear how it's going to pan out, and he doesn't want to burn bridges with Boyle Holdings.'

Mark sat back in his chair and sighed. 'You didn't see the faces on those guys today.'

'Would you ever shut up and listen for a minute?' She hadn't taken that tone with him before, and he was pulled up short. 'Look, Thornley checked you out with Tom Hyland and liked what he heard, apart from some botched deal last year before you left. So how about this: you set up a company in Ireland, and we get Declan to be a silent partner. You go back to the consortium and say that in view of Declan's difficulties, you're going solo on this. They like you. You'll have our backing, which they'll like, and Declan will get a slice of the pie. No bridges burned. And the deal gets the significant equity of Boyle Holdings, rather than the non-existent equity of MT Properties.'

He saw the beauty of it, but he hated her, or Thornley, for thinking of it first.

'Declan won't like it,' he said, as though he cared.

'The way I see it,' Verry said, 'we've no choice. If we do nothing, like you said, the deal could be in trouble. This way gives us a better chance.'

The starters arrived, but Mark didn't notice.

She continued: 'Let's the three of us sit down tomorrow and thrash it out.' And then she picked up her fork.

§

When he walked into the office early the next morning, Mark's heart sank. Declan looked a wreck. He'd cut himself shaving, stuck a bit of bog roll to his chin and forgotten to take it off.

Verry arrived at 9 a.m. Mark made the introductions, and Verry mentioned that she knew Declan's daughter. Declan didn't seem interested in the information.

Mark had reluctantly agreed with Verry that they would have to downplay the extent of their discussions about the Clonskeagh deal to date: if Declan hit the roof about not having been briefed by Mark, they'd be on the back foot. Now, Verry spoke circumspectly of the events of the past week or so and their possible impact on his business. Declan merely nodded. She then explained that she was financing a very attractive consortium development in Clonskeagh and that she'd seen a possible role for Boyle Holdings. She'd had preliminary discussion with Mark to this end, but in light of recent events she thought it might be in everyone's interest to approach the deal a bit differently. And then she explained what she had in mind. Mark was in pain: instead of his imagined moment of mastery, he had to sit in silent witness to Verry's confident performance.

When she was finished, Declan sighed and looked out the window. Then he turned back to the two young people sitting in his office.

'Good,' he said. 'It all sounds good. I can't argue with the logic of it.'

Mark couldn't believe how easily they were getting off. It was going to work.

'And it's not over yet,' Declan sighed. It took a moment for Mark to realize that Declan was referring to the Tribunal shit storm, and to compose his features into an expression of sympathy.

§

In the middle of all this, a wedding: Liam Creighton's older son. They had to get out of the house in half an hour and Declan was stalled in front of the wardrobe, unable to choose a tie. Sinéad had watched him out of the corner of her eye, standing there now, unmoving, for about thirty seconds. She was fairly certain what he was thinking about.

Guilfoyle had given his testimony to the Tribunal and had answered the questions vaguely and evasively. He could provide no detail or documentation as to how the Boyle donations had been spent. Afterwards he utterly rejected the implications the media were drawing from the testimony. There was no doubt in his mind, he said, that he would be fully vindicated when the Tribunal's findings were published.

Declan, she knew, was expecting some action from Seán Guilfoyle – his resignation as chairman of HibTrak, or worse. It seemed clear that the men couldn't work together after what Declan had done to Seán's brother. If Seán left now, and for a reason that would be obvious to everyone, the disruption would go beyond the need to find a new chairman. If he stayed, Declan's relationship with his chairman might be unworkable.

'Do you want some help, love?' she asked him.

'No, it's all right. Will this one do?' He reached in and fished out a strip of dark silk.

'Don't forget we're going to a wedding, not a funeral. You'll have to try to look a bit more upbeat.'

He focused on her. 'I'll be all right.'

'I know you will.' She rubbed his upper arm gently. 'Come here to me again.'

'What?'

'Just come here.' She took him in her arms. He was unresponsive.

'At this point, your arms should go around me.' She moved her head back to look in his face. He smiled.

'OK, I remember now.'

She breathed in, unsure whether she should articulate the feeling that had just struck her. It might knock him completely off balance. She stroked the hair back from his temples and considered his face.

'I want you to sell the factory,' she said.

He wasn't surprised. He wasn't angry.

'Your relationship with those people and that place has been poisoned. You can't count on the loyalty of your chairman. You knew even before all of this that it made sense to sell. I want you to do it.'

She studied his reaction, but there was nothing, only fatigue.

'All right,' he said.

She breathed out long and hard. They'd be late for the wedding, but it didn't matter.

§

Declan's name had become synonymous with corruption, and every day he got up a little angrier. The balance had to be set right. People had to understand that making money hadn't been the reason for it all. And that his dealings with Guilfoyle were on the level, at least from his end.

Nick Anderson advised him to keep his head down and wait for it all to blow over. Next week there'd be some volcano or outbreak of war or a kitten discovered to have survived in a mine for three months, and the country would forget about him. But Declan felt he had to explain. So it was that when the producer of *Ireland Live* rang his office and asked to talk to him, Declan took the call. The producer offered a thirty-minute interview with the presenter, Mimi Kilmartin. Against the advice of Nick Anderson, he accepted.

When the recording light went on in the studio, it was a relief to begin talking and at last explain how things really were. Kilmartin's questions didn't draw him up short, but nudged him on. Not that he needed encouragement. Even after all that had happened, he was amazed to think that people on the west coast of the country, in the remotest villages, were listening to him.

After about ten minutes, there was a commercial break. When they came back, Kilmartin took a new tone.

'Declan, you have to admit that when people saw you and your wife coming out of your house in Blackrock, they saw a man who'd done well, was driving an expensive car, and lived in a large house in a good area, and the question they want answered is: how did your friendship with Guilfoyle . . .'

'If I could just interrupt you there, Mimi. The thing about the car I found hard to understand. I only bought it a few months ago, and before that I drove the same car for twenty-odd years. I virtually ran it into the ground . . .'

'Declan, you now own a new BMW 750iL. But there's nothing wrong with success – that's not the point here. The question is: what did you get back from Mick Guilfoyle?'

'I never received any favours. I was setting up a business in Connemara, a deprived area with hardly any industry and high unemployment. Mr Guilfoyle was an elected representative anxious to make his constituency prosper. We had a common interest and, more importantly, it was the public interest also.'

'It's hard for people to believe that you gave so much money over twenty years to Mick Guilfoyle and can't tell us what you got out of it.'

'What I got out of it? First off, the money often went towards sports facilities in the area. A cultural centre was set up. You can't do that sort of thing unless you work with your local TD. Those amenities catered for the growing population of Ardnabrayba. The growing and, I should say, *prosperous* population of the town.'

'But it was clear at the Tribunal that you hadn't looked too closely at where your money went and asked whether it contributed to the culture of corruption in Ireland . . .'

Only now, too late, did Declan realize that he had walked of his own free will into Mimi Kilmartin's territory and was at her mercy. It was not personal and it was not vindictive, but she intended to humiliate him publicly as a matter of professional procedure. Even at that moment, he did not hold it against her.

His frustration was compounded by the memory of many evenings of humiliation when debating at the Commerce and Economics Society, when he knew that he was better informed and more intelligent than his opponent, but not as wily, not so intent on winning regardless of the truth of the issue. He was sure that if he talked with Mimi Kilmartin quietly for an hour over coffee and explained each of the major steps of his career, she would understand. But he could not retreat to a private place for a quiet word. He could not slip off unnoticed and work things out with the people of power and influence.

How had he arrived at the position? That was a stupid question. He knew exactly how. He needed to explain to this woman and to the country what it was like to grow up in Ireland in the 1940s and then graduate from university and come of age in a place with such dismal prospects. He needed to explain what it was like to have entered the Civil Service out of the desire to change things, and not for a cosy position. And then to have left that same job to take a risk on something big that would make things move faster and better, that would transform a town like Ardnabrayba, make people prosperous and happy to live there. If he could get that point across then he would be satisfied.

'When I was a young man . . .'

Mimi Kilmartin smiled, then gently broke in. 'Declan,' she said, not unsympathetically, 'our listeners have heard many times over what it was like back then. Even I remember it a bit. But that can never be a justification for what's been going on in this country with businessmen – and it's usually business*men* – and politicians.'

'I never wanted to justify . . .'

'Didn't you?'

He did. Of course, he did. He wanted the whole country to understand him, to sympathize with him, and Mimi Kilmartin was now breaking the news that there was no sympathy for people like Declan Boyle.

Twenty minutes later he got into his BMW and checked his messages on his phone. There was one from Issie wishing him a happy birthday.

§

He turned instinctively towards town when leaving the car park, forgetting that he'd arranged to have a talk with Patrick Sutherland about Max starting at Deerpark College in mid-term. Issie's patience with the newfangled school had snapped.

He swung left at Eglinton Road and threaded his way back. Beyond the gates of Deerpark, five rugby fields spread out in front of him, interspersed with cedars. In the middle was the old manor house, and beside it the gymnasium and the new wing of classrooms.

When he was admitted to Patrick Sutherland's office, he was struck by how little had changed when he first walked into it with his father in 1946, to meet the then headmaster, Hugh O'Neill. The men had exchanged jokes, and James Boyle had given O'Neill a contribution to the school's building fund. Then the headmaster had turned to Declan and asked him what he was going to do when he grew up. The man's eyes were friendly, but his bushy eyebrows curled up towards his temples, making him seem like a forbidding wizard. He wouldn't release Declan from his gaze and yet Declan found himself unable to answer.

Now Patrick Sutherland – who had left the priesthood shortly after standing as chief celebrant at Owen's funeral, and married within the year – got up from his desk and came over, his hand outstretched.

'Declan, I've just been listening to you on the radio,' he declared.

'Oh.'

'Don't be down in the mouth about it. You did fine. And there's few people that can survive the onslaught of Mimi Kilmartin.'

The business with Max was dealt with quickly. It would not be a problem. Then Sutherland rang for tea, and a young man in his mid-twenties came in with a tray a few minutes later. His accent was foreign, but Declan couldn't place it.

Declan took a sip of his tea and felt its refreshment in the deep core of his body. He'd only had a glass of water at the *Ireland Live* studio, and nothing else since breakfast. The sugar in the biscuit also helped.

'How are you doing?' Sutherland asked, his eyes intently on him.

'Terrible, to be honest.'

'It's a huge amount of pressure you're under at the moment.'

He appreciated Sutherland's words, but wasn't looking for pity. Outside the window, the boys were on break and a group of them were kicking a ball around.

'How's the team doing?' Declan asked.

'The Senior or the Junior?'

'I suppose I always think first of the Junior . . .'

'Because of Owen?'

'Yes. All this spring I've found myself thinking of him more and more.'

'Yes?'

Declan looked at Sutherland. It seemed he wouldn't mind if he, Declan, talked about Owen. Most people preferred to steer clear of the subject, as though doing him a favour, when really they were looking out for themselves. And who could blame them? The prospect now of saying words about his son, of reminding himself and someone else that Owen had walked the earth, indeed had breathed the very air about this school, drew him forcefully.

'Nothing like the first two years, of course, after he was killed. But I often wonder what he'd be like at such and such an age.'

'That's completely natural.'

'And I also can't help wondering what he would make of all this.'

'You mean the Tribunal?'

'Yes.'

'From what you told me after the funeral, he wasn't very interested in all that kind of thing.'

'That's just it. He didn't care about money or career or current affairs or public life. But he was a good boy – a good man, I mean. Everyone liked him, and he'd no malice in him.' Declan exhaled deeply. 'I suppose every parent will say that. I tried to get him going, but he always got the better of me. Never head-on – we'd very few actual arguments. I don't know, just through his essential decency. Like in the poem we did for the exams, "so sweet his nature seemed".'

'Yeats.'

'Yes.'

'So what do you think he'd say now, to all this?' Sutherland asked.

'That's just it. I don't know. But of all the people I've known in my life, I'd like to talk to him most of all about it. Somehow not even my father . . .' Declan paused. 'Or I'd just like to sit with him again and know he was beside me, in the car . . .'

The silence that followed again was accentuated by the sound of the boys outside. Sutherland's secretary could be heard taking a call and saying in a low voice that the headmaster was busy at the moment but would definitely call back within the hour.

Declan rose. 'Patrick, I've taken up too much of your time already. You've been good to listen to me.'

'Come on, Declan, you know better than to thank me for that. And I hope we're going to see a lot more of you, now that Max will be with us. A third generation of Boyles, no less. I can see we've got a dynasty on our hands here.'

§

He didn't take his now famous car, preferring to travel by train to Galway. Sinéad would come down in her own car the next day and they'd drive back together. He could have taken hers, but he wanted to try to sleep during the three-hour trip. And although he didn't close his eyes once, he dreamed much. Or rather remembered much, of the times he travelled this same track alone for the summers. A book lay unopened on the seat beside him, and he stared out the window as the midlands rolled by.

A young HibTrak manager picked him up and drove him to Ardnabrayba, where he'd booked a room in the hotel. The Two Widows ran a kind of B&B, but it was full up with Irish college students in August. His first choice would have been to stay with the Poschiks, but Robert had told him that their son was coming for the weekend. Declan wondered if they weren't a little relieved to have that excuse, given the reason for his visit.

He'd flown out to Greenwich, Connecticut, the previous week and the negotiations hadn't been what he'd expected. Rauchmacher Partners confirmed that they wanted to keep HibTrak going. Declan's tractors were 'industry standard', they said, which was due to the high-quality engineering tradition that the Germans had brought with them and inculcated in a younger Irish generation who had been hired fresh out of University College Galway, and further afield. They were considering a slight name-change – H-Trak – but otherwise everything would continue as before. He was also flattered that they'd done their homework on him, remarking what good use he'd made of opportunities in the Irish economy and, into the bargain, how he'd helped a rural community.

He returned to JFK in a black Lincoln Town Car, the dark-suited driver silent all the way. Could it be so easy? He was puzzled. Would it really be profitable for them to keep the company going? Wouldn't it be better for them to sell up and have the land rezoned for holiday homes? He had pushed them on the point, and they'd insisted there would be minimal disruption to the factory, perhaps just labour cut-backs of about five per cent, which he thought more than fair.

He arrived in Ardnabrayba on Thursday afternoon, and Rauch-macher's representative, Amy Limputra, was flying in to Galway the next morning for the meetings that they would conduct jointly with the management and the unions. On Friday evening, he and Amy would talk to the community in the hall of the primary school.

The prospect of staying in a hotel in Ardnabrayba was strange, and marked his new status in the place: he had become an outsider. His closest friends here were the Poschiks, and he had no family left in the village. His cousin Dara, having run the Two Widows for a while, had sold the pub and was living as a retired gentleman of relative leisure in a new estate on the outskirts of Galway city.

Declan's driver, Joby Naughton, said little on the way to Ardna-brayba. Declan wondered if his reserve arose from tact or fear. He knew that it was widely assumed the factory would be closed.

Ardnabrayba had been where Declan's life began: that was how he often thought of it. Here he had learned how to deal with polit-icians, lawyers, accountants, employees; how to drive a project from concept to completion. Nothing prepared you for the moment when you were onsite in a hard-hat and wellingtons with an archi-tect and county councillor, saying, 'This will go there. That will connect here.' He'd stood in an empty field, the Mweelrea Moun-tains in the distance, up to his ankles in mud, and made Hibernia Traktors rise from the ground.

Now, he was feeling his age. His back was chewed up with ten-sion, despite four sessions of physio, and he had a cold that he couldn't shake. When he woke up in the morning his head was full of the details of the deal, and it would take him a minute or two to disentangle them from his dreams, realizing that it was all going ahead. He'd found himself drinking more in the evenings – a third of a bottle of whiskey was about the amount he needed to wind down to sleep.

As they drove through the Connemara villages, Declan tried to imagine away all the accretions of the decades, to remember the journey as it had been when he'd made it with his uncle on the cart. But it was impossible. Ranch houses – canary yellow, candyfloss pink – with green psychedelic lawns announced the outskirts of the villages. Wedged between them, occasionally, were seven-bar gates: a residue of farming land in what were now tiny suburbs. Then a GAA club, a building supplier's yard, a car park, a hotel that said, 'Coaches Welcome!' A service station. Endless signs saying that real-estate agents were hard at work in the area. Then the shops: Londis, Spar, sometimes a local name, yellow gas cylinders and stacks of briquettes out front. In one village, two letters were missing from a shop sign, making it 'McNama 's'.

They were almost there now. A banner was hanging across the road: 'Ardnabrayba welcomes the Connemarathon!' It was three in the afternoon. Joby dropped him off at the hotel, but didn't help him with his bags – an oversight or a deliberate slight, Declan wasn't sure. He checked in and decided to go to the Two Widows for a quiet pint. There was no one in the pub but the proprietor, whom Declan had never met before. He sat at the bar in silence, waiting for the pint to be pulled.

The new man hadn't changed it much. The name was the same and the family photographs were still on the wall, including the one from the great snow of 1947: his two cousins standing proudly beside a snowman, and his uncle behind them with a humorous look on his face. At the end of the bar the old telephone squatted, the cord snipped at the back, there for show only – Irish pub atmosphere for tourists.

The publican placed the pint in front of him softly and said the price. Declan handed him a ten-euro note. The man had a large frame and a white beard. He moved slowly and carefully, pursing his lips at more detailed operations, as when he fished the change out of the till. The voice was ponderous and inflected with a humorous lilt.

'Quiet today,' Declan said.

The man looked out towards the street, as though to test the veracity of the statement, and then turned back to his customer.

'You're right there.'

'No coaches coming through?'

Again, the man looked out.

'No.'

The laconic responses would have been rude if it hadn't been for the tender play in his eyes.

'And yourself? Just passing through?' the man asked now. Declan seemed to remember that his name was McFadden.

He looked around the interior of the pub. He didn't want to mislead the man, but neither could he resist the temptation to say, 'Yes, just passing through.'

McFadden nodded affably.

Declan lifted the pint and impressed his lips upon the creamy head, making a passage for the dark liquid below. Its slight chill and bitterness worked like a balm. He wanted to drink even deeper from this well, long draughts of cool blackness that would lift him out of all the complication and let him rest for a while.

Eventually he told the publican who he was, to which the man answered, 'Oh, right.' He paused, and added in afterthought, 'They all thought you were coming tomorrow, with the lass from the States.'

Two American women in bright red raingear came in, ordered glasses of Guinness and went to a table by the window. After serving them, the publican came over again, making a job of rearranging the slops tray and the glasses on the shelves.

'There's some people . . .'

Declan looked up.

'Some people round here,' the publican continued, 'who aren't happy about it all. It's none of my business, but there were a bunch of lads in last night, full of loud talk and how they weren't going to take it lying down.'

'Who were they? Local lads?'

'I couldn't put names to them, as I'm still settling in myself. I'm sure anyway that they thought better of it all this morning. It's just come as a shock to people, that's all.'

'I can imagine they're worried, but there's no cause. This crowd are going to keep everything going as it was, let me assure you.'

McFadden grunted noncommittally, and rearranged the glasses beneath the bar for a few seconds. Then he looked up at Declan. 'But the fact remains they don't know this place and the people who live here. They're over there in some skyscraper in New York. They wouldn't have a qualm about selling the place up.' He pursed his lips in finality and didn't wait for Declan to reply. He greeted two new arrivals loudly and cheerfully, moving off down the bar to take their order.

Declan drank his second pint alone, as more people trickled in. When he got to the end of his third, he felt tired, though it was only five o'clock. Last week's jet-lag must still be in him, and today's journey. He went to the hotel, asked that he not be disturbed by any phone calls, and slept for ten hours straight, waking at four. Breakfast wasn't served till 7.30, and Amy Limputra wouldn't arrive till nine. There was nothing to read, not even a Bible in a drawer, and anyway he wouldn't have been able to concentrate. His mind was full of the meetings ahead that day.

Outside, there was neither light nor ambient noise. At around five, two or three cars tore along the main street in quick succession and birds began to sing. Towards six his mobile phone rang. It was Joby Naughton.

'There's been some trouble at the factory,' he said.

'What trouble?'

'A couple of lads . . . The Guards are coming to meet you. They'll know more. I'm not sure myself.'

As Declan dressed, he remembered the last time he'd been visited by the Guards in the small hours. He bent down to tie his shoelaces and stalled, his eyes straight ahead, seeing nothing. The varnished wood of the hotel-room door gradually came into his consciousness, its dark swirling grain truncated by the frame and lock. Two uniformed men had come through the front door of the Merrion house fifteen years ago, told him his son was dead and then walked out the same door they had entered. Now he was scared of all the unknown possibilities lurking out there, which suddenly seemed too much for the force he had left in his body.

He recognized neither of the guards who were waiting for him.

'Mr Boyle, we're sorry to bother you like this. But there's been a bit of trouble out at the factory.'

'So I was told. What happened?'

'A couple of lads broke in and gave some of the machinery a bit of a battering. They didn't do much damage, though. A bit of graffiti here and there. We can take you round if you want to come and see.'

Declan got into the passenger seat of the Garda car. Little was said as they drove to the factory. As they approached the gates, he could see that the HibTrak sign had been sprayed with the words 'Yanks Out'. Nearer the main door there was 'Fuck off back to Dublin, Boyle'.

This wasn't the factory he had built: HibTrak had been expanded and given a new shell in the mid-1980s, work that had been overseen by Seán Guilfoyle. He gazed over the large area of white corrugated metal, punctuated by the odd window; it blended in with all the other factories in the country. From the front entrance he could see Doolagar Mountain, and imagined their old bungalow on the other side. After a particularly long day at work, with a few hours still left to go, he sometimes used to come out to this spot for a breath of fresh air, thinking of his wife and children in the house – doing the homework, making the food, Sinéad perhaps with them both on her lap and reading from a book. He could also make out the spire of the church, which had the graveyard beside it: Mamó there beside Séamus and their son, but not his father, who had been buried in Dublin.

Joby Naughton had followed the Garda car, and Declan told him to get to work immediately to remove the graffiti, or at least have it covered up. By the time Amy Limputra emerged from a car wearing a perfectly pressed beige suit and grey silk blouse, plastic sheets had been placed over the sign and a hoarding had been leaned against the defaced wall. She kissed him on the cheek and said, with concern in her voice, 'You look like you could do with a little rest, Declan.' They were entering the boardroom and there wasn't time to respond, so he just nodded, and gestured for Amy to go first.

Of the whole Rauchmacher negotiating team he'd liked Amy Limputra best – born in New Jersey to Indonesian parents, business degree from Villanova, single mother of a two-year-old boy. Who was looking after the kid now? he wondered. Declan tried to concentrate on the agenda for the day, but his mind kept flicking back to this unknown boy. Did he go to his grandparents, or did they come to him? What was it like to be third-generation Indonesian in Connecticut? No matter how he tried, he couldn't focus on where he was and what lay ahead.

Surprise was visible on the faces of the managers around the table when the deal was outlined and Rauchmacher's plans explained. One manager said sarcastically that it all sounded too good to be true. The meeting with the union was tenser. The representatives could not be convinced that the buyers really intended to keep the factory operating. Declan noticed that the union leaders wouldn't look him in the eye, and seemed to ignore his few remarks.

When it was over and the conference room had emptied, Amy closed her laptop and said that it had gone better than she'd hoped.

'What? You thought you wouldn't leave town alive?'

She laughed. 'No, nothing like that. But this kind of change can make people suspicious and hostile. I think they'll come to see that we're serious. What are we going to do now? The community meeting's at seven, right?'

'Maybe you want to get a rest at the hotel?'

'No, best not do that.'

In the end they went for a drink at the Two Widows – a Ballygowan for Amy, two pints for Declan – and then to the hotel for an early dinner.

§

By the time Sinéad arrived at the school hall, the meeting had already started. Declan and Amy were up on the stage; in the seats at the front she recognized one of the GAA coaches, a favourite of Owen's a long time ago, now middle-aged. The school hadn't been built when Owen was small – he'd attended a century-old national school that was now used as a cultural centre – but the pastel shades in the corridors and the light finish on the smooth wooden doors could not distract her from the memories of living in this town thirty years before. She would not be driving up to their old home tomorrow for a nostalgic ten minutes.

The people in the hall wore grim expressions, and Sinéad felt a wave of resentment and anger flowing towards the stage. Amy remained unruffled and sympathetic, reminding the audience that Rauchmacher wanted only the best for the community. They were happy to keep everything going. It was in good shape thanks to the previous management (a nod in Declan's direction) and thanks to all the people here this evening.

A woman stood up at the back and requested the microphone. There was the usual embarrassing pause, as Joby Naughton tried to make his way to her, asking for it to be handed down the row. The woman was dressed professionally – perhaps a restaurant or super-market manager – and when she received the mike, she turned around and picked up a sheaf of printouts from the seat of her chair.

She began to speak, but the mike wasn't working. She examined it and found the switch, and it came on with the sound of its foam head ruffling through the papers the woman was holding. The audience was now getting impatient.

'Thank you,' she said. 'I'm not good at this sort of thing – as you can see,' there was a little laughter, 'but I've done a bit of homework on our American friends here, and it's not quite as rosy as Mr Declan Boyle would like us think.' Another pause while she went through her papers. Then she cleared her voice.

'In 1995 Rauchmacher Partners bought the Ozma Bakery in Milton, Delaware, and three months later shut it down, and as a result turned Milton into a ghost town. In 1998 they purchased

Felton Machine Tools in Passaic Falls, New Jersey, and ended production once again, within the year. In 1999, they became interested in the UK, and made two unsuccessful bids – one for a lawnmower factory in Derby and another for a . . .' She checked her notes. 'A lathe factory in Swindon. They were outbid by another company, which subsequently shut these factories down and destroyed their communities.'

She lowered the papers and looked at the people around her.

'We'd only be fooling ourselves if we believed their old talk. We're next on the chopping block, make no mistake.'

There was a disquieting silence in the hall before Amy Limputra began to speak. She thanked the woman for her contribution and said that it was completely accurate in all details. 'But what you omitted to say is that in none of those cases did we promise workers and management that we'd be continuing. Rauchmacher Partners made it clear at the outset of negotiations that we'd be selling up and moving on. We're successful because we play a straight hand. If we misled people it would catch up with us in the long term, and that's no good for business.'

Sinéad looked around to see the reaction. Some people were shaking their heads in disbelief; others seemed impressed by the confidence of the rebuttal. Some of them obviously wanted to believe her.

When it was over, Sinéad pushed through the departing crowds towards her husband.

'I'm all right, love,' he said, smiling at her. 'Just a little exhausted by it all.'

She told him that Issie and Max were on their way down – with Kasimir Poschik.

Declan looked puzzled for a moment. 'That's the new man?'

'So it would seem. I've arranged to meet them in the Two Widows.'

It was dark when they emerged from the school building, and rain came at them in small bursts. The security light came on in the car park, making them feel as though they were on stage.

§

As Declan reached out to open the pub door for Sinéad, it flew open pre-emptively, releasing a blast of noise and light, and the figure of the Minister for Finance, Mick Guilfoyle TD, with his wife.

'Declan.' Guilfoyle and his wife arranged themselves so that they and the Boyles could fit into the small space under the awning, out of the rain.

'Mick,' said Declan, and nothing more. Sinéad was holding his arm and could feel the tension in his body.

Guilfoyle sighed and looked around the car park. He nodded, as though in agreement with something Declan had said.

'No hard feelings about the Tribunal, eh? My solicitors told me you wouldn't perjure yourself. You had to look after yourself.'

Declan didn't respond.

Guilfoyle continued: 'But this is something else altogether – HibTrak selling out. It's the end of this town.'

'All that stuff back there wasn't just talk,' Declan said. 'Rauch-macher mean what they say.'

'And you believe them, do you?'

'I've no reason not to.'

Guilfoyle nodded again, as though in agreement.

'Well, from what I've heard in Dublin, they'll have the place asset-stripped by spring.'

'I don't know who you're talking to, but they're misinformed,' Declan said.

'Ah no, Declan. You don't want to believe it, because it'll trouble your precious conscience. When you're gone, what'll stop them? You know as well as I do what these people are like. They're not interested in tractors – you know that. I don't know what their angle is, but you can be sure they've got one. You've made your money and now you're getting out while the going's good. Nothing wrong with that. Just don't pretend that you've looked after everyone.'

He paused for a second, then continued: 'Let me tell you now that I'm going to do everything in my power to stop this deal. I care about this town and this constituency a bit more than you seem to.'

Sinéad watched and listened – between them, almost – and was struck by the intimacy of the politician's tone. Declan was leaning on her arm, ever harder.

People spilled out of the bar. Guilfoyle, having said his piece, drew himself up, smoothed out his jacket and gestured to his wife to indicate that she should go first.

Sinéad and Declan watched in silence as the two walked towards their car. Declan was still leaning heavily on her.

'Are you all right?' she asked.

'Yes. I think I just need to sit down for a while.'

'Come on, let's get you inside.'

'A pint would do me a world of good.'

The Two Widows was full of Irish college students, but Sinéad succeeded in getting a table. Declan looked much better after he'd taken a few sips of his pint.

Issie and Caz arrived shortly after, having left Max with the Poschiks. Sinéad, grateful that they'd missed the encounter with Mick Guilfoyle, greeted them effusively. Issie was actually sheepish, a spectacle Sinéad would have enjoyed more under different circumstances. Declan was now up saying he'd get a round of drinks. Then, abruptly, he was sitting down again, with a look on his face as though a terrible realization had ripped across his mind. He put both his hands to his chest.

He said it felt tight. He slumped back on the bench.

Rather than wait for an ambulance, Caz phoned his father to come immediately in the car. They had him in the county hospital within half an hour.

§

They'd put a kind of plastic clamp on his finger, and then the Senior House Officer delivered his diagnosis. Declan was disoriented, but able to absorb the news: suspected myocardial infarction. Heart attack. Patient now stable. Other data that Declan didn't catch.

Sinéad held his hand, until Dr Oja whispered to her that he should be allowed some rest. She kissed Declan goodnight, and as she leaned towards him he inhaled her scent deeply and savoured the stretch of delicate flesh between her cheek and ear. He thought, I have to hang on to this somehow.

He slept fitfully through the night, his dreams riffing off the events of the previous months. At one point the island appeared below him, a jagged green tab of earth in the midst of the ocean. Could he see Ardnabrayba? No. Cables dripped from his naked limbs, somehow attached to him, but no longer his responsibility.

Then it became necessary that he see where his son was buried. Where was he resting on the island? There, near the east coast, among the houses and roads of south Dublin, his flesh and bones already loam – his sweetness transformed to insentient matter. We write small contracts – marriage certificates, purchase agreements – across the darkness of this fact of death. And then give ourselves back to the earth, as he would soon do. He wanted to tell all this to his son. But his son no longer needed help or advice. He tried to dream that he was sitting beside Owen, talking to him, but the dreams were dragging him elsewhere.

Once or twice he surfaced into consciousness. Was he in the same hospital where he'd been as a young man? He tried to remember the architecture of the ward where he'd lain for two months in 1959. Back then, he must have memorized every curve and corner of plastered wall, but now there was no recognition. The nuns' habits swishing down the central corridor, the spiritual illumination in their faces. Sister Colette, without a surname. The young boy, Arthur. Where in the world was he now? Still in Galway? Or further afield? Or in the ground, like so many other people from that time. They go away, Declan thought. They come for a while, and talk, and then they go.

There were five other beds in the small ward and it was windowless, except for the glass door at the end which seemed to give on to a brightly lit corridor. The shadow of a nurse or doctor rippled by in silence, across the tactful distortions of the glass. One of the other patients had a tiny reading lamp, and nodded to Declan in acknowledgement before returning to his book. Declan had no desire to pick up a book or even a newspaper. His mind had been dragged to a halt by his exhausted body, and he wallowed luxuriantly in that inertia.

He thought himself incapable of ever being stressed again – his body simply didn't have the energy. He wanted to lie like this for days, months, years.

Occasionally one of the other sleeping patients turned in his sheets, and then subsided into more regular breathing.

His adult life had merely been the blinking of an eye between that first long stay in hospital and now. He looked around; he felt like the same man who had been taken up and folded into the rhythms of this institution, rendered powerless, woken and told to sleep at appointed times, fed, measured, talked to, moved about, considered, and eventually dismissed to go back out into the world.

He looked at Sinéad dozing in the armchair. That was the difference. That was the proof. She anchored him outside all this.

When he woke again it was morning. The armchair was empty. Then he heard voices. At the end of the ward he saw his wife and his daughter talking to a doctor. Sinéad glanced in his direction. Issie too. Further back was a young man. Could that be Owen? Could he have succeeded in calling him back from wherever he'd been? But it wasn't. He remembered the face of Robert Poschik's son, whose name he couldn't now recall.

The conversation was ending, and the two women began walking towards him. Issie said something to Sinéad, but he couldn't make out what. The two women were now at his bed and looking at him, their independent eyes full of love and worry. They were here.

Acknowledgements

Brendan Barrington, editor at Penguin Ireland, encouraged *Mount Merrion* from the start and profoundly affected its development – from overall trajectory to smallest details. The imagination, precision and creative flair he brought to the work leave me deeply in his debt. My wife, Tereza Límanová, read multiple drafts, and her conversation made me aware at every turn of further possibilities and options. Other readers of early drafts who helped hugely include Robert Cremins and Aisling Maguire. I would like to acknowledge the stories, advice, assistance and sometimes just general encouragement of the following: Tomáš Fürstenzeller, Renata Greplová, Selina Guinness, Sabine Heurs, Ivor McElveen, Josh Mensch, Alistair Noon, Anna Quinn, Finbar Quinn, Jack Quinn, Evan Rail, Richard Ryan, Jill Siddall, Donla uí Bhraonáin and Brad Vice. I would also like to thank Caroline Pretty for her copy-editing.

A novel that covers forty-plus years and touches on details of social life, business and politics incurs obvious debts to works of history and memoir. Foremost among these are Diarmaid Ferriter's magisterial and panoramic *The Transformation of Ireland*, and June Levine's *Sisters*, one of the funniest and most compelling memoirs of recent decades. Also of great help were Garret FitzGerald's *Just Garret: Tales from the Political Front Line*, R. F. Foster's *Luck and the Irish: A Brief History of Change, 1970–2000*, Ann Marie Hourihane's *She Moves Through the Boom*, Wladimir Kaminer's *Russian Disco: Tales of Everyday Lunacy on the Streets of Berlin*, Colm Keena's *Haughey's Millions: Charlie's Money Trail*, Simon Kelly's *Breakfast with Anglo*, David McWilliams's *The Pope's Children: Ireland's New Elite* and Fintan O'Toole's *Ship of Fools: How Stupidity and Corruption Sank the Celtic Tiger*.